# THE HEAT OF PASSION

For the life of her, Tacita didn't know why being mad at Jed made her so unhappy.

"It's a hard 'nother day or so, ma'am," he said now, breaking into her distress, "but then we'll be in Alamogordo and you can rest up."

Her sniff wouldn't come this time. Rosamunda managed a brief snarl, although it came out sounding more like a peep than one of her usual full-bodied growls. Tacita silently honored her for the attempt.

"You can take a nice long bath in the hotel and soak all this rotten desert off you in Alamogordo."

*That* was the reason; Tacita realized it when her eyes began to sting. First he'd led her into this ghastly oven, and now he was being kind to her—even when she was nasty to him. She wanted to hate him, and she couldn't.

What she felt like doing, and abominated herself for, was to ask him to hold her in his wonderful strong arms until she passed from this unendurable mortal coil and made her way to a higher, and hopefully cooler, dimension. One with water and cool, soothing breezes. Tacita could hardly believe it of herself. Not content with being boring, she'd discovered herself to be a despicable weakling as well. The knowledge made her very sad.

# Rosamunda's Revenge

It's A
Dog's Life

# EMMA CRAIG

LOVE SPELL BOOKS  NEW YORK CITY

*Rosamunda's Revenge is for all of us who could probably survive without our furry friends but don't think it would be worthwhile.*

LOVE SPELL®

August 1997

Published by

Dorchester Publishing Co., Inc.
276 Fifth Avenue
New York, NY 10001

# Rosamunda's Revenge

## It's A Dog's Life

# *Chapter One*

Rosamunda took one look at the tall man striding across the lobby floor and knew him for a
man who favored big dogs. Hunting dogs. Dogs
with thick fur and lots of fleas. Dogs with bone
heads. Dogs with little brains, big feet, no social
graces, huge rumbling barks, and bad breath.

So she bit him on the ankle. She would have
kneecapped him, but she couldn't reach.

Jedediah Hardcastle heard a strange, high-
pitched snarl, the clatter of tiny claws against
the wooden floor, felt something bump against
his boot, and heard a rip come from the direction of his trouser cuff. When he looked down,
it was to find a hairy rat attached to his left foot.
Shoot, he already knew New Mexico Territory
to be a wild place; until this minute, he didn't
know about the big rats.

"Hey!" He lifted his foot and shook it. "Hey! Son-of-a-buck!" It was a heavy blasted rat, too; must have weighed five or six pounds. And tenacious. Jed began to wonder if he'd have to shoot it before it would leave go of his trousers.

"Stop! Stop that this instant, you vicious brute! What are you doing to my dog?"

Jed lifted his head when he heard the feminine exclamation, intending to let the officious female know exactly what he thought of hotels that allowed huge hairy rats to run loose in their lobbies. As soon as he saw her, he felt his words dry up and his mouth drop open.

A fairy princess in a fluff of sky-blue ruffles, she was floating down the staircase and headed straight at him. A vision in frills, with hair a mass of blond curls, and a face like an artist's dream in painted porcelain, Jed knew it had to be something unearthly. He'd surely never seen a real, honest-to-God woman who looked like this creature did. If he had, he'd have been inclined to get engaged to her instead of Miss Amalie Crunch back home in Busted Flush, no matter what his parents wanted.

Although struggling to maintain his balance whilst keeping his foot in the air was a perilous proposition, Jed whipped his Stetson from his head. It was an automatic reaction to a woman entering any room in which he stood. He was polite that way.

After a second, he realized his foot still hung in the air with the rat dangling from it. The savage beast was making furious growling noises that might have sounded ominous had they been pitched an octave or three lower. Jed hardly noticed anymore, so busy was his brain in drinking in the sight of the vision in blue. Carefully, he replaced his foot on the floor without stomping on the rat. He'd always heard females disliked the sight of blood, and he certainly didn't want to offend the fairy princess.

As soon as his boot hit the lobby floor, the rat backed up, Jed's trouser cuff still clenched in its teeth, and began snarling ferociously as it tugged. Since the trousers were made of thick, heavy buckskin, the lightweight vandal didn't stand a chance. Jed endeavored to ignore it.

He closed his mouth and gulped. The glorious apparition had finally made its way to him. He could see now that she wasn't a fairy princess at all, but a woman. She was the most beautiful little thing Jed had ever seen in his life, but at the moment she looked mad enough to spit tacks.

"Rosamunda! Rosamunda!"

The incredible female knelt at Jed's feet and put her arms out to grab the maddened rat. Jed thought about protesting. He almost lunged at her, afraid the beast was rabid and might forsake his trouser cuff and turn on her. The words she'd cried as she'd descended the staircase finally penetrated his shocked brain, however, and he blinked instead.

"That thing's a *dog?*"

"Oh, my poor, poor baby. Oh, Rosamunda, darling! Did that awful man hurt you?"

Caught somewhere between utter astonishment and swelling indignation, Jed stammered, "Hurt it? Me? Awful?"

"Ooooh! You horrid big brute!"

She was looking at Jed when she said it. He swallowed hard.

The irate enchantress hugged the rat—that is, she hugged the dog to her breast in a manner Jed would have envied if he'd had his wits about him, and backed up. Her blue eyes crackled fire, and her flawless cheeks glowed pink.

"But—but—"

Part of what she'd said was true: Jed was big. But a brute? Hell, he was the politest man he knew. Of course, since he lived in the relatively uncivilized environs of Busted Flush, Texas, perhaps he wasn't the best judge. Still and all, he tried. Miss Amalie Crunch seemed to find his manners pleasing.

"How dare you try to hurt my dog?

That was enough. Jed could take a lot of abuse from people. In fact, he made a point of it, since to do otherwise would have been unfair to them; but even he could only take so much.

"Now, wait a damned minute, ma'am. That thing attacked me."

"Did you hear that, Rosamunda?" the beauty cried, speaking to the animal in her arms. "The beast is swearing at us! Well, I suppose we might have guessed."

Jed lifted his hat in a beseeching gesture. "I beg your pardon, ma'am, but your—dog—attacked me." He still couldn't quite make himself believe that thing was a dog.

She'd done a good job at attacking the brute, too Rosamunda thought to herself proudly. Because she was still mad at him on an instinctive level, she bared her teeth at him.

He glared back, confirming him as a lout in Rosamunda's estimation. Satisfied that she'd made her point, she subsided into Mistress's arms and put on her best wounded air.

"That's right, sweetheart. You just tell that bad man what you think of a huge, hulking ogre who tries to hurt sweet, precious doggies."

Rosamunda, sensing victory, allowed herself to cease pouting. She smirked at the monster instead. His glare got hotter, but he didn't reach for her. She considered it a rather large victory in her admittedly small life.

Jed was fit to be tied. He also felt an almost ungovernable urge to make this magnificent female cease feeling ill will toward him. "Ma'am, I'm sorry if I hurt your dog. But I was just walking through the lobby, going to the desk to ask about the job I'm here for, when that—dog—up and charged at me and grabbed my trouser cuff. I didn't provoke the attack, either. Honest."

He almost got lost in her big blue eyes. They were the blue of a summer sky. The blue of Luggett Lake on a clear spring day. The blue of bachelor's buttons. Of Texas bluebonnets. Of—Jed's imagination gave out and he merely stared down into them. It was a long way down, as he was a very tall man, but it was worth it. Even if she did still seem mad, and possessed a voice shrill enough to crack glass, she was the most gorgeous female he'd ever seen in all his born days.

She had a sniff that could make a large man feel really stupid, too. She demonstrated it on him now, in fact.

Feeling more sheepish than he had since he'd mistakenly burst in on his cousin Willie and old man Huggenbaker's wife back when he was fourteen, Jed said in the smallest voice he had in him, "I'm truly sorry, ma'am. Reckon I've never seen a dog like that before."

She sniffed again, and Jed tried harder. "You see, ma'am, I'm from Texas. We've got us big dogs in Texas. We don't have no dogs like that."

Rosamunda didn't care for the expression he gave her when he said it, so she growled at him again and had the pleasure of seeing his hands bunch up into fists. She'd already taken his measure, though, and knew good and well he wouldn't use those fists on her. To do so would irritate Mistress and he was trying to make an impression. Or correct the one he'd already made, rather. Humans. They were so predictable.

"Any dogs," Mistress said.

"Beg pardon, ma'am?"

"*Any* dogs. You don't have *any* dogs like this in Texas. Nor, obviously, do you have much grammar." She sniffed yet again.

Rosamunda sneered and was pleased to see the monster's neck turn red. It was a common reaction in human beings when they felt humiliated.

The man didn't have time to defend his improper use of the English language, because Mistress continued, "I'll have you know this is very much a dog. She's a Yorkshire terrier, and she's a direct descendent of the great Huddersfield Ben himself. Her pedigree is impeccable."

Rosamunda thought she heard him mutter, "I'd like to peck her." She wasn't sure, but she snarled anyway. Her snarl earned her a hug and a stroke from Mistress, which made it worthwhile.

The monster finally decided to give up. Clutching his hat in both hands, he said, "Well, ma'am, I'm sorry. I didn't mean to hurt your— your dog. Er—Rosie."

"Rosamunda," Mistress corrected.

Rosamunda snarled.

"Oh. Yeah, whatever you said. Now, if you'll please excuse me."

"With pleasure," Mistress said grandly.

Jed felt like a chastised schoolboy when he finished his interrupted journey across the hotel lobby and finally made it to the registration desk. At least the desk clerk seemed to understand.

"Met the princess, did you?" he whispered sympathetically, casting a furtive glance around Jed's large frame.

With a gusty sigh, Jed said, "Reckon I did."

"Damned dog yaps at everybody. You're the first one I seen it go after," the clerk said.

"It bit my foot." Jed still had trouble believing the stupid hairy rat had done such a thing. He couldn't decide whether its outrageous behavior betokened phenomenal bravery or absolute insanity, although his inclination leaned toward the latter.

The desk clerk nodded in compassion.

"Well, I got other business to attend to besides fighting off pork-chop terriers," Jed told him. "I'm here on a job." He reached into his jacket pocket, withdrew a crumpled paper, and smoothed it out on the countertop. "Lady by the name of"—Jed stopped, drew in a big breath, and said precisely, "Tack-*eye*-ta Grant-ham."

The desk clerk's eyes widened. He murmured,

"Whoo-ey." Then he said, "I'm right sorry, mister."

Jed said, "Sorry? Why—" and got no further because he heard, from directly behind him, a shrill, shrieky, *"Who?"*

He turned, startled, to discover that same magnificent example of feminine beauty he'd so recently encountered. The snot-nose terror was still in her arms, too, and it still smirked at him.

*"Who* are you looking for?" the vision asked.

She sounded horrified, and an uneasy feeling began to slink up Jed's spine. He picked up the wrinkled paper, glanced at it, and tried again. "Tack-*eye*-ta Grant-ham."

"Oh, good heavens! There must be some dreadful mistake." The woman drew herself up to her full height, which must have been all of five feet and an inch or so, and said, "*I* am Tacita Grantham, sir." She pronounced it *Tass*-i-ta *Gran*-tham.

"You?" Oh, shoot; he should have guessed.

"Yes. I. And I don't believe we shall be doing business together."

All in all, Jed supposed he wasn't sorry to hear her say so. She might be pretty, but his first impression of her made him suspect her beauty, like that of most folks, went only skin deep. Still, he was troubled. He pushed his hat back on his head and stared down at the female holding the rat. "Well, ma'am, what do you aim to do instead?"

"I shall find another escort," she said regally.

Now it was true that Jed Hardcastle had a great appreciation of feminine pulchritude. And it was also true that this creature was about the finest example of such he'd ever seen in his entire life. If circumstances were different, and in spite of his standing engagement to Miss Amalie Crunch, he'd delight in spending any number of months guiding Miss Grantham from the wild and woolly territory to the glories of San Francisco. A fellow could generally make a female shut up if he went about it the right way. Jed wasn't a fool, after all.

In this case, however, he wasn't so sure. As gorgeous as she was, he'd already discovered her to be a shrew. And that damned thing she called a dog would be a pain in the ass, too. Or at least in the trouser cuff. He wasn't certain he'd enjoy spending several weeks in the company of a snot and a bitch, no matter how pretty one of them was.

Jed's first impulse was to tip his hat, utter a friendly thank you, and depart, thanking his guardian angel for a lucky escape. Two things prevented him from doing so.

Number one, he was pretty sure she wouldn't be able to find a competent man to lead her from the Territory to San Francisco. Not in Powder Gulch, she wouldn't. Of course, there wasn't another man from Texas to the Arizona Territory as competent as Jed himself, but there were others who were fairly good and could work in a pinch.

Number two was indirectly tied in with number one. No matter how much he didn't like her, his brain rebelled at the image it created of this vibrant, beautiful woman's desiccated corpse lying on the desert floor with vultures perched on those blond curls and pecking at her lovely eyes. He didn't have the same compunction about the animal in her arms, but still . . . He removed his

15

hat politely and held it in front of his lone-star belt buckle.

"Uh, ma'am?" he said, wondering how to advise her of his scruples without being crude.

"What?"

Her scowl rankled. So did her abruptness. As sharply as his drawl would allow, he said, "Ma'am, we may not hold with grammar or bog-hole terrors in Texas, but at least we have us some manners." She stiffened up like one of his grandpa's coon hounds on the scent, but Jed didn't give her time to respond. "I was going to point out to you that it may not be easy for you to find another fellow to guard and guide you in Powder Gulch. This place ain't—isn't—a big metropolis, you know."

He'd obviously struck a nerve when he mentioned manners. Her cheeks blossomed a bright cherry red, and Jed felt a mad impulse to grab her and kiss her silly. He'd never do such a thing. Not even if she asked. Not only was he too polite, but he was so big and she was so small, he'd probably squish her to death.

"Yes, I've already noticed that," she said stiffly, apparently deciding to ignore his barb about her lack of manners.

"According to the letter your lawyer wrote, you've got to get to San Francisco by July."

"Yes. Yes, that's true."

"Then, ma'am, I suggest we start over on a better footing and try again."

Rosamunda didn't care for his choice of words, objecting to the "footing" part, and showed him so by lunging at the big ugly thumb folded over the brim of his hat. She missed his back. He didn't bother to look at her. He found no more weapons.

"I'll help you with your wagon, then," he said when he was through with his search.

The newcomer swept a gallant bow. "I should consider it a favor, kind sir."

"What's your name, stranger?" Jed asked politely. He could feel Tacita's hot glare boring into his back as he headed off with the drummer.

"My name is Cesare Cacciatore Picinisco, my good fellow. And will you honor me with your name, sir?"

"Hardcastle. Jed Hardcastle, Mr. Piskanickle."

Rosamunda's low growl followed them into the trees.

"Well, I don't care what you think. I think it was rude of you to treat that poor Mr. Picinisco the way you did!"

Rosamunda couldn't have agreed with her mistress more unless she'd commanded Jed to leave them now and continued on her way without the fool man. Thanks to this kindhearted Mr. Cesare and his wonderful wagon, Rosamunda hadn't eaten so well since . . . well, since yesterday. Still and all, she hadn't expected to eat well on this journey at all. Not that she begrudged Tacita a single miserable meal of stringy dried beef and water, but it was a pleasure to have partaken of Mr. Cesare's delicious beefsteak.

She sighed as Tacita scratched her little round belly. She'd have glowered at Jed, but she felt too lazy.

"You can never be too careful out here in the territory, Miss Grantham," Jed said stiffly. "I'm surprised you didn't learn that when this gentleman dumped all those weapons at your feet."

"I still think you were a beast to keep your gun trained on him for so long."

"You'd have preferred it if I'd dropped my guard and he'd shot us all?"

"Oh, don't be silly! He's not that type of person."

"Maybe."

Rosamunda, on her back in Mistress's lap, looked over to where the two men had parked Mr. Cesare's wagon. It was a lovely wagon, painted all over with flowers on a red background. CESARE'S GOODS WARES, AND MISCELLANY had been stenciled on both sides in fancy black lettering. It was a pretty wagon. Rosamunda liked it. She liked Mr. Cesare, too.

Although she had little energy to spare at the moment, hers being occupied in digestion, she tilted her head to one side and snarled at Jed. He harumphed.

Then he said, "Miss Grantham," in a measured voice that clearly indicated his strain, "I would appreciate it if you'd let me do the job you're paying me to do, and you just tend to your dog-eared terrier. I know this country and the people who live in it a whale of a lot better than you do."

It looked to Rosamunda as if Tacita didn't want to admit to a thing. "Perhaps," she said stubbornly. "I still don't believe there's any need to be rude to people without provocation."

Jed merely humphed.

Picinisco had propped himself against one shiny black wagon wheel. He smiled now and withdrew a harmonica from his pocket.

"May I honor my two hosts with some music?"

he asked politely. "It's the least I can do for the kind people who allow me to share their company and their fire." He cast an uncertain look at Rosamunda. "And their animal."

"She's a Yorkshire terrier, Mr. Picinisco," Tacita said with pride. "She's a descendent of the great Huddersfield Ben himself, and a prime example of her breed."

Nodding, Picinisco said, "Really." He sounded fairly befuddled.

Tacita gazed down at Rosamunda with love in her eyes. Rosamunda licked her hand. "Oh, my, yes. Why, she's a perfect bitch."

Jed, who had been in the process of swigging his coffee, choked, and some of the coffee spewed out onto the ground in front of him. Rosamunda and Tacita both eyed him glacially for exhibiting such abysmal manners.

Picinisco merely stared harder and said, "Er . . ."

Pointedly ignoring Jed, who had succumbed to a coughing fit, Tacita continued. "She has a splendid coat. Just see how even and straight it is. And look at how neat and compact her body is, too. Her muzzle's not too long at all, and there's not a sooty hair to be found amongst the tan. And see where the tan begins? It's perfectly even. See? Her coloring is absolutely exquisite."

Rosamunda rolled over onto her full tummy, both so that she could exhibit her manifold charms more fully and also to assess the reaction of Tacita's audience. Everything Tacita said was true, of course. Rosamunda was a paragon of her breed. As little as she admired arrogance, still more did she reject false modesty. Rosamunda knew herself to be perfect. She couldn't help it.

Jed Hardcastle was still choking and paid no attention. Mr. Cesare, however, seemed very attentive. Rosamunda honored him with a pleasantly doggy smile.

"Go on, please, Miss Grantham. I am strangely interested in this delightful animal of yours." Picinisco's smile fairly beamed across the fire to Rosamunda and Tacita.

Happy to oblige, Tacita said, "Oh, well, her perfections are legion, Mr. Picinisco. Take her ears, for instance."

Jed, who had finally stopped coughing, choked out, "Huh!"

Tacita frowned. "And her eyes. Why, just look at her eyes. They simply radiate intelligence."

This time Jed said, "Ha!"

Tacita ignored him. "And her legs are straight as a string. See?" She demonstrated, turning Rosamunda over and showing off her legs. Ever eager to oblige her mistress, Rosamunda did so by being absolutely still and holding her legs straight up in the air. "And her coat is as glossy as a newly minted coin. She's just the prettiest thing in the whole wide world."

Tacita nuzzled Rosamunda, who nuzzled her back. Jed looked away in disgust. "And she only weighs five pounds, so she's as dainty as a porcelain rose."

"And is a dog like your delightful pet expensive, Miss Grantham?" Picinisco asked. "I understand some purebred animals can cost a good deal of money."

"Oh, my, yes! Why, if somebody were to purchase such a specimen as Rosamunda, he might expect to pay nearly two hundred dollars."

Picinisco's mouth dropped open.

"Two hundred dollars? For *that*?" Jed's unflattering words precipitated a hot glare from Tacita and a low growl from Rosamunda.

"Yes, Mr. Hardcastle," Tacita said frigidly. "Two hundred dollars. Rosamunda is as close to perfection as you can find in a Yorkie." Peering lovingly at her dog, she added, "Of course, Rosamunda is priceless to me. She was a gift from my beloved parents. They brought her to me all the way from England, and I wouldn't part with her for the world."

Tacita jumped when Jed rose all of a sudden. "I'm turning in." He sounded as though he couldn't do so fast enough.

Eyeing him with irritation, Tacita said, "I'm not through telling Mr. Picinisco about Rosamunda's merits, Mr. Hardcastle. I shall go to bed when we've finished our conversation."

Rosamunda couldn't understand why Jed seemed so angry when he looked down at her and said, "Suit yourself."

He was undoubtedly jealous, she decided, preening inwardly. He obviously couldn't hold a candle to her when it came to possessing sterling attributes of their respective breeds. She was certain that nobody would pay two hundred dollars for *him*. Rosamunda felt quite smug.

Picinisco's mouth closed with a snap. "One moment, Mr. Hardcastle," he said, stuffing his harmonica back into his pocket and standing up. "Before you retire, please allow me to offer you a sip of my very best cherry brandy. A small thank you for allowing me the pleasure of your fire and your company." He smiled at Tacita. "And you, too, Miss Grantham."

Tacita smiled graciously. "Thank you very much. A sip of cherry brandy sounds quite elegant."

Picinisco showed the brandy bottle to Jed and Tacita. The label was indeed elegant, and inscribed in a language Rosamunda couldn't identify. She was quite good at recognizing the way English words used those letters they called the alphabet. He then poured the liquor into two small, heavy glasses and handed one to Jed and one to Tacita.

"Thanks, Mr. Picklewillow. Don't mind if I do." Jed took the proffered shot glass, drained it, and smacked his lips. "That's pretty good stuff."

Tacita, giving Jed a superior look, sipped her brandy demurely. "Mmmm. It's delicious, Mr. Picinisco. Where is it from?"

Smiling benignly and pouring Jed another glassful, Picinisco sighed and said, "From my own beloved homeland, Miss Grantham. From Sicilia." He splayed a beefy hand over his heart. "From Sicilia."

For the life of him, Jed couldn't understand why he found Tacita's recitation of the wonders of that animal so irritating. What did he care if she chose to waste her love on a frog-eyed terrier? It was nothing to him. He couldn't stand the woman anyway. The more attention she paid to the rat, the less she'd pay to him. And that's just the way he wanted it.

He couldn't, therefore, understand why it should gall him so that Tacita, the most beautiful female he'd ever encountered, should be so determined to lavish all of her affections on a dog.

Not, of course, that Jed himself wanted her affection. Far from it. After all, he was engaged to Miss Amalie Crunch, and he was not a man to break a promise, even one made for him by his parents. He couldn't, however, banish the niggling thought that Tacita's love for Rosamunda was a substitute somehow, that there must be something sad in her life if she had forsaken the human race for a five-pound, mean-tempered canine.

Oh, Jed could understand how a body could love an animal. Hell, when he was a boy, he'd loved his hound, Biscuit, more than anything else in the world. But he'd been a boy. A boy and his dog. Why, that was a combination even poets couldn't resist.

Jed could even feature love between a girl and her dog. But Tacita was a full-grown woman. And a well-grown one, too. She should have a fellow in her life, not a dog.

It aggravated the hell out of him that he was beginning to feel kind of sorry for her. Of course, there was that fellow she was going to marry in San Francisco, but she sure didn't talk about him the way she talked about that dog of hers. Contemplating her marriage annoyed him, too, for some reason, so he ceased thinking about it.

But two hundred dollars? She must consider him a pure fool if she expected him to believe anybody would pay two hundred dollars for a dog—especially for a dog that was smaller than a damned rabbit and had a temper nastier than a polecat.

*    *    *

Jed's sympathetic mood didn't last past Tacita's first piercing shriek the following morning. His head pounding and his eyes gummy, he groped for his gun before he realized it was Tacita screeching and not an Indian raid.

Staggering to his feet, he almost fell over again when blackness threatened to send him reeling. Good God, what was the matter with him? Slowly, the words Tacita screamed began to penetrate the befuddled mire of his brain.

"She's gone! Oh, Mr. Hardcastle, she's gone! That fiend kidnapped her!"

Through what seemed like a forest of gunk, Jed's thought processes began to stagger to attention. He peered around the clearing. The wagon was gone. Obviously, therefore, the wagon's driver must be gone, too.

"Don't just stand there! *Do* something!"

Jed rubbed his aching head. Then he rubbed his sandpapery eyes. "Who's gone?" he asked in a foggy croak.

"Rosamunda! Oh, Rosamunda's *gone*! She's *gone*!"

Jed almost fell over backward when Tacita flung herself against his chest and began sobbing onto his long johns top. His gun slipped out of his numb fingers and his arms closed around her and he tried to make sense of everything.

"Oh, Mr. Hardcastle" came, muffled, from the region of his breast bone. "Oh, she's gone! Oh, I'll die if Rosamunda's gone! I'll just die!"

"Don't worry, Miss Grantham," he found himself saying. "I'll find her."

He wanted to kick himself as soon as the words left his lips. It was because he was confused, is all. If his head weren't full of glue and Tacita Grantham's soft sweet body weren't pressed against him, he'd never have uttered such a tremendously foolish declaration.

She pushed herself away from him, and he felt bereft. The sensation was so astonishing, he could do no more than blink down at her. She still clutched his arms.

"You will?"

Her eyes were wide blue pools, swimming with tears. His heart gave an enormous lurch, and he discovered an urge to vanquish tyrants on her behalf. Anything. He'd do anything to make those tears go away.

So he swallowed and said, "Yeah. I'll get Rosie back for you."

He was almost glad for his idiocy when she threw herself against him again and cried, "Oh, thank you, Mr. Hardcastle! Thank you, thank you, *thank* you!"

# *Chapter Four*

Rosamunda was fit to be tied. In fact, she was tied.

She hadn't gone meekly into this dark sack, however. Even though she was still scared to death, the knowledge that she had acquitted herself well in battle made her proud. The perfidious Mr. Cesare would bear scars from this day's dark deed, no matter what happened to her. She might not have slipped through his fingers as she'd tried to do, but she'd at least bitten several of them while making the attempt.

She couldn't deny being worried, however. And she missed Mistress like mad. She was pretty sure she'd be able to find her again once she escaped, though. Her nose was as keen as anything. She wasn't a championship Yorkshire terrier for nothing, after all.

There was no denying, however, that it would

be a daunting journey. This awful territory was very much bigger than she, after all, and it all looked alike. And it was dry as a bone, too, albeit much less tasty. Nevertheless, Rosamunda would not fail. She'd achieve her goal or die trying.

She frowned into the darkness of her burlap prison, her last thought striking her as having been rather unfortunate. She resolved to banish all thoughts of death from her mind as unprofitable. She *would* find Mistress, and that was that.

Of course, first she had to chew through this wretched burlap sack, which she'd been working on ever since the black-hearted, villainous, swindling, cheating, kidnapping Mr. Cesare had succeeded in stuffing her into it. Then she'd have to gnaw through the rope binding her front and back feet together. It would be difficult, but she'd not shrink from her duty. It made her furious to know that she'd actually liked this awful man after dinner last night.

If she'd known what a scoundrel he was then, she'd have eaten *two* of his wretched steaks!

Damn! Jedediah Hardcastle had never allowed himself to be taken unawares like this before. It nettled him to know that this Pisklefletcher fellow had gotten the better of him. Drugged brandy! And he hadn't suspected a thing. Jed could hardly stand it.

The incident was especially galling because he already knew Miss Tacita Grantham didn't esteem Jed's frontiersmanship as she ought. He'd meant to teach her some respect by showing her how masterful a guide he was. Allowing that black-hearted villain to drug him wasn't the way to go about it, and Jed was really annoyed with himself. Masterful, ha!

Not content with allowing himself to be duped by that blasted Gypsy, he'd managed to disgrace himself further in Tacita's eyes by allowing her dog to get napped.

"I don't suppose you can just buy yourself another one of them—those blankety-blank terriers, can you?" he asked as he tried to grope for reason through the drug-induced fog enveloping his brain.

Tacita gaped at him for only a second or two before she burst into tears again. Jed watched in dismay and wished he knew what to do. He couldn't very well put his arms around her again, even though he wished he could. Such behavior would be terribly unprofessional. Not to mention dangerous in ways he didn't care to contemplate.

"Buy *another* dog? How can you even ask me such a question, you horrible beast? Rosamunda is the only thing on earth I have to call my own! The only thing on earth I love! She's the only living creature on earth who loves me!"

Jed stuck his finger in his ear and wiggled it in order to get his hearing to work right. Her piercing screech had almost knocked him out again. But surely he'd misunderstood. Had she just said what he thought she'd said?

"Your dog, ma'am?" he asked at last. "Your *dog* is the only thing you have that you love? That loves you?"

Her face buried in her hands, Tacita sobbed, "Yes! Yes! Oh, *please* find her for me, Mr. Hardcastle. *Please* find her for me!" She looked up, her drowned blue eyes accusing. "You *said* you would!"

Stunned, Jed stared at her for a full minute, her words piercing his thick hide, staggering through the drugged-brandy fog in his brain, and lodging in his heart. That hairy rat was the only thing on earth this beautiful, albeit shrill, woman had to love? The only thing on earth that loved her? He shook his head, bothered more than he cared to admit by the sadness her grief-stricken statement evoked within him.

"I'll find her for you, ma'am," he said at last. "I said I will, and I will." He sucked in a deep breath and added, "Anybody who'd go back on his word to a lady isn't one as I'd call a man." There. That Texas-sized declaration made him feel a little better.

She shook her head and moaned. The dart of sadness that had lodged in Jed's heart twisted, bringing forth another flood of compassion.

Awkwardly, he walked over to her and considered patting her on the back. He was afraid he'd knock her down if he did, though, so he just stood there watching her cry and feeling terrible for a minute, wishing he could think of some other comfort-giving gesture that wasn't so perilous. If only she wasn't so small. Jed was pretty sure he couldn't have knocked Miss Amalie Crunch down with a two-by-four.

What he wanted to do was hold her in his arms and kiss her until she forgot about that damned rat of hers. Jed frowned. Shoot, that brandy must have been spiked with something really potent.

He finally gave up and left Tacita to wring her hands and cry as he set about packing up the mules and saddling the horses. The morning breeze cooled the tearstain blot on his chest and wouldn't let him forget that Tacita had lately been weeping there. His chest still felt oddly empty.

The feeling of emptiness annoyed him. There was no reason he, Jedediah Hardcastle, frontier guide extraordinaire, tough outdoorsman, and staunch Texas male, should harbor anything other than a feeling of disinterested protectiveness toward Tacita Grantham. She was, after all, employing him to do a job. He should, therefore, guide and guard her to her destination; nothing more. Tender feelings were not part of his job description.

The tenderness he was feeling now, however, went way beyond disinterestedness. He didn't like it. He was betrothed to Amalie back home in Busted Flush. Well, he was as good as betrothed to her, at any rate. Granted, he hadn't quite managed to make himself pop the question to her yet. Still, both his family and hers anticipated the match. And so did Amalie, for that matter. She was the right woman for him, too; Jed knew it. She'd been born and bred in these parts; she knew what was what.

And if Amalie had a laugh like a horse and tended to fall over her own size-thirteen feet a little too often for Jed's taste, why, what did it matter? Amalie was a good girl. She was a good *Texas* girl, what's more, and knew what to expect from life out here in the West and what to give back to it, as well. Besides, she could cook up a storm, and Jed knew very well that while beauty faded, a good cook went on forever.

Miss Amalie Crunch wasn't any city girl, as

beautiful and delicate as a hothouse flower and apt to go into hysterics if she lost her dog. If she lost the only thing in the world that loved her.

Aggravated with himself for remembering Tacita's mournful words, Jed commanded his thoughts to "Hush up!"

Tacita uttered a miserable, "I-I'm s-s-sorry, Mr. Hardcastle. I'm just so worried about poor Rosamunda."

Jed whipped his head around to find Tacita trying valiantly to fold her bedroll blanket while tears rolled down her faultless porcelain cheeks, a little splotchy now with emotion and misery. The blasted arrow in his heart gave another vicious twist and he regretted that she should have taken his words, spoken to himself and for himself, as criticism of her and her grief.

"I didn't mean you, ma'am," he muttered, feeling worse than he'd felt in a long time. Only this time the feeling had nothing to do with Cesare Picinisco's cherry brandy.

They drank cold coffee and ate hard biscuits for breakfast, a meal Jed refused to set forth without, no matter how much of a hurry Tacita was in. He knew they couldn't travel on an empty stomach without courting disaster, even if she didn't. Besides, he needed strong coffee, even cold, to etch through the sludge that buzzard's brandy had made of his brain.

There was something about Tacita's unhappiness that nibbled at the edges of Jed's conscience like a rabid mouse. He felt he'd failed her, and it was an uncomfortable feeling for the generally invincible Jedediah Hardcastle to deal with.

He didn't even harbor black thoughts in his

heart when he put that stupid sidesaddle back on the mare. He hoped she wasn't too stiff to ride, and his heart clenched again.

He hated that. It worried him and it didn't seem right. He had no business harboring tender feelings for anything. He was a rugged frontiersman, for heaven's sake. Moreover, the longer he considered what he was about to do— head out across the vast plains after a damn-fool terrier—his tender feelings started to slide downhill.

He had managed to fall into a towering grump by the time they finally set out to follow Picinisco's tracks. The blackguard was aiming vaguely northwest, so at least he wasn't taking them very far out of their way. It was a small consolation, and it didn't assuage Jed's crabby mood.

"Oh, can't we go any faster?"

Even though he'd come to anticipate the question, which Tacita asked every fifty yards or so, Jed cast a beseeching glance at the heavens and wondered what she expected him to do. Fly? No matter how much she valued that blasted rat of hers—the only thing on earth she loved; he wasn't sure he could stand it—he wasn't about to abandon three pack mules and all her earthly belongings in the middle of the desert to hare out after it.

"No, Miss Grantham," he ground out for at least the hundredth time, "we can't go any faster. We've got two horses and three pack mules with us."

He heard her miserable sniffle and felt like a monster for being short-tempered. At least this time she didn't ask him why not. Her restraint didn't make him feel much better. Even though he was still angry at her for making him care, he couldn't refrain from offering her a measure of comfort. "We'll catch him, though. Don't worry."

"But we're traveling so *slowly*."

"He's going even slower than we are, in that wagon of his. It's heavy, 'cause it's full of pots and pans and such. And food." The thought of that food made Jed scowl. Damned bastard, to lure them with beefsteak and brandy and then steal Tacita's dog. It made him mad.

"But what if he hurts her before we can catch them?"

"He won't hurt her."

"How can you know that? Why, she might be in mortal agony even as we dawdle along after them!"

Jed knew Tacita was upset. And he felt bad about it, too. Actually, he felt more than bad. He felt responsible and had a tremendous urge to take all her burdens—every one, including that dog of hers—onto his shoulders, which were so much broader than hers. Nevertheless, he couldn't keep the sarcasm from his voice when he muttered, "For the good Lord's sake, woman, why do you expect he took her, anyway? He ain't—he isn't going to hurt her!"

"But, how can you *know* that?" Her voice had gone squeaky, and Jed winced.

"Bless it, if you hadn't bragged about how much money your blasted dog cost, the idea of taking her would never even have occurred to him!"

Only the clopping of their animals' hooves met his angry declaration. It was almost silence, and it almost made him happy. Actually, he felt both triumphant that he'd finally gotten through to her and more than a little bit mean. She was already upset. He didn't suppose he ought to rub her nose in her foolishness.

At last she said, "Do you really think he took her for the money?"

"Well, why the h-h-harmony else would he have taken her? He sure doesn't need the meat."

"*Meat?*"

Her shriek pierced his still-aching head and made tiny, barbed shards of pain stab the inside of his skull and cling, twisting. Damn, he wished she'd stop screeching at him.

Hunching over, he grumbled, "Pickskinicker wouldn't be the first man on the plains to have to eat a dog, damn—dadblast it. But he won't eat your pet, ma'am."

"Oh, my God. Oh, my God!"

She was in a full-fledged fit of agonized grief again. Jed cursed himself for bringing up meat, and said, "He's got a whole wagon full of food, Miss Grantham. He's not going to eat a two-bite dog when he's got an icebox full of beefsteaks and barrels full of vegetables just sitting there."

He heard her blow her nose and hoped she'd quit worrying now. How she could cry when her head must be at least as sore as his, Jed couldn't fathom. In his experience, which admittedly wasn't large—he was, after all, a man, and men didn't cry—tears only made headaches worse.

He decided not to tell her that some Indians considered dog meat a delicacy. Even if the abominable Gypsy were unlucky enough to meet up with a band of renegades, Jed expected the Indians would prefer beefsteak to inch-high mop-bucket terriers.

"Oh, I hope you're right, Mr. Hardcastle."

Her voice sounded incredibly sad and very thick, and Jed's big heart gave another immense throb. He frowned, wondering if drugged brandy could cause heart palpitations. Surely he couldn't care this much about Tacita Grantham and her pork-butt terrier.

Could he?

His frown deepened, and he told himself not to be stupid. Of course, he couldn't. He had a girl in Texas, one who was as right as rain for him. He just felt sorry for this addlepated female, was all.

"Of course, I'm right." He was surprised by how gentle he sounded.

"Thank you" caressed his ear, feather light and delicate. Jed's heart executed another painful athletic maneuver, and he hoped to God she wouldn't talk any more. Her misery was too hard on him in his hung-over condition.

To ensure her silence, he said, "Better pull that scarf over your mouth and nose, Miss Grantham. It's dry out here, and the dust will get to you if you don't."

He was relieved when she followed his advice. She must have been truly upset, though, because she didn't even argue with him about it first.

Jed and Tacita had been trailing Picinisco for about two hours when they made their way out of a stand of straggly scrub oaks and caught sight of the Gypsy's wagon in the distance.

Yanking her scarf down from her face, Tacita cried, "Oh, Mr. Hardcastle, look!" and Jed cursed himself for not having had the foresight to tell her to keep her mouth shut when they

77

eventually spotted their quarry so as not to alert him to their presence. Not, of course, that an admonition would have done much good, he thought glumly.

"It's probably not a good idea to announce that we're after him, ma'am." His voice was as dry as the dust under their horses' hooves. "I don't think he can get away, but he might try something if he knows we're here."

"Oh. Oh, dear, I'm sorry."

Well, this was really something. Searching his memory, Jed couldn't recall another instance before today when Miss Grantham had apologized for doing something stupid. Today, however, she'd apologized twice, and the morning wasn't even over yet.

Feeling almost gracious, he said, "It's all right, ma'am. You aren't used to the way things are around here. Just, please don't screech anymore. He might hear you."

"I didn't screech, Mr. Hardcastle. I never screech, and don't appreciate your saying I do. I think you're being mean."

Jed shut his eyes and prayed for strength. Then he decided to hell with it, turned in his saddle, and said roughly, "Stay here. Don't even think about moving."

He handed Tacita the mules' lead ropes, nudged poor Charlie in the ribs, and tore out after the wagon.

"You want that blasted dog back, I'll get the blasted dog back," he growled into Charlie's mane, leaning over the horse's neck as the huge animal stretched out into a ground-swallowing gallop.

\* \* \*

78

Rosamunda had just poked her nose out of the hole she'd gnawed in her burlap sack when she heard Mr. Cesare mutter something foul in a language she assumed to be his native tongue. She didn't understand the words, but coupled as they were with the sound of a horse's hooves pounding across the ground behind them and getting closer, she understood their import.

She cocked her ears and listened hard. Although she couldn't be sure, her ears were nearly as sharp as her nose and she thought she recognized the sound as coming from that beastly Jedediah Hardcastle's beastly brute of a horse. Eyeing the thin rope tied around her front paws, she bent to her task and began to chew quickly. Her mouth was dry and her jaws ached, but she knew where her duty lay and she aimed to do it.

Tacita grabbed the lead ropes Jed thrust at her and her mouth fell open. She saw him nudge his heels into Charlie's shiny hide, and forgot the question she'd been about to hurl at him. Holding the ropes in one hand, she gripped her leaping tree with the other, her heart flying to her throat.

"Oh, my land! He's going after him! At last!"

Her nerves jumped and skipping like water beads on a hot griddle as she watched. She saw the ghastly Mr. Picinisco lean over to see who was following him. Even from this distance and despite the beard covering most of his face, she recognized his look of astonishment. Then she saw the wagon begin to pick up speed, churning up a huge cloud of dust, and she feared he might outrun Jed.

"No!" she cried, and kicked her own placid mare's flanks. "No, you wretched man! I won't let you escape!"

The horse grunted and twisted its neck to stare at her. The animal looked aggrieved, and Tacita felt guilty. And frustrated.

"I'm sorry," she muttered.

Still, she needed to get to her beloved Rosamunda, and quickly. She guessed it was silly of her to think she could gallop to the rescue. She couldn't let go of the mules' ropes, after all, unless she wanted to risk all their supplies, and she knew Jed would never forgive her if she did that. Besides, without supplies they might die.

This living-in-the-wilderness-with-the-noble-savages nonsense wasn't at all like Rousseau and some of those other novelist fellows made it out to be. Tacita decided she really ought to write to a few of the ones who were still alive and set them straight on the matter.

"Oh, bother. I guess I'll just have to follow at a fast walk."

So she did, her nerves rampaging like irate buffalo with each jogging step her mare took. The mules looked as irritated as the horse about having to step up their pace. Tacita hoped they'd all forgive her.

The wagon gave a tremendous jerk, and Rosamunda had to scramble for balance, no mean feat with her back legs still tied together. Still, as her center of gravity was fairly low and as she was a naturally graceful animal—she was, after all, a champion—she soon regained her equilibrium. Her teeth also regained the rope binding her ankles together. She chewed doggedly.

She heard Mr. Cesare hollering at his mules, trying to speed them up. Then she heard Jed's rumbling bass voice, carrying over the thunder of crunching wagon wheels and pounding hooves. She realized how worried she'd been when she felt a rush of pleasure at the sound of his voice.

"Pull up, Pickywicker, you damned bastard!"

Although she deplored Jed's language, Rosamunda discovered she couldn't fault his sentiments. Her little heart soared when she realized Mistress must have sent him out to rescue her. She was sure he'd never have bothered on his own.

"Never!" her captor hollered back.

She renewed her efforts on the rope.

Suddenly, the wagon came to a shuddering halt and Rosamunda found herself upended. She tumbled back into her rough burlap prison. Then she felt herself and her bag being lifted into the air, and began yipping in terror and fury. The sack swayed back and forth in the air, and she had to scramble to keep upright.

"I've got the animal!" she heard the villain holler, and gave another shrill yip. She didn't appreciate being called an animal. "Don't do anything stupid and you can have her back again."

"I'm not the stupid one here, Picklepoop." Jed sounded really, really angry. Rosamunda almost didn't blame him, even if he was a beast and a brute. "You hand that blasted dog over, or you'll be breathing lead."

"Ha!" cried Mr. Cesare, in what Rosamunda considered an entirely too-confident manner, considering his foe evidently had a gun aimed at him. "You shoot me, you shoot this dog, too!"

Rosamunda felt herself being jerked forward again. This was really abominably uncomfortable. She didn't appreciate being manhandled any more than she liked being called "the animal." Her yips turned into ferocious growls.

"Put that sack down right now, Picklefellow!"

"Never! Miss Grantham's precious dog is in it, and if you shoot me, you'll shoot it!" He laughed, sounding mildly hysterical.

Rosamunda was feeling moderately hysterical herself. She didn't like being used as a shield. Not one little bit. Particularly since she wasn't sure Jed would honor Mistress's sentiments in this matter and spare her.

Sure enough, Jed said, "Ha! If you think I care about that hairy rat, Peckernapple, you've got another think coming. I'd as soon shoot it as you, so just hand it over."

That was enough for Rosamunda. Furious at both of these ugly, horrible men, she scrambled for the hole she'd gnawed in the sack earlier in the day and wriggled herself free.

"Hey!"

She didn't have time to savor Mr. Cesare's startled cry, or the look of astonishment on his face, before she launched herself at his throat.

# *Chapter Five*

Tacita gave Rosamunda some water and some of the meat she'd demanded from Mr. Cesare—which, in Rosamunda's opinion, was the very least she should have demanded from him. For her money, the scoundrel deserved a noose at least, even if there wasn't a tree handy to hang him from.

Jedediah Hardcastle confiscated all of the Gypsy's weapons, much as he'd done the night before, only this time, he threatened to keep them if he didn't promise not to bother them again. Rosamunda thought it a foolish promise to extract. After all, the fellow obviously possessed not a shred of honor in his soul. Did Jed really expect him to respect such a promise? After that Jed bandaged the fiend's wounds, which Rosamunda considered completely superfluous. Then he gave the kidnapper a good hot lecture.

She figured Mr. Cesare deserved a lot more than a lecture, and would have glared at the both of them if she'd not been so busy slurping up water and eating good beef. The ghastly man had snatched her before she'd even eaten her breakfast!

Jed unloaded Mr. Cesare's guns, promising to shoot him dead if he ever dared show his brisket—whatever that was—on the trail again. Rosamunda figured that would be entirely too late to perform such a service to humanity. She was not in a position to object, however, as she didn't possess opposable thumbs and, therefore, couldn't shoot him herself now, which is what he deserved.

Then they remounted, Tacita settled Rosamunda in her arms, and they continued their journey.

"Oh, my poor precious darling. My sweet, wonderful, beautiful girl. Are you all right, darling?"

No. She wasn't all right. Rosamunda snuggled more closely to Tacita and buried her head in her armpit. Tacita's adoring caresses helped, but Rosamunda was still more shaken up than she liked to admit.

"Rosie'll be all right," Jed said, sounding a little impatient.

Rosamunda jerked her head out of its sanctuary and scowled at his buckskinned back. She'd like to skin him. As if he knew anything about the tribulations she'd just endured! And if he didn't stop calling her Rosie, she was going to chew his arm off.

"Her name is Rosamunda, Mr. Hardcastle. And she's been through a terrible ordeal," Tacita said, her voice throbbing with passion. Rosamunda kissed her for it. "How can you be so callous?"

Even from the sanctuary of Tacita's arms, Rosamunda could hear Jed sigh.

"I didn't mean to sound callous, Miss Grantham." Now he sounded merely resigned. Rosamunda didn't consider it much of an improvement.

They were headed back to the river. When she lifted her weary head, Rosamunda could see it, threading along through the endless brown prairie like a long, shimmering muddy-gray snake. Scrub brush and some stubby trees grew near the water, but even they only looked to be a darker shade of brown against the relentless tan of the plains. This place was unfriendly and dreadful, and Rosamunda couldn't wait until they were out of it. She whined dejectedly.

"I don't know why you let that awful man go, Mr. Hardcastle."

Rosamunda didn't, either. She considered Jed's lenience to a dreadful villain nigh unto wicked. To show Mistress how much she appreciated her, she snuggled into her armpit again. Tacita cooed and petted her some more.

"What do you think I should have done with him?" Now Jed sounded beleaguered. Rosamunda sniffed and didn't feel the least bit sorry for him.

"Well, I don't know. But he's a criminal and a kidnapper, and you should have—have arrested him or something."

"Ma'am, there's no place around here to take somebody I've arrested—especially somebody with a wagon and a whole load of beef he claims he has to get to Fort Sumner—"

"Humph. I just bet he was lying about that, too."

"And, anyway, I'm not a lawman. I can't just go around arresting people for no reason."

"No *reason*? Why, that awful man stole my dog!"

"Well, I can't go around arresting people for stealing dogs, then."

"And why not?"

Jed turned in his saddle and glanced back at Rosamunda and Tacita. His face wore an expression of long-suffering patience. Rosamunda wanted to bite him.

"Hell—hallelujah, ma'am, I figure the man's been punished enough. That dog of yours blasted near chewed his ears off. Not to mention his fingers. And she gnawed a hole in his neck, too."

And quite proud of it she was, too. After curling her lip at Jed to show him what she thought of his reasoning, Rosamunda preened.

Tacita humphed once more. "It's no more than he deserved."

Jed's eyes narrowed slightly. Then he said, "Maybe," and turned around again.

"I don't know why you went to the bother of bandaging his neck, though. After what he did, he didn't deserve such consideration."

"Aw, hell—hello, ma'am, what he did was wrong, but I don't think he's a really bad man. I've met plenty of hardened bandits in my day, and I can tell you that they're a different breed altogether. This Picklenisckle fellow just looks like an opportunist to me. I figure he's suffered enough already." He gave Rosamunda another look, which she returned darkly.

"Well, *I* think you should have either left him to take care of his own wounds or arrested him. Humph. It would serve him right if he'd bled to death."

Rosamunda heartily approved of Tacita's bloodthirsty sentiments and licked her chin to let her know it.

"Ma'am, the only way to get a lawbreaker to justice out here is to shoot him and sling him over a horse. Believe me, if you'd ever smelled a corpse after it's been hangin' around in the sun for a couple of days, you'd wish you hadn't."

Rosamunda swallowed and wrinkled her nose. So did Tacita. Neither of them said anything.

"Even if I tied him up and managed to get him and his wagon and mule to a sheriff somewhere, I don't reckon the law in these parts would care much about a fellow who stole a dog. They got bigger things to worry about. I mean, it ain't— isn't like he took a horse or our food or something important."

Rosamunda heard Tacita gasp and felt her begin to quiver with indignation. She didn't blame her. She was pretty indignant herself.

"Well, I never!" Tacita huffed, and subsided into offended silence. Rosamunda joined her, mostly because she wanted all of Mistress's attention for herself and didn't care to have her wasting any more of it on Jedediah Hardcastle, who didn't deserve it.

Jed was happy when they finally got back to the Rio Peñasco and the shelter of the trees growing along its banks. There weren't very many of them, but they provided a modicum of shade. It was getting hotter than a sun-bathing horny toad as the day progressed. He sighed in satisfaction when the horses and mules trudged into the trees and he felt the temperature drop several degrees. Because he knew one must take care of his animals in this hard land before he did anything else, he decided to let them refresh themselves at the river for a few minutes.

In order to assuage Tacita who, he knew, was still angry at him for a variety of reasons, he said in his best, most conciliatory voice, "Would you like to dismount for a little while, ma'am? I know you want to make sure your dog is all right. I can water the horses and give 'em a handful of grain." In a fit of unfamiliar expansiveness, he added, "Reckon we could eat something, too."

He knew his afterthought had been a mistake when she said, "Well, I'm glad you think about your charges occasionally at least."

The frost in her voice dropped the surrounding temperature several additional degrees. Because he didn't want any more unpleasantness to accompany him on this very, very long journey than was absolutely necessary, he decided to respond moderately. And briefly.

"Yes, ma'am."

His control seemed to have a soothing effect on Tacita. She still sounded stiff, but wasn't nearly as snippy when she said, "Very well." As though the words choked her, she also said, "Thank you."

Pleased to have crossed the hurdle of her displeasure almost easily for once, Jed guessed he'd be wise to continue in a similar manner. "Would you like me to help you down off your horse, ma'am?" He eyed Rosamunda with misgiving, but decided he could weather another bite or two if the animal took it into its obviously addled and extremely small brain to attack him again.

"Thank you very much, Mr. Hardcastle."

Jed expected Queen Victoria herself couldn't have sounded as gracious and condescending as Tacita Grantham did just then. In a way, her attitude tickled him. Showed she had spirit, by damn, even if she was a city woman betrothed to a sissy Englishman. He also didn't mind putting his hands around her waist again.

So he did, lifting her down as if she was as light as a goosedown pillow. Which, all things considered, she pretty much was.

She looked at him with those big blue eyes of hers and honored him with another little "Thank you" that sounded less regal and rather more breathy, and Jed wondered if she found him even a fraction as appealing as he found her.

No. Of course she didn't. Jed told himself not to be silly. That was foolish thinking, and unproductive. Besides, he was an almost-engaged man and she was an almost-engaged woman, and it was ungenteel of him to harbor such thoughts. Not that he'd ever been particularly genteel, but still . . .

"My pleasure, ma'am." Especially since the rat didn't bite him this time.

"Oh, my, it's much cooler in here, isn't it?" Tacita looked adorably flushed as she fanned herself with her hand. The mutt in her arms was eyeing him malevolently, but Jed decided to ignore it.

"Yes, ma'am." He waited until she'd sat herself down on a big thrusting tree root and settled the animal on her lap. Then he handed her some jerky and a hard biscuit.

"Thank you very much," she said in a much softer tone of voice. Maybe she was getting over her huff. He sure hoped so.

"I shall brush my darling's hair after luncheon, too, since she got all ruffled while being such a good, brave puppy."

"Yes, ma'am," Jed said. He did so without even grimacing, and was proud of himself.

Her brilliant smile almost knocked him dead. Maybe she wasn't so hard to take after all. Maybe all he had to do was keep in mind that she was a woman uneducated in the ways of the wild, one who had no experience in the world and who honestly believed that dog of hers was the only thing on earth that loved her. He sure as the dickens hoped he could remember that the next time things got rough and she began screeching at him.

Hope died abruptly when he heard a gruff, growly voice say, "Now what have we here? Why, I do believe I just found what I was looking for."

And, out of the trees on the other side of the river, a lone gunman on a big black horse emerged. The gun in his hand looked as big as a cannon and was aimed directly at Jed's most prized vital organ.

Tacita leapt to her feet and uttered a stifled scream.

Rosamunda yipped.

Jed let his chin drop to his chest and muttered, "Aw, hell."

# Chapter Six

Tacita's mouth had gone dry and her heartbeat sped up as soon as she felt Jed's hands on her waist. When he lifted her from her saddle as if she weighed nothing at all, she had to hold her breath so she wouldn't swoon.

He was *so* big. And when he wasn't making her angry, he made her feel incredibly safe. Of course, she'd never tell him so. He already had an inflated head. Nevertheless, she was impressed that he'd managed to effect the rescue of Rosamunda with so relatively little difficulty.

Tacita wasn't sure what she'd do without Rosamunda. Or even if she *could* do without her. She certainly didn't fancy finding out. But Jed hadn't failed her. He truly was adept at this frontiersmanship nonsense.

Her heart was still fluttering in her bosom when the gunman appeared. Then it stopped fluttering instantly and sank like a stone. Her recoil was involuntary and immediate, and she squeezed Rosamunda so hard, the poor love squealed.

"Oh, I'm sorry, precious."

Tacita didn't dare take her attention away from the armed intruder to comfort her darling, who'd already been through more than any dog should be expected to endure today. She only stroked her distractedly as she cast a frightened glance at Jed. He stood next to her, and she found him shaking his head as if he couldn't believe this latest obstacle the fates had thrown onto the path of their journey. She didn't blame him. If this is what the Wild West was like, Tacita didn't want any part of it. Idiotic place. She couldn't wait until she could set foot in a city again.

"What the hell do you want?" Jed growled.

Tacita, worried lest this latest villain take exception to his rough question, reached out with her foot and kicked him. He barked out an annoyed "Ow!" and glared down at her. She glared back. Rosamunda growled.

"Never you mind what the hell I want, damn it," the intruder said. Tacita deplored the foul language both of these men employed.

"Who in the name of thunder are you?"

"My handle's Farley Boskins, not that it's any of your business."

"Reckon it is my business, Boskins. You just made it my business."

"Be quiet, Mr. Hardcastle!" Tacita hissed. "The man's got a gun!"

Jed looked at her for a second as though he'd just discovered she had two heads. He grumbled, "I can see that, Miss Grantham."

"Well, then, for heaven's sake, don't annoy him!"

Jed rolled his eyes and snorted.

Their captor chuckled. "It don't matter none, ma'am. None of his lip ain't gonna bother me none nohow."

It took her a moment to sift through the words the man had uttered, rearrange them into various grammatical orders, and pick one that made sense. When she'd done that, she determined that he was telling her that he didn't mind if Jed snarled at him. Small comfort. Still, it was better than watching him shoot Jedediah Hardcastle and seeing Jed fall dead at her feet. When the dismal possibility entered her head, she shuddered, wishing her mind's eye's vision wasn't so acute.

Her horror increased when the stranger dismounted and walked over to her, grinning evilly. She scooted away from him until she was flat up against the trunk of a large oak tree.

"Wh-what are you doing?" She was annoyed that her voice squeaked so badly. She wanted to sound brave and Wild Westish and knew she'd failed utterly.

"You got somethin' I want, lady."

Her maidenhood! The virginity she'd been saving—God alone knew why. Tacita already knew she was too boring to attract the attention of any man who'd want to marry her. Except, perhaps, for that sissy Englishman waiting for her in San Francisco.

She shut her eyes and prayed fiercely that she wouldn't faint. Or throw up. Good Lord, she'd read about people like this awful man. Oh, she knew Jed would save her if he could, but she feared he was no match for a loaded gun. She tried to swallow, but her mouth had gone too dry.

"P-please, sir, if you don't hurt me, I'll give you money."

"Yeah?" Boskins sneered. "I'll take your money, lady, but first I'll take what I come after."

Tacita started to tremble uncontrollably.

Well, this was just too much for one Yorkshire terrier to take with equanimity. How much hardship was she expected to endure in a single day, anyway? Rosamunda pulled her head out of Tacita's armpit, eyed the menacing man who was now reaching for Mistress's throat, and decided she'd been through enough already today.

So she bit him on the thumb. It was the thumb resting on the hammer of his gun, which he dropped immediately even as he let out a pained howl. As Jed Hardcastle sprang for the gun, Rosamunda, snarling like a fury, worked her way up from there.

"You sure you're all right, ma'am?"

Tacita had screamed in terror when she feared that awful man was going to hurt her beloved Rosamunda. Shivers still rattled her and Jed was pretty sure she was crying again. Shoot, he'd never known a female to cry so much. She had her head buried in Rosamunda's ruffled fur and she sat in the dirt, having slithered into a heap at the foot of the oak tree after her legs gave out on her.

The gunman had fled, sans gun, leaving behind a string of vile curses and more than a few drops of blood. Jed had raced after him as far as he could, but he didn't dare leave Tacita alone for long enough to track the black-hearted bastard down and shoot him dead. Now he stood over her, still furious and feeling helpless.

What he wanted to do was kneel beside her, gather her to his broad chest, and comfort her. The urge surprised him, as he wasn't used to harboring soft emotions in his Texas-sized breast. He kept feeling them for Tacita, though, and he was dreadfully confused by them.

"Y-yes," she whimpered. "I th-th-think so."

Her wretchedness pierced Jed to the bone. Although he didn't quite dare touch her, he did squat down beside her.

"You sure, ma'am? Maybe we'd better rest here for a little while longer."

She looked up at him, her blue eyes swimming in tears, and he had to fist his hands in order to keep them from grabbing her.

"Th-thank you, Mr. Hardcastle. I was s-s-so frightened. I thought he was going to hurt Rosamunda."

Rosamunda gave a little whine and licked her mistress's hand. It seemed to give her comfort, and for the first time, Jed approved of the little rat. He even went so far as to say, "Rosie's a real scrapper, Miss Grantham. Even though she's small, she has the heart of a lion." There. That ought to earn him a bit of credit, anyway.

"Oh, yes!" Tacita cried, ignoring his use of her dog's diminutive name, and appreciative of his sentiments. "Yes, she does."

Although Rosamunda wanted to bite Jed for calling her Rosie again, she supposed it would do. She didn't relish being likened to a cat, even one as large and ferocious as a lion.

She did not, however, appreciate the look in Jedediah Hardcastle's eyes as he watched Mistress. It was an affectionate look if she'd ever seen one. She was surprised to find it in such an unlikely place, disapproved of it, and what's more, she didn't trust it. Not one tiny bit. That expression boded ill for Rosamunda's future health and happiness, and it worried her.

"Good day to you, sir!"

Farley Boskins was mad as a cougar with a coyote hanging onto its tail when he met up with a strange-looking Gypsy fellow and his flamboyant wagon about five miles away from the scene of his humiliation. He couldn't believe he'd been bested by a five-pound dog. A fancy, five-pound dog. Boskins could hardly stand it.

He was certainly in no mood to exchange pleasantries with the voluble drummer who'd called out the friendly greeting. Reaching for the gun no longer resting on his hip and coming away with an empty hand, he uttered a blistering curse. After consigning all canines to the fires of hell, he managed to grab the rifle from his saddle scabbard and aim it at the bearded gentleman with the white bandage wrapped around his neck and the piece of sticking plaster on his ear.

"Get 'em up," he growled, pleased that his voice at least still sounded ferocious.

Cesare Cacciatore Picinisco, whose day had been ruined already, stared down the barrel of that gun and knew this was it for him; he couldn't take any more. He burst into tears.

Raising his hands in the air, he blubbered, "Shoot me, sir. Shoot me. What good is life to me?"

Boskins was unused to his victims going meekly to their dooms. He didn't like it. He preferred to savor their terror before he dispatched them. It gave him a thrill. This fellow's attitude was no fun at all.

It did, however, give him pause. If he were to follow long-established practice, he'd oblige this strange man, shoot him dead, and then have to root through his wagon to see what, if anything, was worth taking.

Since, however, the fellow's weepy plea had caused him to think before he acted for once in his misspent career, Boskins realized his hand hurt where that damned dog had bitten it. He also realized that if he refrained from shooting this man a little while longer, he might not have to do so much hard work himself with his sore hand. Although it was slow in coming, a decision to spare this victim emerged within Boskins's brain.

Frowning heavily, he said, "I ain't gonna shoot you."

Picinisco bowed his head. "Blast."

Boskins decided the man was crazy, which sent his thoughts tumbling down yet another path. He understood many Indians considered crazy people somehow blessed by God. He wondered if they were right. Farley Boskins didn't have much truck with God on a day-to-day basis himself, preferring to do business with representatives of a lower realm. All at once, however, he decided it might be a good idea not to bait God today. Although it grieved him, he guessed he'd just better let this nitwit live after he robbed him.

Grumpy about having his plans thwarted for a second time in the same day, he snarled, "What the hell you got in that wagon?"

"N-nothing, sir. Nothing at all."

Boskins cocked his rifle and showed his teeth in a feral grin. People hated his grin; he knew it because they told him so. His teeth were broken from fights and discolored from chewing tobacco, and he enjoyed displaying them to people he didn't like. He didn't like most people. He especially didn't like this colorful drummer.

"Like hell. What you got in that wagon?" He drew his horse up so that he was level with the fellow. "Or do I got to look for myself?"

His words were full of meaning, the import of which Picinisco caught in an instant. And, while he was possessed of a small felonious streak of his own, he was not a fool. He understood.

He also discovered, much to his dismay, that while initially he would have welcomed death as a release from life's miseries, after having been granted a reprieve he wasn't so sure anymore. That was the trouble with having time to think. His face bleached of color and he stammered, "I'll look, sir. I'll look. No need for you to bother yourself."

"Damn right," Boskins said, pleased to know he hadn't lost his touch, even if he couldn't kill the bastard.

Picinisco scrambled into the back of his wagon, leaving the bandit chuckling evilly in the hot afternoon sunshine. As far as his own feelings about the matter went, he was both terrified and feeling mighty sorry for himself. If that miserable son of a sow, Jed Hardcastle, hadn't taken his ammunition, he'd at least have been able to defend himself when this latest menace appeared. The fact that Jed had reacted so strongly to his borrowing a mere *dog* was particularly irritating.

As far as Cesare Picinisco was concerned, no dog should be worth two hundred dollars. And if it was and that woman could afford one of them, why on earth couldn't she just go out and purchase another one?

If Picinisco had two hundred dollars, he sure as the devil wouldn't waste it on a dog. A dog, even an expensive one, was merely a dog, after all. He'd never understand some people.

His wounded throat, ear, and fingers took that opportunity to throb in unison, and he acknowledged that perhaps Miss Grantham's demented pet was a trifle different from most of the dogs he'd known in his life. Most dogs were man's best friend. That abominable freak of nature most assuredly was not.

Speaking of freaks of nature, his heart was beating a terrified tattoo against his ribs when he thrust a wooden chest out onto the wagon seat and dared face his newest adversary. Since he'd been denied the pleasure of a quick, merciful death, the thought of being killed by the fiend no longer held much appeal. Unfortunately, he didn't trust the man to spare him.

Wasn't that the way things always worked? Now that he'd lost interest in dying, he wanted to live. The day thus far has been so bad, however, he wasn't sure he would. Glumly, he decided he probably wouldn't now that he wanted to. He wondered if he could file a complaint somewhere.

"Here, sir. Look, it's all yours." He lifted the chest's lid and dipped his hands into it. When he withdrew them, they fairly dripped jewelry. Gold and silver, rubies and emeralds, all were souvenirs from the last several large towns he'd passed through. Long ago, Picinisco had decided not to depend entirely on the fruits of his honest business for his livelihood, as the fruits of this dishonest one paid greater dividends.

His adversary smirked. "Now where in hell'd you get all them things?"

Picinisco shrugged. "I have my ways, sir."

"Damn! You didn't get them things honest."

"Being a drummer on the prairie does not afford the best of livings, my dear sir. I occasionally have to supplement my income."

"Yeah," growled his foe. "Well, I aim to supplement my ink-come today, too. Gimme them jewels. And I ain't nobody's dear."

Picinisco wasn't surprised to hear it. With a heavy sigh, he transferred his hard-burgled goods into a burlap sack. He did not realize it was the same one he'd used for Rosamunda's prison, however, and they leaked out again. He discovered his mistake when the ominous click of Boskins's rifle being cocked smote his ears once more. He looked down and saw with horror what he'd done.

"Oh, my good sir! I am so sorry! This isn't the sack I meant to use."

"Yeah. Right. One more mistake like that and you're dead."

Quivering like aspic, Picinisco stammered, "Really sir, there's no need for violence. I shall

**100**

give you anything I have. Anything."

"I know." Another oily chuckle issued from his foe.

Eventually, Boskins's confidence proved to be well-founded. Not only did he ride away with almost all of Cesare Picinisco's disposable cash and jewelry, but with almost everything else of any real value in his wagon. Some of the meat the drummer had been carrying to Fort Sumner remained, but not much. His bandit possessed a prodigious appetite.

And, as if that wasn't enough, before the foul man left Picinisco to contemplate the wreckage of his life, he beat him up with his good hand.

Picinisco watched through swollen eyelids as the evil gunman trotted away across the desert, headed in the direction of El Paso. His ugly laugh sounded a discordant accompaniment to the ringing in Picinisco's battered ears.

"Thith ithn't fair," he murmured thickly to the uncaring desert and his mule, who didn't care either. "Thith jutht ithn't fair."

Then he made a vow. As he was a coward by nature, there was no way he'd go after the evil gunman. Jedediah Hardcastle and Tacita Grantham were another matter. They weren't exactly evil, but they had left him alone and defenseless on this wild, terrible frontier. He resented them for it. They also had that overpriced animal in their custody and were basically too nice to kill anybody.

A coward he might be. But he was also sly and sneaky and well versed in the art of burglary. He knew he could remove that wretched two-hundred-dollar dog from its present owners.

And he would.

\*    \*    \*

"You were certainly not exaggerating about the evils to be found in the territory, Mr. Hardcastle. It's a simply dreadful place."

Jed decided not to push them on today's leg of their journey. He figured neither Tacita nor her pet were up to being pushed. Nor was he, for that matter. He was mortally glad she'd stopped shaking and crying, however. He was also determined to be kind to her, no matter how unflattering she got.

Therefore, when she disparaged the home of his birth, he only remarked mildly, "It's not always so bad, Miss Grantham. We met up with a couple of hard cases today, but most of the people who live here are honest, even if they aren't real civilized."

He saw her shudder and the same urge to comfort her that he'd fought earlier in the day trampled through him. Damn. These soft feelings of his were getting to be a real pain in the butt.

She drew the brush through Rosamunda's silky fur again. She'd been brushing that stupid rat of hers off and on all day long. "I hope you're right. This journey has been terrible so far."

"Don't reckon I'd argue with you on that score, ma'am."

He couldn't figure it out, either. Picinisco he'd already written off to a quirk of a devilish fate. But that other fellow, that Farley Boskins, didn't sit so easily in Jed's memory. Sipping his after-dinner coffee from his battered tin mug, he reviewed the encounter in his mind. No matter how often he did so, it remained an enigma.

After he'd thought for a while he asked, "I

don't suppose you ever met up with that last fellow before today, have you, ma'am? Farley Boskins?"

Her head jerked up and she stared at him as if he'd asked her if she wanted to feed poison to her dog. "That ghastly gunman? I should say not!"

Unfazed by her vehemence, Jed persisted. "You sure? You ain't—haven't ever met up with him in Galveston? San Antone? He never worked for your pa or anything?"

"Good gracious, no! Why, I imagine I'd remember such a despicable character as Farley Boskins, Mr. Hardcastle."

"Yeah," Jed agreed, discouraged. "Reckon you would."

"I should say so. Besides, my father would never hire such a man. He only employed men of the highest character."

"Glad to hear it." Jed took another sip of his coffee and studied the fire. It had burned down low now and the branches he'd piled up earlier glowed red hot in the dark night. Trees circled the clearing he'd chosen and gave it a comfy, secure feel. The trees smelled good, too, their piney fragrance mingling with wood smoke and the leftover aromas of their cooking. Jed had opened a can of Picinisco's peaches and roasted another couple of Picinisco's steaks, and they'd dined well this evening. Through the branches overhanging his head, Jed could make out about a million stars, bright in the night sky.

The campsite was right pretty, actually, although Jed seldom allowed himself to dwell on anything as unproductive as nature's beauty, particularly when he had mysteries to resolve.

"What about your uncle, ma'am? Do you suppose he might have hired Boskins?"

"No! Why on earth are you even asking such questions? That man today was a—a thug. Neither my father nor my uncle would have anything to do with him."

Jed eyed her in silence for some minutes, pondering. He savored the silence as conducive to heavy thinking.

Tacita Grantham, however, as he'd noticed before, didn't take much to long stretches of quiet. She got twitchy and broke into them as if they made her uncomfortable.

Sure enough, she did it again this evening before he'd finished sorting through his thoughts.

"Why on earth do you seem to be insisting that my father or my uncle employed that creature, Mr. Hardcastle?"

"I'm not insisting on anything, ma'am."

She seemed to be puffing up, and Jed knew she was getting mad. He'd noticed before that when she got huffy she took a bunch of little breaths and kind of expanded. If he wasn't otherwise occupied he might have taken time to think it was a cute characteristic. He guessed she wanted an explanation and sighed heavily, unused to having to explain everything; most people took him on faith—and for good reason.

"You see, ma'am, Boskins appeared to be after something in particular."

She shuddered and hugged Rosamunda. "I should say he was."

Jed rolled his eyes and tried again. "No. What I mean is, he seemed to be after something specific. You remember what he said when he first saw us?"

"No, thank heavens."

"Well, he said something like, 'I've found what I was looking for.'"

"Did he?"

"Yes."

Tacita pursed her lips, an activity that made ungentlemanly ideas caper into Jed's head like a troupe of prancing dandies. He shook them off, annoyed, and stared into the fire again.

There was obviously something wrong with him. He'd never been plagued by irreverent thoughts about his employers before. Granted, he'd never had an employer who looked like Miss Tacita Grantham; still, he was sure he must have a tic or something.

He wished he were home; his mama would give him one of her evil-tasting tonics and he'd be right as rain come morning. Of course, she'd also begin to pester him about setting a date with Amalie Crunch. A shiver rattled him, and he hunched over his coffee cup. He jerked to attention when Tacita's voice penetrated his black musings.

"I *said*," she uttered, evidently not for the first time, "what do you suppose that means? What on earth is the matter with you, Mr. Hardcastle? You seem to be lost in a fog this evening. I do wish you'd pay attention."

Jed glanced across the fire. He saw both Tacita and her mean-tempered pet frowning at him. What a surprise. He sighed again and reminded himself that he was supposed to be feeling sorry for them.

"Beg pardon, ma'am. I'm not sure what it means, but it sounded to me as though he knew who he was after."

Crinkling her brow in a way that made Jed look away and groan, Tacita murmured, "How strange."

"Yeah," crept from his throat. He gave himself a mental punch in the jaw and told himself to keep his mind out of his drawers and on the matter at hand. "He looked to be reaching for your neck, too."

"I thought that was just because he was going to strangle me, or—" She stopped speaking abruptly and turned a deep red. Even across the coals of their campfire in the dark of night, Jed could see her blush, and realized what she must be thinking.

Wonderful. Jed's indelicate thoughts had apparently managed to transcend space and silence and lodge themselves in her head, too. Only she obviously wasn't thinking of them fondly, as he was. She was thinking of them in terms of rape and savagery. He wasn't surprised; the woman was a complete innocent.

Thrusting all of those irrelevant notions aside yet once more, Jed said stolidly, "No, I don't think he had lovin' on his mind, ma'am. I got the feeling he wanted something you was—were wearing or something."

Tacita lifted a delicate hand to her throat. "Something I'm wearing? How can that be? I'm not wearing anything."

Oh, Lordy. If only that were so. Jed administered another mental punch upside his head, this one more violent than the last. "I don't suppose you showed anybody any jewelry or anything in Powder Gulch, did you?"

"Of course not! I'm not a fool, Mr. Hardcastle, no matter what you think of me."

He refused to get mad. He was going to help her whether she wanted him to or not. "Hmm," he mused mildly. "Were you wearing anything that somebody might want?"

"Certainly not."

"Didn't ask the sheriff or the hotel clerk to hold any jewelry for you?"

"Of course—oh."

Sitting up straighter, his attention caught, Jed didn't even harbor a lustful thought for a second. "You mean you did?"

Tacita pursed her lips again, and his second's reprieve ended. He tried not to think about it.

"Well, actually, I guess I sort of might have."

She looked troubled, her big eyes going round. He couldn't make out their color tonight; they only seemed big and dark and sort of glowy by the light of the gleaming coals, kind of like Luggett Lake on a moonlit night after he'd been fishing all day and was feeling tired and relaxed and happy. Or the way his mama's chocolate cake looked after she'd iced it with that dark, dark frosting he loved so well. Her eyes were shiny like that. Only Tacita looked sweeter than any cake.

He had to swallow before he could force out the words, "What do you mean, 'you sort of might have,' Miss Grantham?"

"Well, Rosamunda has a pretty collar with some sapphires on it. I bought it for her because she's such a perfect little lady, and I wanted her to have something as beautiful and precious as she is."

She rendered her little speech into Rosamunda's beautiful, precious fur, and Jed's insides rebelled. Damn it, it wasn't fair that a vicious little rat should be the object of this splendid female's undivided affection. A *man* should be the recipient of her love, not some fat-nosed terror who was about as big as a minute and nastier than a nest of riled yellow jackets. Of course, Jed wasn't thrilled by the thought of Tacita in the arms of another man, either, but he elected not to contemplate why.

Teeth clenched, he asked, "So, who'd you show this collar to anyway?"

"Well, I guess I asked the hotel clerk where I could keep it first."

First? Oh, Lordy.

"And then, when he couldn't help me, I guess I asked the nice gentleman at the telegraph office."

Great. Jed shook his head slowly.

"And then he suggested I ask at the newspaper office."

"The newspaper office," Jed repeated, wanting to make sure he'd heard her correctly.

"Yes. Because the telegraph man said the newspaper man hated everybody else in town and probably had a safe." She frowned. "And he did, but he hated me, too, and wouldn't let me use it."

"I see."

"So then, I went to the sheriff, and he locked it in his desk drawer." She looked brightly at Jed. "But that's all, really. That's not many people, and I can't imagine any of them following us in order to get a dog's collar."

"Or hiring anybody to get it for them?" Jed thought about asking her why she hadn't just posted their itinerary in the *Powder Gulch Gazette* in order to make it easier for anybody who wanted to follow them, but decided he'd better not.

"Oh, I don't think any of those men would hire anybody." Her gaze searched his face, and she looked the tiniest bit guilty. "I—I didn't think of that, you see."

"Yeah, I see," said Jed, who did. "Well, isn't this just dandy?"

Tacita frowned at him. Jed wasn't surprised.

# *Chapter Seven*

"Do you really think that awful man found out about Rosamunda's sapphire collar because of something I did in Powder Gulch, Mr. Hardcastle?"

Tacita had been troubled by the possibility all night long. Even though the prior day's activities had worn her to a nub, her sleep had been restless. When she wasn't having frightening nightmares featuring horrid men carrying off her precious darling, she'd been dreaming about Jed Hardcastle's hands on her waist. And other places. This morning, she couldn't have told anybody which dreams had caused her more aggravation.

"I don't know, Miss Grantham."

She looked up from folding her bedroll, hoping he'd expand on his answer. At the moment, he was preparing breakfast, a task he went about

110

as he went about everything: deliberately, unrushed, but with no wasted motions. He didn't seem inclined to grant her unspoken hope, and Tacita felt a spurt of irritation.

"Oh, I do wish you wouldn't be so taciturn, Mr. Hardcastle!"

He did look up at that. He even spoke.

"Beg pardon?"

Feeling a little silly—after all, he hadn't actually scolded her for telling so many people about her wealth—she murmured, "I said, I wish you weren't so taciturn."

His eyebrows lowered into a quizzical "V" and Tacita realized he didn't know what she was talking about.

Feeling slightly superior, she said, "Taciturn. Close-mouthed. It's from the Latin, *tacitus*. It means silent. It's the same root my name came from. Tacita. *Tacitus*. Taciturn."

"*Your* name?" Jed grinned. "Silent?"

Tacita frowned.

Rosamunda growled.

Jed's grin got bigger. "Your folks didn't know you very well, did they?"

Tacita had opened her mouth to sling a hot retort at him when the truth of his words struck her, right in the heart. She swallowed and looked down at her bedroll again.

"No," she said shortly. "They did not." And she went on about her business.

Puzzled, Jed felt his grin fade and die. Although he didn't believe what he was about to say, he said it anyway. "It might be that Boskins wasn't really after us, ma'am. He might have just happened on our camp."

111

She only nodded, and Jed wondered what on earth he'd said to hurt her feelings. That her parents didn't know her? That had been meant as a joke, for heaven's sake. He squinted hard, trying to decipher her expression. Rosamunda lifted her lip in a snarl, but Tacita didn't say a word. Nor did she look at him.

Finally, he shrugged and went back to boiling the water for coffee.

"What do you mean you didn't get it?" Luther Adams Williamson stared at Farley Boskins, horrified.

"It ain't my fault," Boskins said sulkily. "You didn't tell me that dog of hers was crazy."

"The dog?" Luther was sure he hadn't heard correctly. "The dog's smaller than your average house cat, Boskins. What did the dog have to do with it?"

Boskins shuffled his feet and looked uncomfortable. "Well, its bein' small don't matter; the thing's crazy."

He had sought out Luther in the El Paso honky-tonk that Luther had usurped for his headquarters. It was the only place in town where he could be assured of a steady supply of calming liquids. Even though he'd consumed a number of such refreshing beverages already today, Boskins's news precipitated the need for another. Luther lifted his beer mug with a shaky hand and downed its contents.

"So the dog bit you and you failed in your mission." He could hardly believe it. On the other hand, why shouldn't he? Everything else had gone wrong in his life lately. Why not this?

Oh, if only Tarkington hadn't had the bad

manners to die! Tarkington Daugherty Grantham, Luther's brother-in-law, had more or less kept Luther afloat for years. And then he himself had sunk, along with Luther's sister Madeline. Luther hadn't had a lick of luck since. A little more than a year since the death of his sister and brother-in-law, he'd managed to get himself so deeply in debt, he was actually trying to steal from his own niece. The truth made him feel guilty, which made him need another drink, so he took one.

"It did more than just bite me," Boskins said sulkily.

Luther frowned up at him. "Well, you're not getting your bonus until you get the Eye. Agrawal's patience is wearing thin, and so is mine."

Boskins plopped himself down in a chair, making Luther's frown deepen. "Now you looky here, Williamson, I think I deserve that there bonus. You didn't tell me that animal was loco. I'd'a charged more if I'd'a known. Why, I might coulda got hydrophobia." He looked sorely aggrieved, which didn't add to his overall appeal.

Recognizing a vulnerable spot in a man who scared him, Luther prodded it. He even gave an experimental derogatory snort before he said, "That dog isn't big enough to spit on. If that's all that kept you from doing your job, I expect a whole lot of people would like to know about it." He also gave an experimental sneer. "Wouldn't want any of them to put you up against a bigger animal. For instance, I reckon a cow'd about do you in, wouldn't it?"

Boskins leapt up from his chair again, knocking it over backward and startling a small squeal from Luther, who feared he'd gone too far. He closed his eyes tightly and started to shake.

"Don't you tell nobody, you hear?"

Luther's eyes popped open when Boskins's whine smote his ears. He stared up at the vicious criminal, whom Luther knew had slain any number of enemies, and almost gasped to encounter the pleading expression on his face. Because he was still too scared to form coherent words, he gulped and didn't answer.

"Please, Mr. Williamson?"

The whine was more pronounced this time, and Luther came to the astonishing conclusion that Boskins feared for his reputation as a stalwart and violent hired assassin. The knowledge emboldened him. Although he was still too frightened to produce another sneer, he did manage a cocky head toss.

"Well, I might be persuaded to keep it to myself if you go back and finish the job."

Boskins sat down and proceeded to look surly once more. "Hell, Mr. Williamson, there ain't no way I can get to 'em now before they reach Alamogordo and board that there train."

Contemplating his beer, Luther made some quick calculations in his head and moaned mentally when he realized Boskins was right. He decided he'd better not risk aggravating his companion by pointing out that it was his own failure that had caused the problem. He didn't quite trust Boskins not to shoot him should he get angry enough.

He said, "Hmmm." Then he said, "Mmmm."

Boskins kept his own counsel.

When a silky voice floated over them like an exotic fabric, Boskins looked up, intrigued. Luther uttered a little scream and spilled his beer.

"I see you are consulting with your minion, Mr. Williamson."

Although Luther had squeezed his eyes shut and begun to pray, sure his end had come, after several seconds passed and he was still breathing, he dared to open them again. He peeked up. Then he shut his eyes once more.

"M-M-Mr. Agrawal," he stammered, sounding more like a strangled chipmunk than a man.

Agrawal bowed, an elegant gesture oddly out of place in the beery honky-tonk. "As you see, my dear sir."

He nodded to a large fellow standing directly in back of him who was garbed in the Indian fashion. The man pulled out a chair, and Agrawal eyed it with distaste. His employee then pulled out a handkerchief and flicked it over the chair. After inspecting it once more, Agrawal sat.

"So, do you have the Eye, my good Mr. Williamson?" He spared a smile for Boskins, who stared at him, his mouth hanging open.

Luther knew he had to gather his wits together and come up with a plausible answer. He had to be smooth. He had to be urbane and dignified. He had to show this Agrawal fellow that he was every bit as sophisticated as he was. Besides, if he fumbled, he was a dead man.

Unfortunately, that last thought was the one he carried with him when he screeched, "No!" He swallowed convulsively several times. "No! This idiot couldn't get it. Said that dog attacked him and ran him off."

Boskins's mouth shut with a clack of teeth. "Well, it did."

Agrawal tutted several times. "What shall we

do, then, my dear friend? I know I needn't remind you of the promise you made to me." He smiled a smile that was slick enough to set Luther's heart to rattling like a hailstorm in his chest. "Not to mention the quite large sum of money I've already paid you to secure the Eye."

"I know. I know," Luther muttered. He wished he hadn't spilled his beer. He needed a drink desperately. Since Boskins seemed to be ignoring his own glass, Luther grabbed it and downed the contents.

"Hey!"

Wiping his mouth with the back of his hand—something he'd never done before in his life—Luther muttered, "Sorry. Thought it was mine."

Agrawal put his hands together in a gesture Luther had most often seen used in prayer. He wasn't entirely sure, but he feared Agrawal wasn't praying.

"So, you have failed to secure the Eye again. Whatever shall we do about this problem, my dear Mr. Williamson?"

"I'll get it," Luther said quickly. "I was just thinking of ways to get it. I'll get it. Honest. I'll think of a way."

Silence—and a tiny smile that made his blood run cold—greeted Luther's stuttering promises. After fully long enough for Luther to get lightheaded from hyperventilating, Agrawal said, "Ah." Then he said, "Hmmm." Then he said nothing at all for at least three minutes.

To Luther, those minutes might have been hours. He discovered himself sinking lower and lower in his chair, until Agrawal's hired man plucked him by the collar and tugged him upright. He screamed again.

Shaking his head, his face a mask of spurious sympathy, Agrawal said, "Tut, tut, my dear friend. You really should do something about your nerves."

"I am," Luther declared, grabbing his empty beer mug.

"That's not what I meant," Agrawal said gently.

"I'll get the Eye," Luther choked out. "I'll get it. Honest."

Agrawal shook his head. Luther nearly cried.

"Oh, I will! Honest. Just give me another little while, and I'll get it. I promise."

Agrawal's smile could have been used by an artist to depict pure evil, as far as Luther was concerned.

"Ah, my friend. Please do not believe that I do not trust you. Why, I know you would not attempt to—what is that quaint expression you Americans use? Weasel out? Yes, I believe that is the one. I know you would never attempt to weasel out of our little bargain."

Luther shook his head so hard his hat fell off and said, "No. No, never. I'd never do that!"

"Just so."

Luther sighed with relief.

"However . . ."

Luther's relief died.

". . . I believe that perhaps you are not equipped for this type of operation, my friend. No, indeed. Not by—what is it you Americans say?—not by a jugful?—yes, that is it. You are not equipped by a jugful, sir. I believe that I should step in and direct matters."

Luther stared at him, wondering what this new wrinkle meant.

"No, my friend, I fear you are not furnished with the necessary endowments for this sort of exploit at all." He turned to Boskins. "Is it possible to secure a private train to San Francisco in this town, my dear sir?"

Boskins pulled on his lower lip, frowned, and concentrated on Agrawal's question for a moment. The expression made him resemble a gargoyle Luther had found particularly repulsive the last time he was in Paris, and he looked away.

After a few seconds Boskins said, "I expect so, if'n you pay enough."

"Money, my friend, is no object. We have a holy artifact to return to its home."

"That so?" Boskins looked almost interested.

Agrawal smiled again, reminding Luther of cobras and cougars and other sneaky, deadly things.

He croaked out, "What about me?"

Agrawal's glittery gaze seemed to bore into him. He got so nervous, he forgot about Agrawal's man standing behind him and he tried to rise from his chair, only to encounter a large, beefy hand pressing down on his shoulder.

"You will come with me, Mr. Williamson." Agrawal nodded, never taking his gaze from Luther. "Yes, indeed. I believe it would be best for you to come with me."

This time, Luther did faint.

Jed, Tacita, and Rosamunda resumed their journey early in the morning, traveling alongside the river once more. This path was much more pleasant than jostling across the prairie had been, although Rosamunda still considered the territory a certain kind of hell. Thank goodness for rabbit fur.

"You know, Rosamunda, darling, I'm beginning to like Mr. Hardcastle, after a fashion. He's actually rather sweet underneath all that smelly buckskin and rough frontier nonsense."

Rosamunda stared at her mistress, confounded. She was, in fact, too shocked even to snarl when Jed gave Tacita a warm smile over his shoulder.

Oh, no! Rosamunda huddled down in her rabbit fur, stunned. This was terrible.

As a pup, she'd been warned about human beings. She'd been told they were fickle creatures, the lot of them. Her mother had explained to her how inexplicable was the behavior of humans. She'd also been cautioned that they often adopted strange allegiances, allegiances that were baffling to more sensible creatures, like Yorkshire terriers.

Why, even her mother, the most magnificent female in the history of the breed, had been forced to endure the attentions of a inferior human male when her own mistress had married. He'd *claimed* to be interested in Yorkshire terriers in general and Rosamunda's beloved mother in particular, but he'd only said so to steal his way into Rosamunda's mother's mistress's foolish affections.

Beasts. They were all beasts. Rosamunda was so upset, she was almost unable to eat her dinner that evening. Almost, but not quite.

Thank the good Lord and Jed Hardcastle, Tacita thought, nothing further untoward threatened them after Farley Boskins beat his ugly retreat into the trees. They were making good time and would surely reach San Francisco when Tacita needed to be there. Having finished their supper, they now rested by the fire.

"Your dog all right, ma'am?"

Tacita had been contemplating the unfamiliar emotions she'd been subjected to for the past several days, and started when Jed's deep voice intruded on her musings. Looking up quickly, she found him watching her from across the campfire. Her heart immediately began performing the same alarming acrobatic exercises that had puzzled Tacita for those same several days.

"Yes, I believe she is." A little shyly, she added, "Thank you for asking."

Rosamunda growled. Tacita, wondering what the matter could be, petted her.

"She don't—doesn't seem to be as pig—that is, she don't seem to be as interested in her food as she usually is, is the reason I asked," Jed explained.

"Do you think not?"

"Just seemed to me, is all."

Tacita inspected her adored pet more closely. She didn't see anything amiss, thank heavens. Tacita wasn't sure what she'd do without Rosamunda. She couldn't even bear contemplating the possibility. "No. No, I do believe she's fine, thank you."

"Good. That's good."

She offered him a tentative smile, still stroking Rosamunda. Really, even if Jed was a bit rough around the edges, it was sweet of him to ask about Rosamunda. After all, Tacita knew he didn't much like the dog, although the reason for

his distaste eluded her. After all, Rosamunda
was a paragon among Yorkies. And who
wouldn't simply adore such a darling, cuddly
dog? She nuzzled Rosamunda's soft, albeit
somewhat dusty-smelling, fur.

Still, Jed had proved himself to be more than
competent when it came to this awful trip. Oh,
granted, she'd been annoyed with him at first.
Yet since that second day out when he'd rescued
Rosamunda from the dreadful Mr. Picinisco,
her feelings about him had undergone a change.
Tacita had even begun to wonder if perhaps it
had been she who was a trifle hard to please, and
not he.

Why, he'd not even made a fuss when she finally gave up on her sidesaddle, even though
he'd made it plain at the beginning of their trip
that he considered sidesaddles ridiculous.
Granted, his sigh had been somewhat heavy, but
at least he hadn't scolded or, worse, said "I told
you so." He'd merely changed the saddle on her
mare and lifted her into it.

It had taken her a while to get used to riding
astride, since it was such an indelicate way for
a lady to travel, but he hadn't fussed about that,
either. She appreciated his forbearance.

As the days wore on, moreover, Tacita was becoming ever more keenly aware of Jed's manly
graces. He was a truly handsome man, in a rugged, rough-hewn sort of way. Besides, he'd
started being nice to her ever since Rosamunda
attacked that second vicious criminal, and she
was grateful to him for it.

"Well, I'm glad she's all right," he said.

"Thank you," she said back, feeling oddly reserved. She chucked Rosamunda under her chin with her finger.

Rosamunda bit it.

"Ow!" Tacita looked down at her darling pet, shocked. She found Rosamunda wagging her adorable little tail, so she chalked up her lapse in manners to a flaw in her own behavior. "Oh, my poor dear darling. Did I pet you too hard?"

"Did she hurt you, ma'am?"

At Jed's growl, Tacita glanced up from her contemplation of Rosamunda to find him looking annoyed, but quite concerned. She thought that was sweet.

"Oh, no. I think she was just telling me to stroke her more gently."

Jed grunted. "Don't hold with dogs who bite the hand that feeds 'em myself."

Sweeping Rosamunda up into her arms, Tacita said, "Oh, my precious darling would never bite me." She kissed her head. "Would you, sweetheart?"

When she looked at Jed again, he was rolling his eyes, a gesture she resented.

"Well, she wouldn't," she told him stoutly.

"She just did."

With a small frown, Tacita said, "That wasn't really a bite." She kissed Rosamunda, who sighed contentedly. "Was it, sweetheart?"

Jed grunted again.

Tacita, who had always deplored grunting and eye-rolling as rude behavior confined to the lower social orders, began to revise her softened opinion of him. As she considered whether or not to take him to task, she gazed into the trees surrounding their camp and petted Rosamunda—very softly.

They'd climbed into the mountains by this time, and the scenery appealed to something deep in Tacita that had until now remained untouched. Stately pine trees towered over their heads, while shorter oaks and junipers fluffed out the rest of the landscape nicely. Patches of pretty wildflowers bloomed here and there, looking delicate and strangely out of place in the otherwise craggy countryside. The low-growing wildflowers shared space with the everlasting greasewood and scrub brush that seemed to be part and parcel of this wild land. The weather was dryer here than in Tacita's home along the Gulf of Mexico, although these mountains were much greener than the desert they'd left behind.

A fragrance both sharp and sweet surrounded them in the forest. It was very much to Tacita's liking. She'd never smelled anything quite like this pungent tang of balsam, pine tar, wildflower, and dusty soil. The combined effects of the scenery and the aroma and her guide's large presence gave her a tingly feeling of excitement.

This was an adventure. She was conquering the wilderness. Sort of. With the help of Jedediah Hardcastle, of course. In truth, except for the occasional unpleasantness brought about by thieving drummers, vicious outlaws, and the odd snake or thorny plant, she was enjoying herself immensely, even if she did miss warm baths. And gas lighting. And full meals with fresh vegetables. Well, and toilet facilities and clean underthings.

Still and all, she guessed this could be considered "roughing it." Or, perhaps, it more nearly resembled "camping out." Either way, the experience was a thrilling one. She knew people back home who did things like this for fun. Near as she could figure, Tacita had never done anything for fun in her life. She frowned, deciding it was probably best not to think about that aspect of her life, which was just one more boring thing about her.

"How about you, ma'am?" Jed asked, once again startling her out of her thoughts and into a tiny jump.

"How about me, what?"

"Are you feeling all right? Do you need to start a little later tomorrow morning in order to rest up or anything?"

Why, how sweet! Tacita took note of his complexion, which seemed to have darkened a bit. On the other hand, it was hard to tell by the light of the campfire. Besides, it would be totally out of character for this hard man to be blushing, wouldn't it?

"What about our schedule, Mr. Hardcastle? Aren't you worried about falling behind?"

"Not yet," he said, and Tacita was reminded once more about his terse conversational style.

Inhaling a deep, refreshing breath of clean mountain air, she said, "It's very kind of you to ask, Mr. Hardcastle."

Jed mumbled something incomprehensible.

"I beg your pardon?"

He looked up and cleared his throat. "I was just sayin' as to how my ma and pa always told me that if I was responsible for something, it was best to treat it as kind as I can."

Tacita was positive he blushed this time. She was perfectly astounded. And charmed. Yet again, Jed Hardcastle had managed to shoulder his large way into her good graces. Heaving a big sigh, she said, "That sounds like good advice."

"My ma and pa always gave us kids good advice, ma'am. I expect all parents try to do their best by their kids."

"Yes. Yes, I suppose they do." Tacita frowned down at Rosamunda, thinking about her own parents, remembering how they seldom gave her any advice at all. Or anything else of a verbal nature, for that matter. It was difficult to converse with people who weren't there.

Jed cleared his throat again and she lifted her gaze. As though he were making an effort to relax, he shifted himself and leaned back against the trunk of a huge pine. "What about you, ma'am? Your folks give you any tips to live by?"

Had they given her any tips? Tacita chewed her lower lip as she pondered. Casting her memory back to her childhood, she recalled several "don't touch that, darling's," one or two "not now, dear's," and about a million "we'll write to you as soon as we get there, sweetheart's." For some reason, thinking about her childhood always made her sad. For some other reason, she didn't want Jed Hardcastle to know it.

She said lightly, "Of course they did."

He nodded. "Reckon all folks do."

"Yes."

Jed picked up a twig and twirled it between the fingers of his right hand. He'd draped his left arm over his knees, which he'd drawn up when he sat. The casual pose suited him. His buckskin breeches drew taut against his knees, and his fringed shirt hugged his form in a manner Tacita had never seen until she'd met him. She enjoyed looking at him and wondered if it was depraved of her to do so. He seemed relaxed and comfortable and as if this outdoorsy atmosphere fit him to a T. In spite of her pleasure in it, Tacita knew that, deep down, it didn't fit her at all. She wished it did.

"So, you told me your folks had an import-export business. They travel a lot?"

His eyes looked dark and faintly mysterious from across the campfire. He shaved every morning before they set out for the day, but tonight a beard shadowed his cheeks, giving him a rugged, outdoorsmanlike appearance. Of course, he *was* a rugged outdoorsman. Tacita felt warm all of a sudden and couldn't account for the sensation by any logical means, as the evening air was quite chilly. It was she who cleared her throat this time.

"Er, yes. Yes, they did. They traveled a lot."

"Must have been an interesting life. You must have seen lots of places the rest of us only read about."

"Oh, I never went with them." She'd spoken before she'd thought about it, and wished she hadn't when she saw one of his eyebrows lift in inquiry.

"You mean they didn't take you with them?"

"Er, no."

"Never?"

"Well—well, I was too young. You know how much trouble youngsters can be."

He didn't answer for fully long enough for Tacita to feel like squirming. At last he said, "I kind of like bein' around kids myself."

"Oh, well, of course my parents *liked* being around me. They *loved* me, for heaven's sake." Her giggle came out high pitched. She shut her

126

mouth and cleared her throat again. "It's just that taking children along on long sea voyages can be"—The word that sprang to mind was tiresome, which sounded wrong. She struggled for a moment before she came up with—"dangerous."

His other brow lifted to join its brother, giving him the look of a man who was trying to understand something that made no sense. "Dangerous?"

"Yes. Why, anything could have happened to a little girl along on trips like that."

He cocked his head. "Yeah?"

"Yes."

"Wouldn't your folks have looked after you, ma'am?"

Now she was getting peeved. "Well, of course, they would have! It's just that my mother found looking after children on long voyages—tedious."

After a moment, Jed said, "Oh."

Tedious? Jed kept watching Tacita, searching for any sign that she considered her parents' attitude toward their little girl unusual. She looked serious, and he had a feeling she didn't. And that made his heart hurt something fierce.

His parents had hollered at him and his brothers and sisters to beat the band, but that was because they cared about them. They'd sure as hell never found them *tedious*; he'd take bets on it. Tedious? He could hardly stand it.

Hell, he'd also take bets that the child Tacita Grantham used to be was about the prettiest, sweetest little girl in the world, with all her fluffy blond hair and big blue eyes and the longing to please. Criminy, if Jed ever had a little girl like that, he'd never want to travel. Damned sure, if he did travel, she'd go with him because he'd never want to be separated from her. He'd sure as the devil never trust anybody else to look after her the way he would.

Because he was so angry at Tacita's parents, he said, "Well, ma'am, I reckon that if a body finds children tedious, he might ought to consider not havin' 'em in the first place."

The look she gave him was so eloquent of distress that Jed felt like a big cruel beast and mentally swatted his own rear end much as his mother used to do when he misbehaved as a boy. Even though he still resented her parents, he said, "Although maybe your folks had their reasons."

She sighed, a mournful sound that sliced through him like a knife. "I'm sure they did," she said softly.

The rat on her lap licked her wrist, and she smiled down at it tenderly. He guessed maybe that idiot animal had the right of it this time; at least it seemed to sympathize in a manner Tacita understood. Jed appreciated it for that.

He didn't suppose Tacita'd approve of the kind of comfort he wanted to offer. What he wanted to do was pluck her up off the ground, settle her on his lap, and hug her and pet her and kiss her until she forgot all about her stinking parents and that stupid animal. He'd probably crush her if he did—and she'd undoubtedly hate him for it, too. Not that she didn't hate him already, he mused glumly.

"What about you, Mr. Hardcastle?"

Her question startled him out of his brown

study of the twig twirling in his hand. "What about me what?"

She gave him a brittle smile. "It doesn't sound as though your parents considered you tedious."

His laugh caught him by surprise. "Tedious? I reckon they didn't have time, ma'am. There were so many of us, they didn't have time to catch their breath, much less get bored."

There was a small pause. "Perhaps you and your siblings were more interesting than I." Her voice was as tiny as the dog in her lap.

"Huh?"

What was she talking about, interesting? Kids were kids. They weren't interesting or not interesting. They were kids and, therefore, of intense concern to their parents.

She pinched her lips together in a gesture Jed recognized as one of disapproval. He guessed she didn't appreciate his "huhs." Too bad. He was seriously beginning to dislike Tacita Grantham's parents.

"Ma'am, I don't think I understand your question. I don't guess kids are supposed to be interesting. Parents love 'em and raise 'em and that's that, I reckon. There's eight of us," he added and grinned, remembering episodes from his past. "I'm the oldest, and when my ma and pa were too busy, I whupped my brothers and sisters for them."

Her eyes went big and round and reminded Jed of some of those fancy Christmas ornaments he'd seen once in a big-city mercantile store in Houston. "You struck your siblings?" She sounded horrified.

"Sure did."

129

"My goodness." It looked to Jed as though she disapproved.

"Nobody ever smacked you when you was—were a kid, ma'am?" Of course, she was so tiny, maybe they'd been afraid to.

"I tried very hard never to give them a reason to want to," she said.

Then she sniffed, Jed guessed to show her superiority. She didn't have to do that. He already knew she was superior.

"You mean you was—were good all the time?"

"I tried to be."

"Didn't that get awful dull, ma'am?"

"Being good? Heavens, no." She looked away, as if embarrassed. "Well, maybe just a little bit."

"Hmmm. Maybe you ought to have misbehaved some every now and then." Grinning, he added, "Your folks might have paid more attention to you."

Jed was sorry he'd said it when he saw the stricken expression on Tacita's face. Her rat growled at him, too, which he recognized as being its normal behavior when he'd insulted her mistress.

With a sigh, he said, "I didn't mean that, ma'am. It was a joke."

Her smile looked anemic. "Yes. Of course."

"Miss Amalie Crunch—back home in Busted Flush?—she's told me more than once that I ought to think before I talk. Reckon she's right."

Tacita looked up quickly. "Miss Amalie Crunch?"

"Yeah. Miss Amalie and me—well—er—I reckon we're promised. Sort of."

"Oh!"

Her pretty rosebud mouth fell open when her

startled exclamation tumbled out, and Jed felt himself get warm again. Shoot. He couldn't remember the last time he'd blushed, but this evening he seemed to be blushing every other second or so. "Kind of like you and that Mr. Jeeves fellow, I reckon," he muttered.

"Mr. Jeeves? Oh! You mean Mr. Reeve. Yes. Yes, I suppose so."

After fumbling around for a moment in the mush that used to be his brain, Jed asked, "So, you expect you and that Mr. Reeves fellow'd want kids someday, ma'am?"

Tacita got a faraway look on her face for a minute. Jed found it enchanting.

"Oh, my, yes, Mr. Hardcastle. I'd love to have children."

"Wouldn't find 'em tedious?" He grinned and was sorry to see her expression change into one of sadness again.

"Oh, no, Mr. Hardcastle. I'm sure I wouldn't find my children tedious. I suppose only people who are interesting themselves find boring people dull."

It took Jed a moment to process the meaning of Tacita's unusual statement. When he did, his heart took to throbbing again.

"Don't reckon most folks think their children are dull, ma'am. I'm pretty sure Miss Amalie wouldn't think her kids were dull."

Tacita sighed. "No, I don't suppose she would."

He read more into her short sentence than the words said. Tucking in his chin and looking at his twig, he mumbled, "I know, ma'am. Reckon Miss Amalie's not getting much of a bargain in me."

"Oh!" Tacita exclaimed, obviously startled by Jed's interpretation of her words. Then she said, "Oh, no, Mr. Hardcastle. I didn't mean that. Why, I believe Miss Crunch is getting a fine bargain!"

Jed was sure he hadn't heard her right. Because he didn't want to ask her and discover he was right and he hadn't, he didn't say anything. He only offered up another one of his grunts and hoped she'd take it right. They didn't speak again before they turned in for the night.

Rosamunda was distressed, and chalked up her short temper to having been kidnapped several days earlier.

Or maybe she was suffering what her mother used to call "Preparental jitters." She was, after all, being carted to San Francisco in order to meet the Yorkie of her dreams. If she'd known it was going to be such a tiring trip, she'd have put up more of a fuss to begin with.

Nevertheless, she knew it was out of character—and dreadfully wrong of her—to have sunk so low as to have bitten her mistress. Even if Tacita had galled her past endurance by making moony eyes at that wretch, Jedediah Hardcastle.

Yet Rosamunda knew, no matter how idiotic Tacita became over That Man, she should not—ever—bite her. Not that it had been a hard bite. Actually, it had been more of a love nibble. And, it must be noted, it *had* served its purpose.

Not only had her mistress begun paying Rosamunda the attention that was her due; she'd also paid less attention to their guide. For a while, at least.

Tacita's sensible behavior hadn't lasted very

long, though. Soon she'd begun talking to him again. This time, however, she hadn't ignored her duty to Rosamunda.

Still, Rosamunda didn't like the way her mistress looked at Jed. Even less did she like the way Jed looked at her mistress.

As she lay on her back in Tacita's lap and allowed Tacita to scratch her tummy, Rosamunda wished she could do something about what had all the earmarks of a burgeoning friendship between the two humans.

Unfortunately, she hadn't a clue as to what to do.

# Chapter Eight

Tacita hated this country. She hated it with a loathing that she'd not believed herself capable of until now.

No longer did a merry river caper beside them. No longer did trees tower overhead, graceful and sheltering her in their serene beauty. No longer did birdsong kiss her ears and leaves rustle like fairies' wings at her side. No; those halcyon days were over now.

During their travels through the mountains, Tacita had believed her only deprivations to be of a luxurious nature. She'd believed the only commodities she lacked as she undertook her trek were hot baths and soap. Well, and decent meals and proper toilet facilities.

She'd been dead wrong. She knew it now as they made their way to Alamogordo across the desert. Across the burning sands of the territory, the only signs of life were the remains of those who'd given their last to the elements. Buzzards circled overhead, waiting, Tacita was certain, for her own corpse to join those old bleached bones that mocked her from the ground. She feared they wouldn't have a long wait.

She was going to die before they got to Alamogordo; she knew it. She was *so* hot and *so* exhausted—so dreadfully weak and thirsty, so enervated—that she would have given herself up to tears if she hadn't perspired all the moisture out of her body long since.

Not that she'd show her tears to Jedediah Hardcastle anyway. What a fiendish brute he was to bring them through this wretched desert. She scowled at his horrible broad back and sniffed, surprised to discover even that much liquid still left in her.

She stank, too. She'd never smelled her own body odor before, and hated it. This wasn't fair.

"It won't be too much longer now, ma'am."

Jed's voice carried to her over the waves of shimmering, shivering heat, along with another gust of dust that seared her skin, grated her eyelids, and burned her nostrils. Actually, the burning sensation might have been due to the heat, although the dust was certainly not a product of Tacita's fevered imagination. Rosamunda sneezed in her fur-lined saddlebag, and Tacita managed to form the soothing words, "Poor baby." She had to unstick her tongue from the roof of her mouth in order to do so.

She hoped her darling would forgive her for dragging her into this furnace. Rosamunda didn't deserve it. Neither did she, Tacita thought miserably.

They'd ridden out of the mountains three evenings ago—and straight into the jaws of hell. The misery had been going on for two days now. Last night, when she'd almost frozen to death after the day had gasped its last and taken the insufferable heat with it, Jed even had the nerve to remind her that he'd told her how it would be. She hadn't spoken to him since. Not that she could have done so if she'd wanted to, since her mouth was too dry.

For the life of her, she didn't know why being angry at him made her so unhappy.

"It's a hard 'nother day or so, ma'am," he said now, breaking into her distress, "but then we'll be in Alamogordo and you can rest up."

Her sniff wouldn't come this time. Rosamunda managed a brief snarl, although it came out sounding more like a peep than one of her usual full-bodied growls. Tacita silently honored her for the attempt.

"You can take a nice long bath in the hotel and soak all this rotten desert dust off you in Alamogordo."

*That* was the reason; Tacita realized it when her eyes began to sting. First he'd led her into this ghastly oven, and now he was being kind to her—even when she was nasty to him. She wanted to hate him, and she couldn't.

What she felt like doing, and abominated herself for, was to ask him to hold her in his wonderful strong arms until she passed from this unendurable mortal coil and made her way to a higher, and she hoped cooler, dimension. One with water and soothing breezes. Tacita could hardly believe it of herself. Not content with being boring, she'd discovered herself to be a despicable weakling as well. The knowledge made her very sad.

"You'll feel better when we get out of the desert, ma'am."

If she'd had the strength, Tacita would have said something cutting to him for daring to utter such a patently clear observation aloud.

"It's real hard going. I don't reckon a lady like you's ever been through anything this bad," he added, confirming Tacita's belief that he was the world's most wonderful man. Except when he was being the world's least wonderful man. She was surprised her emotions could fluctuate so wildly in this heat; she was sure the rest of her wouldn't have been able to move at all if it weren't for the horse under her.

Unless, of course, she perspired so much that she slid clean out of the saddle and landed in the dirt. She wondered if Jed would pick her up and decided he would. Then she decided he wouldn't, because her temper had been so uncertain lately and he'd been the recipient of its abuse. Then she decided he'd pick her up anyway, because he was the most wonderful man in the world. Then he spoke again, annoying her because he'd interrupted the flow of her confusion.

"This is the worst of it, ma'am. After we get to Alamogordo, things won't be so bad."

She tried to say "Thank you," but couldn't get her mouth to work.

Jed had never been in such a pickle in his life. Until now he didn't know he could be such a damned fool. But he couldn't deny it any longer.

He had to acknowledge the truth. Face the music. Pay the piper.

His heart—an organ he'd never had reason to be concerned about before—was in peril.

Yup. He slumped lower in the saddle, his big body dripping sweat, his heart heavy, and felt grumpy as all get out. How on earth could he have allowed himself to get all mushy about a frilly little city woman?

Just because she was pretty and tiny, possessed a surprising gritty streak, and made him feel big and brave and strong was no reason to be so addlepated. Shoot. She also suffered from delusional thinking, and Jed wasn't pleased to know he was on the verge of falling in love with a lunatic.

Her *dog* was the only thing on earth that loved her? Sweet Lord, give him patience. Jed had never heard anything so crazy in all his born days.

Besides that, the whole thing was impossible.

Even if he were to do such a damn fool thing as court her, what would his mother and father say? What would the folks back home in Busted Flush think? What would Miss Amalie Crunch do? Poor Amalie. Everybody knew she was waiting for Jed, and Jed had never gone back on a promise in his life—and never would.

Not that they were promised, exactly. They weren't really and truly, officially, marked-down-in-a-book or shouted-all-over-town engaged. It's just his ma and pa and her ma and pa and everybody else in Busted Flush expected them to get hitched. He guessed he'd kind of promised his folks. A long time ago. A really, really long time ago.

Still, Jed Hardcastle wasn't a man to go back on his word; not for anything. His word was his honor, and his honor was his life. Well, his honor, and his job. And maybe the new ranch he'd just built in Busted Flush. And his family. Some of his horses, he guessed. Maybe a couple of his old buddies.

At any rate, Jed's honor was very important to him, and he didn't think anything as trivial as falling in love with a female ought to interfere with it. Falling in love. The very phrase gave him a stomachache.

He slid a glance over his shoulder and wished he hadn't done anything so stupid when he saw how miserable Tacita looked. His endangered heart gave a twinge that was almost as big as he was when he took in her face—brick red in the sweltering heat—and her stringy, drippy hair. Shoot, her frock, which she'd donned fresh—or as fresh as it could have been, after it had been hauled on a mule for several hundred miles— looked like she'd dunked it in water before she'd put it on.

She wasn't cut out for this; Jed knew it. And he wanted to rescue her, to pick her up in his big arms and carry her to safety. Which, after a fashion, was exactly what he was doing.

With a sigh, he decided none of his bitter musings mattered. His foolish heart didn't stand a chance. Even if he were to do something as outrageous as throw Miss Amalie Crunch over and ask Miss Tacita Grantham to become his bride, she'd never consent. Hell, if he were to do such an irrational thing, Miss Grantham would probably laugh at him. Or slap his face, if she could reach it.

What on earth would a tiny porcelain goddess like her want with a big lug like him? The thought might have made him laugh if it didn't make him want to cry.

Besides all that, she had that sissy Englishman waiting for her in San Francisco, and she was going to marry him. The thought made Jed's stomach ache even harder and his endangered heart throb.

"It's all right, darling. This will soon be over."

It wasn't all right, and Rosamunda resented her mistress for saying so false and foolish a thing.

Rosamunda was prostrate. When they'd finally stopped for the night, she'd been so debilitated she could barely hang her tongue out and pant. She was too done in to do more than sprawl on the rabbit fur in her saddlebag. She was too tired even to glare at Jed, much less snarl at him as he deserved.

Any human being who would put a world-class Yorkshire terrier through this torture was a cruel monster. Rosamunda felt very put upon.

"Oh, you poor, darling sweetheart. Poor, poor baby."

Rosamunda went limp when Tacita gently lifted her from the saddlebag. She let her head loll to emphasize the state of her unhappiness, and only swallowed some water when Tacita squeezed it into her mouth from her own handkerchief, which she'd wet with water from her flask.

"Oh, Mr. Hardcastle! Do you think she's permanently injured?"

There were tears in Tacita's eyes. Rosamunda

140

felt almost—but not quite—guilty for exaggerating her state of collapse. Truth to tell, she did feel fairly collapsible. She'd never endured such abominable heat, and didn't care to do so ever again.

Any human being who would put a Yorkie through this torture should be horsewhipped. Not that she blamed her mistress entirely. No. For the most part, she blamed Jed Hardcastle for her misery, and resented Tacita for asking him for assistance. She slitted one eye open and squinted at Jed.

He ignored her.

"I don't know, Miss Grantham. Want I should check her over for you?"

Horrified that her Mistress might actually hand her—*her, Rosamunda!*—over to such a brute, Rosamunda whimpered.

"Oh, this wretched territory!" Tacita cried, hugging Rosamunda to her bosom. Rosamunda sighed, glad someone knew who was important around here.

"It's mighty rugged, all right."

Rosamunda opened one eye wider in order to view Jed's countenance, but discovered herself in the dark, since her head rested on the cushiony softness of Tacita's breast. She'd been hoping to see the guilty look on his face.

"Yes." Tacita sounded sad. "Still, I suppose one must endure hardships in order to achieve one's goals in life."

What? Rosamunda frowned. That's not what she wanted to hear.

"I reckon that's so, ma'am. My ma and pa used to tell me and my brothers and sisters that all the time."

Rosamunda would have rolled her eyes in disgust had she been able to do so. This human fool talked about his "ma and pa" as if they were fonts of wisdom. They sounded like idiots to her. Her own mother had told her that the most important thing a Yorkshire terrier could do to assure her rightful place in the universe was to hold her ears at an alert angle, lift her tail to show off its feathery perfections, and never mess on the carpet. Rosamunda had learned her lessons well and had carried them honorably into her adult life. They'd served her well, too. Until recently.

It was a crying shame more human beings didn't stick to the basics and save themselves the interminable trouble they were always putting themselves through. Traversing hostile territories indeed! Rosamunda would like to tell these people a thing or two. She would have done so, if she'd been able.

A watery sniffle and a "Yes. Yes, I imagine they did. They sound like such sensible, kindhearted people," greeted Jed's banal pronouncement.

Rosamunda was aghast to realize her mistress actually believed that hogwash about having to endure hardships in order to achieve frivolous goals. Sensible people, her hind leg. And kindhearted? To actually approve of journeys like this? Absurd. She heaved a little sigh in order to divert Tacita's attention from Jed.

"Oh, my poor sweet precious!" Tacita cooed, which pleased Rosamunda.

"Do you think maybe you should dump some water on Rosie, ma'am?"

Although she'd been languishing quite beautifully, Jed's brutal suggestion made Rosamunda jerk to attention. Dump water on her? She pulled away from Tacita's bosom and stared, horrified, at the dreadful man who had dared to threaten her with *water*.

For once Tacita ignored Jed's shortening Rosamunda's name. "Oh, look, Mr. Hardcastle! She seems much more chipper now. I don't think we'll need to revive her with water."

"Good. We don't have much to spare." Jed's voice was as dry as the landscape.

Taking in the look of patent disbelief on his face and the slight curl of his lip, Rosamunda knew she'd given herself away. To make up for it, she lifted her own lip and snarled at him.

"Maybe you ought to introduce that dog to one of them—those actor fellows, Miss Grantham," Jed muttered. " 'Pears to me she'd do pretty good on the stage."

Tacita missed Jed's point, for which Rosamunda could only be thankful. As she stroked her lovingly, Tacita murmured, "Oh, yes. Why, my darling would grace any stage in the world."

Jed rolled his eyes.

Rosamunda honored Tacita with a rather dry kiss.

The next day, Tacita had to abandon one of her suitcases to the merciless desert.

"The mule's not going to make it unless we lighten its load, ma'am."

Tacita put a hand to her mouth and nibbled on the end of her finger until she tasted the dust. Then she spat it out and tapped her cheek instead. "Oh, dear. I hate to throw anything away, Mr. Hardcastle."

"Well, ma'am, like I said before we left Powder

Gulch, this is a hard trip." After a moment, during which it looked to Tacita as though he were struggling with himself, he added, "I told you how it'd be."

Tacita hung her head. "Yes. I know you did." She felt very sad that she'd given him such a hard time in Powder Gulch. He'd been right and she'd been silly to believe he was merely trying to frighten her. "I remember it well."

"Do you want to go through one of them—those bags and see what you can stand to part with, ma'am? I don't want you to have to throw out something you especially need or anything."

"Thank you, Mr. Hardcastle."

So she'd ripped into the two bags she'd brought with her and ruthlessly sorted through her belongings. In truth, the bags primarily carried clothing, and Tacita knew she could always replace them. They were mostly fancy clothes, anyway. She'd brought them to wear in San Francisco, and they were all heavy with boning and other materials designed to torture women into loveliness. When she flung them aside, she actually experienced a moment of freeing exhilaration.

Of course she kept the beautiful emerald necklace her parents had given her right before they departed on what was destined to be their last ocean voyage. She'd scarcely taken it off, in fact, since her father had clasped it around her neck. She smiled sadly, remembering, then shook off her mood. Yes. She'd definitely never part with her necklace; besides, she wore it.

She also kept the photographs of her mother and father. And Rosamunda. And Edgar Jevington Reeve's wonderful Yorkie, Prince Albert, with whom Tacita planned to breed Rosamunda.

She even found her lost smile when she stared at Prince Albert's picture. He looked alert, well groomed, and handsome—and quite cool—in Edgar's arms.

Frowning, she also considered Edgar's countenance, and decided he looked thin and pasty. Prince Albert, though . . . Well, Prince Albert was truly a prince among Yorkies. Looking up, she saw Jed staring at her, his expression unreadable.

She packed the photographs away in her second, smaller, suitcase and padded them carefully with her flannel nightgown. The thought of flannel made Tacita feel almost physically ill.

"There. Can the mule handle that much, Mr. Hardcastle?"

"I think so, ma'am. You done—did a good job."

Jed still looked kind of sad, and Tacita thought it was very sensitive of him to care about her lost belongings. Although she knew she must look a perfect sight, she gave him her sunniest smile. Jed smiled back.

Rosamunda, watching the two of them, wanted to heave.

That afternoon, Tacita saw in the distance a sea of snow shimmering under the relentless sun. She knew it was snow, because there was nothing else so white and nothing else that could cover so much territory. Since she knew it couldn't be snow even though there was nothing else it could be, she knew she was seeing things that weren't there and rubbed her eyes to banish the vision. When she opened them again, the snow was still there.

Oh, dear. She'd lost her mind at last; she knew it. The blistering heat had boiled her brains. Wasted her wits. Incinerated her intelligence. She was now a lunatic. She wondered when she'd start to rave and hoped Jed would be kind to her. In spite of her dried-out state and her determination to be strong, she whimpered.

At once, Jed turned Charlie around. He was at her side in an instant.

"What's the matter, ma'am?" He sounded scared.

She shook her head, too miserable for words. Jed persisted.

She resisted.

As usual, he was stronger than she was. Feeling utterly defeated, she murmured helplessly, "I'm hallucinating."

He stared at her, apparently too overcome by her disturbing declaration to respond. She stared back, too wretched to elaborate.

At last he said, "Huh?"

Tacita frowned. "Hallucinating," she repeated. "Having visions. Seeing things."

"Oh." Scratching his chin, Jed asked, "What makes you think so, ma'am?"

"Because—" Oh, dear, this was so embarrassing. Tacita took a deep breath and regretted it immediately when it burned her lungs. After a brutal coughing fit, she tried again. "Because I see snow on the horizon."

Bracing himself on his saddle, Jed turned and looked toward where she pointed. "Oh, that."

Oh, that? Tacita frowned again. Then she became hopeful. "You mean you see it, too?"

"Sure. That there's the White Sands."

"The White Sands?"

"Sure. That's the White Sands. They're—white."

She frowned again. "I can see that. But what are they?"

"Well, they're sand. White sand."

Although she deplored the gesture, Tacita allowed herself to roll her eyes. She deserved it, given the circumstances. "Yes, I can see that. But what *are* they?"

Jed shrugged. Tacita wanted to pummel him. He said, "I've heard they're gypsum deposits that the wind's scraped into powder. They're one of them—what do you call 'em—natural phenomenons. They're nothing to worry about."

Nothing to worry about, he said. And here she'd believed herself to be insane. Tacita might have shrieked if she'd had breath and spit enough. "I didn't think for a minute somebody'd hauled them out here, Mr. Hardcastle."

He chuckled. "Reckon not, ma'am."

Tacita didn't speak again until suppertime. It took hours and hours for the White Sands to pass from their view. Tacita had never seen anything like them. If they hadn't caused her such real distress, she might have appreciated their pristine beauty. As it was, she wished the shimmering gypsum dunes had decided to take up residence in Arabia or somewhere. Anywhere she wasn't, in fact.

# Chapter Nine

They arrived in Alamogordo the following evening.

*Thank God*, thought Rosamunda.

"Thank God," said Tacita.

Jed bowed his head and looked like he was praying. Rosamunda hoped his prayer was one begging forgiveness for having led them through the last several hellish days. *She'd* sure never forgive him.

"I'll get us some rooms at the hotel, ma'am."

"Thank you, Mr. Hardcastle."

Tacita looked extremely fatigued. Rosamunda wished she'd lift her down from her saddlebag so she could bite Jed's ankle and punish him for torturing them in this way. Poor Mistress. Poor Rosamunda. She didn't have a chance to bite him because he lifted her mistress down before

148

Tacita took her from her saddlebag. She resented Jed for it.

Nevertheless, she rested patiently in Tacita's lap while Jed spoke with the hotel clerk. Her opportunity for revenge would arrive one day. Rosamunda knew it, and she was willing to wait. She'd heard it said once that revenge was a dish best served cold, and she believed it. Of course, Rosamunda would have appreciated anything served cold at the moment.

At least this hotel wasn't quite as dismal as the one in Powder Gulch, Jed decided, even if it did sit in Alamogordo, in the middle of New Mexico Territory. Alamogordo was a relatively civilized place, all things considered. It had been here for years, probably settled by the Spanish in their quest for the fabled City of Gold, damn fools that they were. They'd missed it here, although it wasn't a bad place. Exactly.

Jed eyed his room, trying to see it through the eyes of a tiny, wealthy, sheltered city woman, and sighed heavily.

"Hell. It's a damned dump."

He knew she'd hate it.

That didn't stop him, though. Before he unpacked, before he asked the hotel staff to draw his bath, before he did more than sniff under his armpits—an activity that nearly made him pass out—Jed went shopping.

"Oh, Rosamunda, I've never felt anything so wonderful in my entire life." Tacita sank back into the bubbly water steaming in the tin bathtub and sighed blissfully.

149

Rosamunda, drying off by the fire, did not even turn to look at her. Her ears drooped, her tail sagged, her chin rested on her damp forepaws, and she projected the very image of a sorely abused Yorkie.

Tacita smiled, understanding that her precious darling was in a towering sulk for being forced to take a bath. She didn't mind. At least her sweetums was clean again, and her prizewinning coat would glisten as it ought to once Tacita had an opportunity to brush it. Besides, now that they were out of that appalling desert, Tacita didn't think she'd ever mind anything ever again in her life.

She'd survived unscathed, too; or at least relatively so. Oh, perhaps she'd bear freckles to remind her of her ordeal, but Tacita didn't mind freckles too much. It's not as if she had a sweetheart who might take exception to a flawed complexion, after all. She grimaced and decided not to think about that.

It felt *so* good to relax in a real bath. Comfortable and soon to be clean for the first time in what seemed like years, Tacita let her mind wander. Immediately, it wandered to Jed Hardcastle, and she allowed herself another tiny frown.

"I wish I didn't think about Mr. Hardcastle so often, Rosamunda. I know such thoughts are not good for me. After all, we shouldn't suit one another at all. He's a rough, uneducated Texas fellow and I'm from the city. Besides, the man is engaged to be married." She gave a tiny sniff. "Miss Amalie Crunch. What on earth kind of name is that?"

Rosamunda lifted one furry ear, but didn't

deign to turn and look at her mistress.

"I can't seem to stop thinking about him, though." Tacita heaved a sigh so big it almost made water slop out of the tub.

Rosamunda's ear cocked back an inch.

"I don't suppose he ever thinks about me at all. Except as a nuisance." Tacita's frown deepened. "I'm not sure what it is about him that's so appealing to me. He's an argumentative man, and I don't generally care for obstreperous people. Perhaps it's because he's so big. You must admit that such largeness of frame is rather comforting. He does give one a safe feeling."

Tacita thought for a moment. "There is one other thing in his favor, Rosamunda darling. He seems to be interested in what I have to say about things."

The latter attribute was the one that most astonished and gratified Tacita. In her entire life, nobody had been interested in anything she'd done or said. The way Jed seemed to focus on her when she spoke—indeed, seemed almost to stare at her—thrilled her.

Her parents, who were brilliant, witty, charming people, had traveled the world over and boasted numerous brilliant, witty, charming acquaintances with whom to amuse themselves. They'd had no patience for the timid little daughter who longed for their attention. When they were home, which wasn't often, Tacita had felt rather like a stranger: tongue-tied and clumsy, a pallid nobody who faded away to a vapor in the reflected luster of her mother and father.

Even now, as she enjoyed her bath, she sighed, remembering her childhood. Oh, how she'd wanted to shine as her parents did. And oh, how she'd failed. She was just too boring for words. Even Uncle Luther, who paid her some mind, was generally impatient about it. He had worries, he said. Although he never said so, Tacita knew that his worries were infinitely more important than his niece.

But Jed . . . It was different with Jed. Of course, it might just be that he paid attention to her because she was the only other person around, but he didn't give her that impression. He seemed truly interested in her.

Tacita sucked in a deep, lavender-scented breath. "You know, darling, it sounds silly, but I believe I could come to care very deeply for Mr. Hardcastle."

Rosamunda's other ear shot up. This was, possibly, the worst thing she'd ever heard spoken in English. Even that horrid Mr. Cesare's, "Here, doggie, doggie," when he'd been luring her away from camp hadn't sounded so awful to her ears. Of course, he'd been holding a piece of beefsteak at the time, too, which had helped.

But this! From her own dear mistress's lips! This presaged disaster. Rosamunda knew it.

"Not that I shall allow myself to do anything so foolish, of course."

Whew. Rosamunda allowed her ear to lower, although she still wasn't easy in her mind.

"And not that he'd ever pay any attention to me, even if I did allow myself to care for him. I already know that most people find me too dull to bother with." Tacita sighed again. "Besides, he thinks I'm engaged to Mr. Reeve."

Tacita splashed her hand in bath water cloudy with desert dust.

"Of course, when he discovers the reason for our journey, it won't make a particle of difference how we feel about one another. Even if he learns to like me by the time we get to San Francisco, he'll hate me once he knows why I hired him to take us there."

Rosamunda cocked her head to one side, wondering what her mistress meant by that. Why should that monster hate her for such a sensible purpose as undertaking a journey in order to breed Rosamunda to Prince Albert?

Tacita picked up the lavender soap she'd carted all the way from Galveston and began to lather her arm, grimacing when she saw the river of muddy soapsuds dripping from her elbow.

"I know he'd never understand our imperative, darling." She smiled at Rosamunda.

Rosamunda still wouldn't look at her. She did agree with her, however. Jedediah Hardcastle was not a man who appreciated life's finer things. He'd already proven it countless times.

"Mr. Hardcastle would undoubtedly consider me foolish beyond hope for undertaking this arduous journey in order to mate you to Mr. Reeve's Prince Albert. He simply doesn't understand."

Rubbing the cake of soap vigorously up and down her other arm, Tacita wrinkled her brow. "Of course, he's always had a large family at his command. I've only had you."

Rosamunda's chin lifted from her paws. She didn't turn her head. She did, however, wonder at the slightly sad tone that had crept into Tac-ita's voice.

"He's right, of course." Raising one leg and soaping a long white trail through the crusted dirt, Tacita frowned and said, "Imagine, having only a dog to love! Why, how perfectly pathetic I must seem!"

That brought Rosamunda to her feet, fury compelling her.

Startled, Tacita dropped her soap. "Good heavens, darling! Why on earth are you growling so ferociously?"

Tacita answered Jed's knock at the door clad in a dress he'd never seen her wear. He supposed that by her standards the gown was a mere noth-ing—a flutter of blue calico with a scrape of lace edging at the high collar and cuffs, simply made, and with nary a ruffle or a ribbon in sight. By Alamogordo, or Busted Flush standards, the gown was a work of art.

In the space of an hour or two, Miss Tacita Grantham had gone from looking like a bedrag-gled kitten to looking like a fairy princess again. Jed, observing her from his superior height, felt his mouth drop open, his eyes open wide, and his brain rattle.

"Evening, ma'am," he managed to choke out.

"Good evening, Mr. Hardcastle."

For the life of him, Jed couldn't think of any-thing else to say. His mind had shriveled up. Scolding himself for being a fool, he made a monumental effort, constructed another sen-tence, and spat it out.

"I—I picked up the train tickets, Miss Gran-tham."

His mouth was so dry, his lips stuck together. He tried licking them and discovered his tongue was dry, too. His voice came out squeaky when he added icing on the cake of his hard-won conversational contribution. "We'll leave tomorrow morning."

Lord on high. He'd forgotten how Miss Tacita Grantham could knock his guts and gizzard about when she was all spruced up. Not for the first time since they left Powder Gulch, he felt big and brutish and out of place. Come to think of it, he'd felt this way in Powder Gulch, too. As soon as he'd met her. At least he didn't stink anymore.

"Thank you very much, Mr. Hardcastle."

She looked up at him, thick eyelashes fluttering. They partially shaded her spectacular blue eyes and gave her a flirtatious expression Jed knew she didn't mean. Not aimed at him she didn't, anyway. Maybe at that sissy Englishman. The thought made him want to punch something, which seemed to unstick his brain and make his words flow more easily.

"You're welcome ma'am."

He shuffled his feet and fidgeted with his hat. Then he noticed the semicircle of tooth marks in its brim, recalled the time that damned rat had lunged at his thumb, and dropped the hand holding his hat. Keeping an eye on Rosamunda in case she got any other crazy ideas, he said, "You want to have some supper in the hotel dining room, ma'am? It'll be better'n what we've been eating on the trail." He tried to smile and failed.

"Yes, I expect it will be. Thank you, Mr. Hardcastle. I'd enjoy a good meal." A brief smile visited Tacita's lips. Jed had a hard time trying not to stare at them.

"Reckon they got pretty good fare here in this hotel—better'n what you'll be getting on the train, anyway."

"Really? I've always dined well on trains, Mr. Hardcastle."

She sounded short of breath. Jed wondered if the trip was finally getting to her. Until now, she'd held up remarkably well for such a little, inexperienced thing. "I expect you have. This ain't—isn't a New York special or anything, though. It's just a trunk line to Santa Fe. They don't have no—any fancy cooks on this train. It'll be beans and beefsteak until we get to California, I reckon."

"Oh."

Jed had begun to read all sorts of meanings into that one breathy syllable until disgust at his own absurdity overcame him. He silently hollered at himself to stop being stupid. She was promised to that damned ridiculous Englishman and didn't give two raps about a big Texas lummox like him. Besides, he was promised to Miss Amalie Crunch and that was that.

Hell, even if neither one of 'em were promised to anybody, it wouldn't make any difference. There was no way on God's green earth this fairy princess would ever think of him as anything but an uncivilized country hick. He reckoned he could be useful to her, maybe, and she might appreciate him for it, but he could never hope for more than that.

She'd sure as blazes never think of him in anything even resembling a soft or cordial light. Romance—the very word made Jed's rugged, no-nonsense Texas innards rumble around unpleasantly, unless that was because he was hungry—was totally out of the question.

"So, shall we go on in and have some supper, ma'am?"

"Yes. Thank you, Mr. Hardcastle."

"It's nothin', ma'am."

In a gesture that would have done his ma proud—she'd tried her blessed best to teach him manners—Jed crooked his elbow and gulped when Tacita placed her teensy hand on his forearm. She tucked the bad-tempered terrier under her arm on her other side, for which he thanked whatever gods might be lingering over this crude territorial town.

"You look—you look very handsome this evening, Mr. Hardcastle."

Jed resisted the impulse to shake his head and say "Huh?" He did find himself staring down at her bouncy blond curls—clean and shining again under a silly little flowery nothing of a hat—his eyes wide open in shock, before he managed to choke out a "Thank you, ma'am."

"I've never seen you in a suit jacket before. Why, I believe I've only seen you in those fringed buckskin clothes you wear so handsomely."

This time Jed did shake his head—hard. He refrained from uttering "Huh?" only because his dry tongue was glued to his equally dry teeth. He recalled the shopping expedition he'd made earlier in the day, rushing through the shops in Alamogordo as if the demons of hell were after him. Then he considered the worn and stained buckskins he'd peeled from his dirt-caked body this evening and remembered conversations

he'd had with his mother back home in Busted
Flush.

"Jedediah Hardcastle, these britches are a
pure disgrace," his ma had told him more than
once. "And this shirt stinks to high heaven. Why
don't you wear real clothes? I'm sure no deer
gave his life to a less worthy cause than these
filthy, smelly things"

Invariably, Jed had laughed, proud of his
buckskins as a badge of his calling. He figured
those lived-in 'skins were what a city slicker
wanted to see on a frontier guide. The good Lord
knew, those city folks paid him enough to do the
job. He figured the image went along with his
employment. He also figured he owed it to the
folks who bought his services to play his part to
the hilt. Why, he already had a brand-new house
and the beginnings of a fine horse-breeding operation established in this, his thirtieth year, because city folks were so blasted picky—or
gullible—about such nonsense.

Of course, the fact that he'd studied business
economics at Texas U. didn't hurt his business
prospects, either. Jed was a whiz when it came
business matters. Thanks to his shrewd invest-
ments, his money was multiplying like rabbits
even as he strolled to the dining car with Tacita
Grantham. His buckskins had helped him earn
that money. He'd always loved them for it.

This afternoon, though, when he'd held his
worn buckskins up to the light, he'd wrinkled his
nose and pretty much decided ten years of use
was enough for any self-respecting garment.
One thing a body could say about buckskins:
They never gave up on a man. But shoot, his
britches could almost stand up by themselves by

this time. And ripe? Sweet Lord have mercy. He guessed his old buckskins were due for retirement, even though he'd kind of miss 'em.

He'd decided, however, that he no longer wanted to appear—or smell—rough and frontierish around Miss Tacita Grantham. He was glad he'd taken the time to go shopping. He had a hankering for her to view him in a more refined light. If there could ever be anything refined about a six-foot-four-inch former Texas Ranger and present-day frontier scout from Busted Flush, Texas, who was more at home camping out on the prairie than escorting a beautiful lady in to supper. Even in so wild a place as Alamogordo in the New Mexico Territory.

With great effort, he forced out the words, "Thank you kindly, ma'am."

"You're more than welcome, Mr. Hardcastle." She twinkled up at him like his own personal star. He'd been about to compliment her on her own appearance, which was spectacular, but after her smile hit him he couldn't remember how to talk. By the time they made it to the hotel dining room, Jed's brain was a complete blank.

Supper passed without incident, except when Rosamunda attacked the waiter and then lit into a patron for perceived slights to her person or that of her mistress.

Jed would never understand that dog as long as he lived. He didn't even want to, except he had a notion that if he could somehow unravel the mystery of why Tacita liked it—loved it—he'd be closer to understanding Tacita herself.

Such understanding had become very important to him in the last several days. He wished it hadn't. And he knew it was foolish even to hope, but he couldn't help but harbor a tiny wish—a mere flicker, actually—that he might replace that animal in her affections one day.

He went to sleep that night cursing himself for an addlepated fool.

# Chapter Ten

"Mmmph."

Cesare Cacciatore Picinisco winced as he nudged his chin up another notch and lathered his cheeks. His bruises were but pallid blue-green memories by this time. His tooth still hurt when he poked it with his tongue, but his split lip had healed nicely. He hoped that after he shaved off the last of his beautiful black beard, neither Jedediah Hardcastle nor Tacita Grantham would recognize him as the drummer who'd snatched their ridiculously expensive dog.

With the few dollars remaining of his funds—they were hidden right above the wheel well on his fancy wagon and, therefore, ignored by the unimaginative Farley Boskins—Picinisco had purchased a ticket on the trunk line from Ala-

161

mogordo to San Francisco. He was going to get that animal back or die trying.

He frowned, misliking the latter portion of his resolve. He was going to try very hard to get that animal back, is what he meant.

He'd had to burgle a mercantile establishment in a small Mexican settlement a few miles south of Alamogordo in order to provide himself with money enough to store his mule and wagon in a livery and buy food on the train during his journey. He resented having to go to all this trouble to secure an animal that, if there were any justice in the world, would have been his long since.

Breakfast in the train's dining car would be his first big experiment. He figured Jed Hardcastle and Tacita Grantham would take their meals in the dining car. "After all," he grumbled, feeling dreadfully abused, "*they* don't have to worry about money." If Jed and Tacita didn't recognize him at breakfast, Picinisco had every expectation of being able to perpetrate his latest scheme to snatch the dog with impunity.

If they did recognize him, he'd have to jump off the train. He decided not to think about it.

"I'll get that dog," he muttered as he carved a path through the thick stubble on his cheeks. He'd already scissored away the bushy part of his beard. Big hairy clumps of it rested in the wastepaper basket at his side. He resented parting with his beard. He resented having to lay aside his colorful clothes and wear the uninspiring brown suit of an ordinary person. He resented every fading bruise on his cheek. He resented the almost-healed puncture marks made by that miserable dog's teeth. He resented

162

his still-bulbous nose. He resented the tooth he'd left behind in the desert.

"I'll get that dog," he repeated, blaming it for his losses.

He decided to leave at least a remnant of his formerly beloved mustache. It was his last link to manhood, the one personal artifact standing between Cesare Cacciatore Picinisco and abject humiliation.

"Reckon you get to see an Indian on this trip after all, Miss Grantham."

Startled by Jed's words, which were spoken quite wryly, Tacita clutched at his arm with one hand and tightened her grip on Rosamunda with the other. "What? Where?" Oh, dear, the train wasn't being attacked, was it? Why, they hadn't even left the Alamogordo city limits yet.

"Yonder."

Glancing in the direction of Jed's terse nod, Tacita felt her mouth drop open. She shut it again and didn't know whether to smile at Jed's little joke or be annoyed with him for teasing her. She decided to await circumstances before she did either. She did find herself gritting her teeth, and made an effort to relax.

She said, "So I see," and left it at that.

Jed led her to a table in the dining car directly opposite the one occupied by the Indian to whom he'd referred. The fellow, his head wrapped in a tidy turban and his swarthy countenance animated, was seated across from a gentleman wearing a uniform Tacita did not recognize, although it seemed almost excessively military.

"But you're wrong, sahib, and I'll tell you why

that is the case." The Indian man poked the table between himself and his traveling companion with a long brown forefinger. His expression was intense and his voice adamant. Tacita thought his accent was rather musical when compared to the rough drawls she'd been subjected to lately.

"You'll never get me to believe you," said the other man, in an accent almost as aristocratic as the one belonging to Edgar Jevington Reeve. Tacita's heart fluttered for an instant when she thought about Edgar, then stilled almost at once. Odd. She'd been used to delighting in long daydreams about him.

Although she'd been reared to shut her ears to the conversations of others, her parents having warned her in particular about the rudeness of eavesdropping, Tacita couldn't help but strain to listen. After a minute or two, she came to a conclusion that piqued her interest and made her listen even harder.

Why, that fellow in the uniform was a British army officer; she'd stake her life on it. She'd read Mr. Rudyard Kipling's wonderful stories, after all. And the other fellow was obviously an Indian—she shot a resentful glance at Jed, who was reading breakfast suggestions from a tattered menu and missed it—from India.

A small dart of pain lodged in her heart when she thought about India. Her parents had been returning from a business trip to India when their ship had sunk in a storm. She sighed and decided eavesdropping, however rude, was preferable to unhappy reflections. Besides, it wasn't every day a body got to listen to an Indian and an Englishman converse on a rustic trunk line train in the Wild West.

"Self-rule is the God-given right of all men, sahib. We have labored beneath the tyranny of the British for centuries. It is time for us to take our country back!"

"Tyranny? Nonsense! You people proved yourselves incapable of self-government long since. Why, you weren't even a unified country, but a mishmash of independent states constantly at war with each other before we brought you together as a nation. You lived in chaos. We British imparted a sense of order and unity to your benighted homeland."

"Not benighted, sir! Never benighted. We lived as we wanted to live."

"In filth and squalor?"

"Squalor, my good fellow, is in the eyes of the beholder."

"Nonsense. You lived like heathens!"

"I beg to differ. Not heathens, sir. We honor— we have honored for centuries and continue to honor—our own ancient and revered religions. Besides, heathen is as heathen does."

"Burning women on the pyres of their dead husbands? I call that heathen."

"Suttee is a sacred religious ceremony. Our women love the custom."

Tacita frowned and opened her mouth to refute the Indian fellow's absurd assumption. Then she remembered she was eavesdropping and shut her mouth again.

"Ridiculous! No woman would choose to die like that."

"That is where you are very, very wrong, sir." The Indian man poked the table again. "Dying in such a venerable fashion assures a female's place in eternity with the gods. It is a sacred custom and honored by our people. Besides, how else are women to atone for their stupidity and uncleanliness? They must do as they are told, being foolish creatures and unable to think for themselves." He shrugged. "How else can such a silly thing as a woman reach Nirvana?"

Tacita was beginning to dislike the Indian fellow a good deal.

The Englishman said, "There. You see? Women are certainly foolish, prone to lunacy, and unable to think beyond breakfast, but that's why they need us to protect them. Not to throw them onto funeral pyres."

She decided she didn't like the Englishman any better than the Indian.

"At any rate," the Indian continued, "our customs are our own and are holy to our own religions."

"Ha! Religions? Kali! You call that a religion?"

Tacita, who had read about the sect of Kali in several stirringly bloodthirsty novels, shuddered and listened harder.

The Indian fellow screwed up his face. "Just because our philosophies differ from yours does not make them wrong."

"Philosophies? Superstitions, rather."

"The followers of our beliefs are as devout as those who adhere to yours, sahib."

"Followers? Bloody assassins, is what most of them are," muttered the Englishman. "We British brought order to the place."

"Against our will! Forcing us into your kind of governmental order against our will is tyranny and will not be tolerated forever. Mark my words."

The army officer shook his head and looked superior. Tacita decided his expression was entirely too smug for her taste. She frowned as she stroked Rosamunda's once-more-silky fur.

"Anything the matter, ma'am?"

Jerking her attention away from the argument being carried on across the aisle, Tacita found Jed eyeing her with concern. She smiled, thinking how truly amiable a man he was, in spite of his great size and his tendency to bully those weaker than he. At least he wouldn't toss a female onto a funeral pyre, Tacita felt sure; nor did he seem to believe that women were intrinsically of less value than men.

"Oh, no. Nothing's the matter." She lowered her voice and leaned forward. "I was only trying to decide whether it was the accent or the uniform that makes that English fellow seem so arrogant."

Jed peered at the two men for a moment before he muttered, "My money's on the accent." Another second's hard through brought forth, "Although that sissy uniform don't—doesn't help none."

Her own little giggle surprised Tacita. "I expect you're right, Mr. Hardcastle."

The train had left the station in Alamogordo at dawn's first light. Jed had suggested taking breakfast on the train, before the supply of fresh eggs ran out, and Tacita had agreed readily. Her tummy grumbled, and she eagerly anticipated a good hearty meal. Renewal of the hostilities across the aisle drew her attention once more.

"Don't be absurd, my good man. Perhaps

you'll be so kind as to tell me how introducing plumbing, refrigeration, and sanitation to a backwards country like yours can be construed as evil."

Cocking her head, Tacita thought the British fellow might just have a point there.

"But we did not *ask* for your sanitation! We did not *ask* for your plumbing! These things were forced upon us. If we had wanted sanitation and plumbing, we should have invented them for ourselves."

She decided the Indian fellow had a point, too, although she did think he might be stretching it a bit.

"Besides," the Indian added, "You didn't give us those things. You stole our natural resources to satisfy your own greed and brought plumbing and sanitation into the country for the use of the British. In return you treat us like slaves. We natives can go hang for all the British care. In fact, many of us do." He nodded as if he'd just made the most important point so far uttered in the conversation.

Tacita gave her order to a harried-looking waiter in a stained apron, then leaned over the table to whisper to Jed, "Do you suppose that man is telling the truth, Mr. Hardcastle? Do you think the British really care nothing about the native Indians, but only about themselves?"

Jed shrugged. "I reckon."

Blinking, saddened by such an assessment of her revered ancestors' motivations—an assessment as unflattering as she suspected it was accurate—Tacita sat back and petted Rosamunda more thoughtfully. Jed surprised her when he continued speaking. She was used to his phlegmatic utterances and was unaccustomed to hearing him explain himself without having to be asked first.

"Reckon folks are pretty much the same the world over, ma'am. Don't none of 'em—that is, I don't expect there's many of 'em care about other folks as much as they do their own kind." He took a sip of coffee and shrugged again. "I 'spect we're just as bad. Hell—er—I mean, shoot, just look at the Indians in our country."

He watched her from across the table, his gorgeous brown eyes somber. She picked up her teacup, sipped, and wrinkled her nose. She hoped she'd be able to find a decent cup of tea in San Francisco. She expected she would, since San Franciscans carried on so much commerce with the Chinese, and Chinese tea was almost as good as tea from India.

"Yes. I remember a conversation we had once about Indians, Mr. Hardcastle."

"Yes, ma'am."

"It seems like such a long time ago now." Tacita smiled, recalling that day in Powder Gulch. It seemed a decade or so ago, although not even four weeks had passed. That was back before she knew Jedediah Hardcastle and still thought him rude, crude, and unpleasant. She knew better now, and wasn't altogether happy about having found out she'd been mistaken.

"Yes'm." Jed slumped a little, and appeared discouraged. Then he sat up straighter, his attention caught by something in the back of the dining car. "What the . . . ?"

Tacita's heart plunged wildly and she turned to look, too. "What is it, Mr. Hardcastle?" She didn't notice anything alarming, thank goodness.

Jed didn't answer for a second or two. When Tacita returned her attention to him again, he shook his head and frowned.

"Nothin', I reckon," he said at last. "That fellow at the back table looked familiar for a minute is all."

Turning to peer over her shoulder once more, Tacita stared hard at the man whom Jed had indicated. She didn't recognize him. Hunched over his table, glaring at the menu, he didn't appear familiar at all. A chubby fellow with dark, almost black hair, he had on those dark-lensed spectacles people with poor eyesight were apt to wear in sunny climates. He'd wound a long scarf around his neck and drawn it up over his chin, and he'd pulled a derby hat low on his head. He also sported a thin mustache and wore an extremely crabby expression. Tacita frowned.

She disliked those thin mustaches. They seemed silly to her, and always looked like somebody'd drawn them on a gentleman's upper lip with a pencil. Her own father had been clean shaven—he said it was easier for a man to keep clean with as little hair on his body as he could get away with, particularly when traveling in exotic locales where the bathing facilities were not the best. Lice, he'd said more than once, were not a man's best friend. Her uncle Luther sported praiseworthy, somewhat bushy, whiskers that joined his sideburns and made him look quite elegant in Tacita's estimation.

Those skinny mustaches, though—well, Tacita just didn't care for them. Glancing at Jed, she was charmed by his well-scrubbed, clean-shaven appearance. Not, of course, that his whiskerless chin meant much. Jedediah Hardcastle would look marvelous in anything. Or nothing.

She quickly turned to stare out of the window and hoped Jed wouldn't notice her blush. "I don't believe I've ever seen that man before, Mr. Hardcastle."

After another frowning moment, Jed said, "Reckon you're right, ma'am."

When he first set eyes on the odd fellow at the back table, Jed got an itchy, uncomfortable feeling that crawled across the back of his neck and made his scalp prickle. Jed had felt that prickly sensation before and he didn't like it. He generally paid attention to it, too. It had rescued him from a tight spot more than once. This one prickled at him like nettles.

He kept staring at the man throughout breakfast, but the fellow didn't do anything but look cranky and eat his eggs and hash.

After breakfast, however, when Jed walked Tacita and her mouse-hole terrier out of the dining room, Rosamunda took one look at the man with the thin mustache and tried to leap out of Tacita's arms and attack him. Tacita held her in check only with difficulty. Jed wondered if the dog had lunged at that particular man for any real purpose or if, as usual, it was just being irrational and nasty.

The animal's behavior was worth thinking about, though, especially when added to Jed's already funny feeling about the fellow. After he left Tacita and the rat in their stateroom to rest, he took himself to the smoking car, where he planned to sit and observe his fellow passengers.

Somebody was following Tacita Grantham and her dog. Jed knew it in his guts. He didn't know who it was any more than he knew why, but he'd bet anything he owned that he was right. Mr. Piskywhiskle and Farley Boskins hadn't just appeared out of nowhere within hours of each other for no reason. Jed didn't believe in coincidences. Besides, Boskins had all but admitted he was after something specific, even though he hadn't said what it was or who'd sent him after it.

Jed's money was on the uncle, although he couldn't imagine why Mr. Williamson should be after Tacita. He suspected, however, that if he was right, Uncle Luther wasn't doing his own dirty work, but was hiring others to do it. That would account for both Boskins and Piskerwhinkey. Jed figured that if Luther had already gone to that much trouble, he wouldn't give up just because the first two attempts to get at Tacita had failed. Maybe Luther stood to inherit a lot of money if Tacita died. Or maybe he'd taken out an insurance policy on her. Both possibilities made him shudder.

Then again, he thought grimly, maybe it wasn't Luther at all. Whoever was pursuing them might be some person from Powder Gulch, thinking to cash in on that damned jeweled dog collar of hers. Tacita'd pretty much advertised her wealth all over the whole town. Shoot. Without half trying, city folks could be such blasted fools.

That man in the dining car, though . . . Jed decided the man, even though he couldn't place him, bore watching. He was glad they were on the train and he didn't have to keep guard over Tacita and her hell-bound terrier all the time, but could leave 'em tucked up securely in a locked room.

Unfortunately, he didn't learn much during his day spent in the smoking car. The Indian gent and the British fellow retired there after breakfast and spent the entire day arguing. The man with the pencil-thin mustache buried his face behind a newspaper and didn't lift it once.

By late afternoon, when Jed finally gave up, his lungs were about to burst from a surfeit of stale cigar smoke, his eyes were watering, and he'd learned more than he ever wanted to know about Indian politics. He'd learned nothing whatever about the man behind the newspaper.

"I don't understand, darling. Why are you in such a temper lately? I know our journey across the desert was difficult, but we're on the train now, sweetheart, and things won't ever be that hard again. I promise."

If Rosamunda could have expressed herself in English, her mistress would undoubtedly never recover from the blistering she'd get. Hadn't she *recognized* that man with the silly mustache as the craven dognapper, Mr. Cesare? Good Lord, even a human being ought to be able to sniff out an enemy better than that! Rosamunda's own sharp nose had recognized his scent in an instant.

Rosamunda, who had always considered Tacita a pearl among the generally swinish lot of human beings, began to have serious doubts about her. First she'd developed a fondness for the monster, then she'd failed to discern so des-

173

picable and unmistakable a fiend as Mr. Cesare.

Since Tacita couldn't comprehend Yorkshire, Rosamunda tried to explain matters to her in a way she could understand. She grabbed the flounce of Tacita's petticoat in her sharp little teeth and yanked hard. As soon as she heard it rip, she released the fabric, pattered to the door and whined, shaking her head and uttering a series of short, sharp barks to add emphasis to her message.

"Rosamunda! You tore my hem!" Completely ignoring Rosamunda's obvious intent, Tacita lifted her skirt and frowned at her torn petticoat hem. "My goodness, darling, I've never known you to be in such a state. Are you nervous about train travel? Is that what's wrong?"

If Rosamunda'd had hands, she'd have wrung them in frustration. Since she didn't and couldn't, she barked out one of her loudest, shrillest Yorkshire alarms. She also stamped her tiny feet, which clicked out a warning tattoo on the shiny floorboards of their sleeping compartment.

Instead of instantly rushing to the door to chase down the vicious criminal about whom Rosamunda was alerting her, Tacita strolled over to the door and picked her up.

"There, there, darling. Let me take you to the baggage compartment. That nice porter told me I could spread some newspapers on the floor just for you."

Rosamunda could hardly believe it when Tacita marched her out of their room, down the aisle, through two more railway cars, and made her squat on the newspapers in the baggage compartment.

Humans. They were simply impossible.

\*    \*    \*

Cesare Picinisco leapt out of sight when he saw Tacita Grantham step out of her stateroom on the arm of Jedediah Hardcastle. She was holding the animal under her arm. Drat. That meant he couldn't get it while Jed and Tacita were away. Didn't that woman ever let the animal out of her sight? Picinisco didn't approve, because such a course of action on her part would make his job more difficult. Well, why should that surprise him? She and that wretched guide of hers had been making his job difficult since the first moment he'd seen them.

On the other hand, they were undoubtedly heading for the dining car right now. That meant Picinisco would have an uninterrupted period of time in which to reconnoiter in her sleeping chamber. Since he was apparently going to have to snatch the dratted dog while Tacita slept, he could use this time to his advantage.

The mutt growled when she passed the curtain behind which Picinisco had hidden himself, but Tacita didn't let go of her.

"My goodness, sweetheart," Picinisco heard Tacita murmur. "Whatever can the problem be? You're as grouchy as an old bear today."

"What's the matter, Rosie?" Jed asked.

Tacita said, "Rosamunda."

Rosamunda yipped twice.

Jed muttered something Picinisco couldn't make out very well, although the words "bear" and "betwaddled" were clear.

Because he hated them all so much, Picinisco thrust his head between the curtains and stuck his tongue out at the dog. Rosamunda continued to snarl at him from her mistress's arms, but

175

couldn't do anything else because Tacita wouldn't let her go. Picinisco felt a surge of triumph.

He fairly swaggered to Tacita's stateroom, where he picked the lock with the ease of long practice. He planned to investigate the arrangement of her belongings thoroughly, so that he wouldn't bump into anything when he sneaked in that night to grab the dog.

Several minutes later, he was concentrating so hard on memorizing the layout of the stateroom that he didn't hear the door open. His first clue that he was no longer alone came in the form of a loud gasp.

Sure that he'd been discovered, Picinisco whirled around. "Aaaaargh!"

"Sir! Sir! Do not shoot me, please!"

Shoot him? Picinisco glanced down at the perfume bottle in his hand and wondered if it really did resemble a gun or if the Oriental-looking fellow clutching at his heart in the doorway possessed an overactive imagination. He wasted little thought on the matter, deciding he didn't care.

He pointed the perfume bottle at the intruder. "Who are you?"

It was the fellow who'd been sitting with that man in the red uniform, Picinisco realized. He remembered them well because he'd felt a faint stirring of jealousy that the two should be enjoying such an animated conversation. He, Cesare Cacciatore Picinisco, never got to chat for hours with his friends like that, undoubtedly because he had no friends. Because he resented this man's ability to make and keep friends when he couldn't, he shook the perfume bottle in a menacing manner and growled, "What do you want?"

The interloper shrank back, the arms he held in the air quaking like the branches of an aspen tree. "Oh, please, sahib, do not shoot me. I, Virendra Karnik, am but a poor passenger on this train. I am but a miserable creature who has been hired to perform a deed. I—I must have entered the wrong cabin. Yes, yes! That is what the problem is. I have entered the wrong cabin! Dear me, how foolish I am, to be sure!"

His dark eyes narrowed. "Although, it must be admitted that you do not look as though you belong here, either, my good fellow."

Picinisco, uncomfortable with the penetrating stare Mr. Karnik was directing at his perfume bottle, jammed it into his coat pocket and thrust it forward to give the impression he was holding a weapon in the pocket.

It was too late. The interloper allowed his arms to drop even as his eyebrows dipped into a disapproving V. Drawing a wicked-looking dagger from a hitherto unsuspected scabbard secreted somewhere on his person, he began to advance toward Picinisco.

"All right, my friend, why are you sneaking around in Miss Tacita Grantham's first-class cabin?"

Abandoning his perfume bottle, Picinisco backed up in rhythm to Virendra Karnik's advance. "D-d-don't hurt me! Don't hurt me! I was just leaving."

"That may well be so, my good fellow, but why were you here to begin with? Tell me" Karnik shook his dagger in Picinisco's face.

\*   \*   \*

Picinisco came to when he felt a cold liquid splash his face. Shaking his head, he opened his eyes to discover himself being loomed over by Virendra Karnik, whose dagger looked positively enormous from this angle.

"Don't kill me with that thing! Don't stab me." He began to weep, visions of his own precious blood staining Tacita's sleeping room overpowering the remains of his ever-precarious courage.

"I shan't kill you if you tell me why you were rummaging through Miss Tacita Grantham's stateroom, sahib."

"I-I-I only want her dog," snuffled Picinisco.

Karnik frowned. "Her dog? You want her dog?"

"Y-yes." Picinisco squeezed his eyes tightly shut, bracing himself to feel the sharp blade of Karnik's knife slide between his ribs.

After a moment's pause required to digest the information Picinisco had delivered, Karnik said, "Why would you wish to possess such a useless creature as Miss Grantham's very small dog, sahib? Does your desire to take the animal involve ritual sacrifice?"

Picinisco's eyes popped open. "S-sacrifice? Goodness gracious, no! She told me the animal was worth two hundred dollars. I want the money."

"Two hundred dollars?"

Karnik's frown deepened and he seemed to be studying Picinisco's face for evidence of his veracity or lack thereof. After a moment, during which Picinisco did not so much as breathe, Karnik lowered his dagger. "I am not altogether certain I believe you yet, sahib, although your story is so absurd that only a fool would invent it."

Picinisco sucked in a deep breath and almost dared renew hope for his future. "It's the truth, nonetheless," he whispered.

Karnik shrugged. "Ah, well, then. I have no interest in her dog."

"You—you don't?"

Standing, Karnik tucked his dagger back into its mysterious hidden home. "No. My desires as regards Miss Grantham are infinitely more lofty than mere money."

More lofty than money? Picinisco had never heard of such a thing. Cautiously, he pushed himself to his feet, eyeing Karnik the whole time. "What are they then, if I might ask, sir?"

Karnik pinned him with a dark, brooding look. "The Eye, my good fellow. The Delhi Hahm-Ahn-Der Eye, stolen from the Great Goddess at the Temple of Hahm by a worthless English infidel and sold, years later, to an equally worthless American infidel."

After a moment, during which he waited for Karnik to expand on his story and was disappointed, Picinisco said, "Oh."

"And," Karnik said, his expression brightening, "I think it would be a good thing were we to combine our resources, my dear good fellow. Two, after all, can more expeditiously execute a plan than one."

Recalling the dagger, Picinisco uttered an eager, "Yes!"

"Pinkeywinkle!" Jed's fist hit the table, making his steak bounce on its plate, Tacita jump in her chair, and Rosamunda yip shrilly.

Her hand pressed to her thundering heart, Tacita squeaked, "I beg your pardon?"

"That's who that fellow is. It's Pinkeywinkle!"

Wondering if Jed had gone 'round the bend and hoping he hadn't because she not only still needed him but had grown immensely fond of him as well, Tacita leaned forward and said cautiously, "I—I—who? What fellow?"

"That fellow with the little mustache. He's that drummer fellow who stole your dog, Miss Grantham. I *knew* I recognized him!"

Tacita sat up straight again, frowning. "Nonsense. Mr. Picinisco had an enormous beard, Mr. Hardcastle. Surely you remember that."

Tacita petted Rosamunda. Rosamunda nipped her finger. Tacita drew her finger away instantly and glowered down at her dog. "Whatever is the matter with you, Rosamunda? I can't believe you did that!" Rosamunda glowered back.

Jed ignored them both. "Don't you see, ma'am? He shaved his beard off. That's why he's trying to keep his face covered, it's 'cause if he didn't, we'd be able to see the lower part of his face isn't as brown from bein' out in the sun as the rest of it."

Forgetting her dog's unusual behavior, Tacita peered at Jed in thought. "Do you really think so?"

"I do, ma'am. I think that's why Rosie tried to attack him, too."

"Rosamunda," Tacita said absently.

Rosamunda growled.

Tacita furrowed her brow and thought harder. "It seems quite unlikely to me," she said after a moment, hoping Jed wouldn't take her words amiss.

"Maybe," he said. "I think I'm right."

She thought he was wrong, although she decided not to belabor the point. She knew Jed never seemed to want to give up an argument, no matter how right she was. In order to placate him without giving up her position on the matter, she said, "Well, why don't we observe him more closely the next time we see him. If you still believe that man with the silly mustache is Mr. Picinisco, then I think we should have him arrested."

"For what?"

"Why, for stealing my dog, of course!"

"Haven't we already covered that ground, ma'am?" Jed rolled his eyes and took a sip of coffee. Tacita glared at him. Rosamunda growled again.

Jed figured not much had changed in his life.

# *Chapter Eleven*

An hour or so later, Tacita gasped in horror.

"Told you so," Jed murmured softly.

Rosamunda snarled.

They stood in the door of Tacita's stateroom, Jed holding his hat in his hand. He felt a certain amount of satisfaction, even though he wasn't happy to see her room all torn up and her things scattered about. He didn't like her reaction to finding them thus, either. In fact, it made him want to slay the perpetrator—after he'd comforted her in dubious ways, all of which flickered through his brain in the space of a very few seconds.

"Oh, dear. Oh, my goodness. Oh, heavens." Staring about with dismay, Tacita hugged Rosamunda close. Jed wished she were hugging him.

"I guess you were right, Mr. Hardcastle." She sounded very sad.

Rosamunda uttered a sound that was something between a growl and a purr, and Jed got the strangest impression she was muttering her version of "Told you so." He shook his head to dislodge the ridiculous thought.

"I 'spect I was, ma'am. I think that fellow is Mr. Piskeywhickle, and I think he's still after you. Or your dog."

This time he had no trouble deciphering Rosamunda's yip.

"Oh, good heavens, we can't allow that to happen, Mr. Hardcastle. We simply can't!"

When she turned those huge, worried blue eyes upon him, Jed felt his knees turn to jelly, his nether regions stiffen, and his resolve to be a gentleman wobble. Mentally knocking himself about the head and shoulders, he stiffened his resolve and commanded his manly parts to unstiffen and behave themselves.

"I won't let anything happen to you, Miss Grantham. Or your dog." He looked at Rosamunda, who scowled at him as if it had been he rather than Mr. Pickleflickle who'd ransacked Tacita's room. "I'll take a look through the train to see if I can find him."

"I'll go with you."

"No, you won't." Jed frowned heavily at her. "You stay here. That's all we need is to have Rosie start yapping and warn him off."

"Rosamunda," Tacita corrected, although her voice lacked conviction.

Rosamunda lifted her lip in a sneer.

183

"I—we—well—are you sure it's safe for us to stay here by ourselves?"

Tacita's voice was very soft, as though she feared appearing foolish in Jed's eyes. Jed thought she was merely showing uncommonly good sense in asking such a practical question. The urge assailed him to declare that he'd never leave her side, that he'd guide and guard her into the jaws of hell and out the other side, should she ask it of him. Sanity prevailed and he refrained.

"I'll leave you my derringer, ma'am. Keep the door locked and make sure you don't open it to anybody but me."

"Oh, my," whispered into his ears, tickled his brain and made him go giddy for a moment.

Shaking off the feeling, he drew the tiny gun out of his breast pocket and handed it to Tacita. The derringer, which had almost gotten lost in his own palm, looked about normal sized when Tacita lifted it up with two fingers, as though she were afraid it might decide to shoot her of its own accord.

"Is—is it loaded?"

"Wouldn't do much good if it wasn't, would it?"

She cleared her throat. "It's just that I've never had anything to do with firearms before, Mr. Hardcastle. I'd hate to wound anybody by accident." Her expression darkened when she added, "Although I think I'd enjoy shooting Mr. Picinisco."

"Just don't pull the trigger, ma'am, and you won't hurt anybody. But you can sure point it at anybody who tries to break in. Even a tiny gun like that will make most men think twice before they do anything the person holding the gun doesn't want 'em to."

Looking dubiously at the derringer, Tacita murmured, "I suppose so."

Rosamunda eyed the tiny weapon as if she'd like to have charge of it. Jed didn't expect the dog would have as many scruples as her mistress about who it shot, and spared a moment to be glad dogs didn't have hands that could grip things.

Striving to be as inconspicuous as possible—no mean feat for so large a man—he searched through every car on the train. When he was through, he searched them all again the other way. Twice he thought he'd spotted Pickywiggle, but both times the man he saw vanished in a flash. He didn't like the idea of Tacita sharing space on the same train with a man who'd caused her such distress. He didn't like it at all. Unless and until he found the blackguard and tied him up, though, he guessed he'd have to settle for protecting her.

He began to wonder if he should spend the night in Tacita's bedroom in order to protect her should Pinkerninker attempt a break-in overnight. Almost immediately, he realized his imagination was becoming overheated.

The good Lord knew, the rest of him became overheated at the idea of sleeping in a closed room with her. He wasn't sure how much more of Tacita Grantham's intimate presence he could stand without succumbing to his base impulses. They were getting baser and more difficult to resist as the hours passed. Although, he admitted unhappily, Tacita might have something to say if he attempted anything untoward. The knowledge did little to cool his ardor.

Rosamunda scowled as she stared out the sooty window of Tacita's stateroom and watched the dark night whiz past.

It was about time somebody besides herself recognized the villainous Mr. Cesare. She was only sorry it had been Jed who'd done so. She didn't like being beholden to him for anything. Nor did she like having to give him credit for anything.

Her mistress was upset, too. At the moment, she was pacing back and forth in the tiny room, looking worried and wringing her hands. The derringer Jed had given her rested on the washstand in the corner because Tacita didn't want to handle the deadly weapon unless she had to. Rosamunda guessed she didn't blame her, since Tacita was so squeamish about such things.

Rosamunda herself would have had no compunction about protecting the both of them with a gun, which just went to show that the resolution of a Yorkshire terrier female was far superior to that of a human female, even though human females were much better at slicing up thin strips of sirloin into bite-sized pieces than were their Yorkie sisters.

Tacita's restlessness was making Rosamunda's nerves jump. She lifted her head and uttered an admonitory growl then squeaked in surprise when Tacita swept her up and into her arms.

"Oh, darling, I'm worried, too. I'm just terrified that something might happen to Mr. Hardcastle. What if that awful man hurts him?"

While she appreciated Tacita nuzzling her neck in such a comforting manner, Rosamunda couldn't understand how she'd managed to misinterpret her admonishing growl to mean she was anxious about Jed Hardcastle's welfare. Rosamunda? Not bloody likely, to use an epithet borrowed from an infancy spent in Great Britain.

"Do you suppose that dreadful man will try to shoot him?"

In Rosamunda's opinion that wasn't very likely, either, since Jed Hardcastle could easily overpower the chubby Mr. Cesare. Since she couldn't communicate her opinion to Tacita, she was unable to reassure her.

Rosamunda resigned herself to being carted back and forth across the room, as Tacita didn't seem inclined to relax. With a sigh, she settled herself into Tacita's arms. At least she could still look out the window, for all the good it did her. She couldn't see much but the telegraph poles as the train raced past them. She'd heard somebody say the train was traveling at the alarming speed of thirty-five miles an hour, a speed almost beyond belief, and one that wouldn't even have been attempted if Yorkies ran things.

All at once, something beyond the window caught her eye. Her ears shot up even as she yipped to capture Tacita's attention.

"What is it, darling? Oh, dear, I hope it's nobody trying to break into our room."

Rosamunda almost bit Tacita again to get her to focus her attention on the obvious. Fortunately, after only a few seconds, Mistress noticed what Rosamunda had noticed, so she didn't have to.

"Oh! My goodness, what on earth is that?"

To Rosamunda's way of thinking, it was obvious what it was. Every now and then she regretted the physical limitations separating humans from canines, as removal of those limitations would make the human race simpler to communicate with. Most of the time, of course, she didn't want any more to do with humans than absolutely necessary.

Striding to the window, Tacita leaned over and pressed her face against the glass. There, outside their window, another train was passing on the tracks running beside the ones their own train rode upon.

"My goodness, that train's going fast. Why, I do believe it's going even faster than ours."

It was true. As she watched, Rosamunda saw the train, a short, sleek model with only five cars, draw alongside the one they were on.

Suddenly, Mistress uttered a sharp shriek, which hurt Rosamunda's ears. She barked to tell her so, but Tacita didn't seem to be paying any attention to her, which hurt her feelings. Then Tacita spoke, sending Rosamunda's grievance flying right out of her head.

"Good grief, darling, isn't that Uncle Luther?"

Rosamunda sat up straight in Tacita's arms and stared into the window of the passing train. When she saw Luther Adams Williamson shooting past in the other train, she was shocked to her daintily trimmed toenails.

"Are you absolutely sure, ma'am?"

Troubled, Jed peered at Tacita over his coffee cup. He'd searched the train from stem to stern several times over, but had been unable to catch another glimpse the man who might or might not have been his quarry. He'd finally gone to sleep sitting with his back against Tacita's door. Since he'd fallen over sideways every time the train rocked, his night had been far from restful. This morning his eyes felt gritty, his head ached, he was exhausted, and he wished they were already in San Francisco.

This latest twist in Tacita's tale struck him as all too possible. Who else but her uncle would have sent Piskaniska after Tacita? Even though Jed couldn't fathom what the man would want with the pothole terrier. Because he felt rotten, he scowled at Rosamunda. She bared her teeth back at him.

"I'm as sure as I can be," Tacita said. "Mind you, it was dark and the train was moving very fast, but there was a light on in the other car, and I swear it was Uncle Luther at the window. Almost as soon as I saw him, he turned away from me, but I know it was him."

"Hmmm."

"I wonder what he's doing headed north. The last I knew, he was on his way back home."

"I 'spect he's on his way to San Francisco," Jed muttered.

"Oh, do you really think so?"

Tacita's smile was entirely too cheerful for Jed to take on an empty stomach and no sleep. He wished the waiter would bring his breakfast. Irritated, he asked, "Well, don't you?"

Her face innocent of guile, she said, "Why should he be on his way to San Francisco, Mr. Hardcastle?"

Jed chuffed out an exasperated breath. "For Pete's sake, Miss Grantham, he's the one causing you all this trouble. Don't you see that yet?"

She blinked several times before her lips parted into an expression of hurt. Those lips were far too enticing for him to contemplate in his weakened condition, and Jed had to look away. He used the time to scan the dining car. Of course, Piskywisky wasn't in it this morning.

The Indian fellow and the British gent had renewed their argument. As the two men walked past their table and out of the dining car, deep in conversation, Jed frowned after them because he felt grumpy.

"Oh, Mr. Hardcastle, not Uncle Luther. You can't still believe him to have sent that man after me. Surely you must be mistaken."

Uncomfortable with Tacita's distress, Jed shifted his shoulders into a hunch. "I don't think I'm wrong, ma'am."

Tacita followed a small silence with, "Oh, dear. But—but what does he want? What could I have that he can't just ask me for? Except Rosamunda, of course, but I can't imagine why he'd want to take her. He never seemed to pay any attention to her at all."

"Well, that's one thing in his favor, at any rate."

Rosamunda growled. Jed growled back.

"Mr. Hardcastle! How can you say such a mean thing?" She hugged Rosamunda to her bosom, and Jed had to look away.

He didn't like the suspicious glitter in her eyes, though. If there was one thing he didn't need this morning, it was a weepy female. Especially one he'd like to comfort in questionable ways.

He grumbled, "Sorry, Miss Grantham," and didn't mean it.

"But what can he want?" Tacita persisted. Her face screwed up into an expression of intense concentration. Jed had an almost overwhelming urge to divert her attention in an all-too-physical manner.

"I don't know, ma'am." He took another gulp of scalding coffee and hoped the pain would keep his mind on higher matters. "What about that dog collar?" He eyed Rosamunda with loathing; she returned the look with one equally scathing.

Tacita glanced down at Rosamunda, who rested beside her on another chair. "I'm sure that's not it, Mr. Hardcastle. He never commented about the collar or paid any attention to it. In fact, as I said before, he never paid any attention to Rosamunda at all."

"How'd he manage that?" Jed regretted the sarcasm he heard in his voice. He chalked it up to his state of weariness.

"Whatever do you mean, Mr. Hardcastle?"

Tacita looked at Jed as though she'd never even heard about her dog attacking anything that came within three feet of it. He shook his head when he realized she honestly didn't get it. "Nothing, ma'am. I didn't mean a thing."

Things came to a head that morning after breakfast. Jed was looking forward to falling asleep on the floor of Tacita's stateroom, an arrangement Tacita suggested as preferable to him propping up her door. Jed had objected but ultimately agreed, as he needed to catch up on his sleep or he wouldn't be good for anything.

As he stood in the hallway and Tacita unlocked her door and pushed it open, his eyes were already closing, in fact.

A duet of sharp screams made them open back up again in a hurry.

Tacita followed up her scream with a shrieked, "Who are you?"

"Oh, my goodness gracious, I must have found myself in the wrong compartment! How terribly foolish I am, to be sure!"

It was the Indian fellow who had been arguing for the past two days with that sissy Englishman. Jed, in no mood to play games, was not amused. He picked the fellow up by his collar and slammed him against the wall.

"What the hell are you doing here, mister? And don't tell me you made a mistake, either!"

"Oh, please be careful, Mr. Hardcastle. Don't kill him!"

"Why not?" Jed growled, furious.

Apparently Tacita could think of no good answer, because she remained silent and only clutched Rosamunda, who looked as if she'd gladly help Jed dispatch the intruder. Jed lifted the man higher, shook him hard, and took pleasure—which he knew to be unkind—in the fact that the fellow was slight enough to be shaken. By this time, Jed was in a really bad mood.

"What the hell are you doing in this room?"

The man uttered a gurgling sound, which only made Jed angrier.

"Answer me, damn it!"

The fellow choked out an incoherent "Grrmmph."

"What the devil does that mean?" Jed shook him again and glared down at Tacita, who had tapped him on the shoulder. She had to stretch to do it, and he would have thought that was kind of cute if he hadn't been so peeved. "What?" he asked her roughly.

"Er, I think you're choking him, Mr. Hardcastle. I don't think he could answer you if he wanted to."

"Oh." Jed dropped the man, who sank into a heap of arms and legs on the floor. Jed didn't feel sorry for him.

"What were you doing in Miss Grantham's cabin?"

The man didn't answer immediately, but lay there gagging and clutching his throat. Jed, in no mood to pamper an interloper, drew back his booted foot, and was about to kick the fellow into compliance, when Tacita clutched his arm. He glowered down at her, annoyed that she'd interrupted again.

"Don't kick him, Mr. Hardcastle. Please don't kick him. Let him catch his breath."

"Harumph."

Since she'd asked—and since she looked scared—Jed guessed he'd comply. He didn't want to. When he got tired like this, he got mean. His ma used to warn him about his temper. She'd made him promise to get a good night's sleep at all times. His ma, however, hadn't anticipated the perils inherent in guarding Miss Tacita Grantham.

"Please?"

Her voice was sweet and pleading, and Jed realized he was still scowling. Her dog, he noticed, was growling and watching the villain on the floor as if she was only waiting for a chance to tear his throat out. He felt a sudden spirit of affinity with her, and realized he must *really* be tired.

"Oh, all right." He knew he sounded grudging. He felt grudging.

"Thank you."

Jed continued to glare balefully at the Indian man. The fellow had stopped gagging by this time and merely wheezed as he struggled to his hands and knees. Although Jed guessed he wouldn't strangle him or kick him to death, his compassion didn't reach so far that he felt sorry for him or offered to help him to his feet.

"What are you doing in here?"

The man gasped.

"Are you the bastard who tore up Miss Grantham's room yesterday?"

He wheezed.

"Answer me, damn it!"

Tacita tugged his sleeve again. "Er, Mr. Hardcastle, I think he needs another moment or two."

Jed transferred his glare at Tacita. Her sweet expression served to alleviate his fury a little, but not much. He heaved an exasperated sigh. "Oh, all right."

Tucking Rosamunda under her arm, Tacita knelt beside her fallen foe and assisted him to his feet. "Here, let me help you, sir." She guided him to her bed.

Immediately, the fellow sank down onto the soft mattress and buried his head in his hands.

What really aggravated Jed—besides the fact that she'd let the bastard sit on her bed, where he had absolutely no business whatever—was that she seemed to feel some kind of compassion for him. He could tell Rosamunda shared his own sentiments, and decided that as soon as he'd questioned the trespasser he *would* sleep. Any time he found himself in agreement with that animal about anything at all, it was time for a nap.

The fellow finally managed to gasp out, "Thank you, miss."

"Sit here, and I'll get you a drink of water."

"You are an angel of mercy, madam."

Jed snorted. Rosamunda made a lunge for the fellow's wrist as Tacita let it go. Jed didn't blame her.

"Tut, tut, darling. I'm sure this gentleman is sorry for his misdeed."

Jed rolled his eyes. Rosamunda yipped.

The man said, "Oh, yes. Yes, indeed, madam. Yes, sahib. I, Virendra Karnik, am a well of sorrow about the dastardly deed I have performed."

Jed muttered under his breath. To Karnik, he said, "You should be a damned well of sorrow, mister. Now what the hell are you doing here, and who hired you?"

"Really, Mr. Hardcastle! Can't you see Mr. Karnik is still feeling poorly?" Tacita handed Karnik a glass of water, which he downed greedily.

It was too much for Jed. Forgetting his mother's admonition to count to ten before he gave in to his temper—particularly when he was suffering from lack of sleep—he whacked the glass out of Karnik's hand with the back of his own and sent it crashing against the stateroom wall. It shattered with a sharp explosion of glass, precipitating a shriek out of Tacita and another from Karnik.

Tacita was so startled that she loosened her grip on Rosamunda. The dog immediately took advantage of her mistress's lapse by leaping onto the bed and heading directly for Karnik's turban. Grabbing his earlobe between her sharp teeth, she shook her head violently.

Karnik screamed in pain and terror. Tacita put her hands to her cheeks and watched, horrified.

For the first time all morning, Jed smiled. "If you want to do some real good, aim for the jugular, Rosie," he advised mildly.

"Rosamunda! Rosamunda, stop that!"

"Aaiiiiieeee!"

Jed crossed his hands over his chest. "Let her be, Miss Grantham. Maybe the bastard'll think twice about busting into other people's staterooms if your dog chews his ears off."

"Rosamunda! Rosamunda!"

"Get her off me! Please! I beg you!"

Rosamunda apparently deemed Jed's earlier suggestion to be a sound one. Leaving Karnik's ear alone for the nonce, she pounced on his neck. Karnik's hands closed over the vulnerable spot a second before she did so, and she only managed to close her jaws around a couple of fingers.

"Good dog," Jed said, his smile broadening.

"Aaiiiiieeee!" Karnik shrieked again.

Daring to reach for Rosamunda, Tacita said, "Mr. Hardcastle!" in a reproving voice. It took some doing, but she eventually managed to pry her dog's teeth from Karnik's fingers.

Jed sighed. He appreciated that little rat this morning. He guessed it was only because he was tired, but he truly appreciated her. He admired her grit, too, especially in light of her mistress's misapplied bleeding heart.

Although it went against the grain, he complied when Tacita demanded that he wet a towel and hand it to her. He guessed it was a good idea to bind Karnik's wounds so he wouldn't keep bleeding all over Tacita's bed. He scowled when he thought of the nasty little burglar on her bed.

Jed glowered all the time Tacita was dressing the wounds on Karnik's earlobe and hand. Rosamunda had to be tied up during the operation because she kept lunging at the intruder. She'd done her level best, but she hadn't managed to inflict much damage, in spite of the bloody mess she'd left behind. Jed appreciated her efforts, even though he wished she'd shut up about it now. The damned dog's yapping was about to bust his brain.

"There," Tacita said after a while.

She stood aside and straightened, pressing a hand to her back as though it ached from having been bent for so long. Jed resented Karnik for that, too. And for Tacita's subsequent question.

"Do you feel better now?"

"What do you care how he feels, damn it? He was rummaging through your private compartment."

She turned to frown at him. "Well, I believe he's been punished adequately, Mr. Hardcastle. After all, you and Rosamunda both tried to kill him."

Rosamunda gave a particularly vicious growl. Jed didn't blame her.

"He deserved it."

With her lips squeezed into two tight lines, Tacita snapped, "Perhaps he was wrong to break into my stateroom, but if you expect to discover the reason for it, I believe you'd better wait to kill him until after he tells us why he did so."

Karnik whimpered. Jed hated to admit that Tacita was right. Rosamunda subsided into a sulky heap of Yorkie fur.

Feeling about as crabby as he'd ever felt in his life, Jed said, "All right. I'll question him." He stalked over to Karnik, who cowered away from him. As well he should.

"Who hired you?"

Jed's snarling question made Karnik hunch up further, until he looked like one of those gnomes from the Grimm's fairy tale book Jed remembered from his childhood. A gnome with white sticking plaster on his ear and a hand swaddled in gauze. That turban he wore only added to the effect.

Before Karnik could answer, Tacita asked, "How do you know anybody hired him, Mr. Hardcastle? Perhaps he's operating on his own."

At her interference, Jed's temper soared until his blood nearly boiled and his head roared. Clenching his fists and trying not to let them get away and thrash the man cowering in front of him, Jed said through gritted teeth, "Let me handle this, please, Miss Grantham."

Tacita sniffed. "Well, it seems to me you're going about it entirely wrong, Mr. Hardcastle."

Rosamunda growled. Jed knew the dog was on his side. He wasn't sure he'd thank her for it if he ever caught up on his sleep, but right now he approved.

"Please," came a quavery plea from the bed.

Jed and Tacita ceased glaring at each other and transferred their frowns to Karnik, who shrank back even further.

"Oh, what do you want?" Tacita snapped.

"I want to confess."

"Oh." Tacita's annoyance seemed to evaporate in a puff of surprise.

Not so Jed's. "To what? Make it clear and quick if you don't want that dog all over you again."

"Really, Mr. Hardcastle!"

Tears began to leak from Karnik's eyes. "Please," he whimpered. "Please, anything but that."

"Talk fast, then." Jed ignored Tacita's hot glare.

"I only came for the Eye. The Delhi Hahm-Ahn-Der Eye, sahib. That is all. The Eye. Which rightly belongs to the Great Goddess of the Temple of Hahm in Delhi, sweet madam. It is one of our most revered treasures, you see. Surely you will not continue to deprive the people of their treasure now that you know how very much they miss it."

Tacita and Jed exchanged a blank look, then returned their attention to Karnik.

"I beg your pardon?" Tacita asked politely.

Karnik said, equally politely, "The Eye, madam. The Great Delhi Hahm-Ahn-Der Eye."

"What ham-and-rye?" Jed demanded, furious. "I thought a ham-and-rye was some kind of sandwich. What the hell are you talking about?"

"A sandwich?" Karnik looked as if it was taking all his strength not to cry. He clasped his hands together, but they must have hurt because he unclasped them again immediately. "No, no." His voice was pathetic, pleading. "Not a ham-and-rye. The Hahm-Ahn-Der Eye. The Eye"—he pointed a swaddled finger at his own frightened eyeball—"the eye which was stolen from the

Great Goddess residing in the temple in Delhi."

Tacita cocked her head to one side. "The Eye? I don't believe I've ever heard of this Eye, Mr. Karnik."

"What the hell are you talking about, mister?" Jed took a menacing step toward the bad, sending Karnik scuttling back into a corner. His eyes began to leak tears.

"The Eye. Surely you know about the Eye, sir. Madam?" Karnik almost whimpered. He cast a pleading look at Tacita, who had proved more amenable to his distress thus far than had Jed. He apparently wasn't encouraged by her expression, because he began to cry harder.

"I don't know what you're talking about, sir. Perhaps if you were to explain what this Eye is, we might be able to help you."

"Ah, to hell with it. Why don't I shake him up a little more. He's just trying to stall for time, Miss Grantham."

"Indeed I am not doing any such thing! Please, sahib! You must believe me! I was hired to fetch back the Eye from the delightful Miss Grantham here! I have no other purpose in the whole world! My entire life is devoted to the holy endeavor."

Rosamunda's head appeared out from where she'd buried it in her front paws and she snorted. To Jed, it sounded like she didn't believe Karnik's story any more than he did. Not for a minute.

"Bull," he said, eliciting a gasp from Tacita. He scowled at her for being such a priss under the circumstances.

"Indeed, it is not bull, my most revered sir. It is the truth."

"Do you know what this fellow's talking about, Miss Grantham?"

She shook her head. "I'm afraid I don't, Mr. Hardcastle. I'm sorry, Mr. Karnik." She gave the fellow a sympathetic smile.

Jed decided the time for both sympathy and diplomacy had passed. He grabbed Karnik by his unswaddled ear and dragged him upright. Karnik's scream shot through his head like a gunshot and irritated Jed. He shook him.

"What the hell is this Eye you're talking about and who the hell hired you to find it?"

"You're going to snap his neck, Mr. Hardcastle, and then you'll never learn anything!"

Although the tug she gave his arm wasn't strong enough to do much more than annoy him, her words gave Jed pause. He dropped Karnik like a sack of potatoes. The fellow rolled himself up into a ball on Tacita's bed and sobbed.

"Please, Mr. Karnik," Tacita said after giving Jed another good hot glare. "We don't understand. I know nothing of any Eye. If you'll explain it to us, perhaps we can help you."

"Help him? I'll help him!" Jed muttered.

"You're not helping at all, Mr. Hardcastle. Go away."

Indignant—after all, *he* wasn't the intruder here—Jed did as she asked. Since the room was small, about the only place to go away to was the corner in which Rosamunda had been confined. Unthinking, his feelings hurt, Jed squatted down and decided if that's the way Tacita was going to be about it, he'd just let her handle everything.

"Here, Rosie," he said in a hurt voice, and began to pet Rosamunda. He only realized what he was doing when Rosamunda's soft growl penetrated his sleep-deprived brain. Immediately, he stopped stroking the dog, who had evidently inherited her peppery disposition from her mistress. Nevertheless, he listened, sulking along with Rosamunda, while Tacita interrogated her uninvited guest.

"Now, please, Mr. Karnik, stop crying and talk to me."

Sniffling, Karnik did as she asked. After fifteen or twenty minutes of eavesdropping from his corner, Jed came to the conclusion that the little Indian really was after this Eye, whatever it was, and that he really did want to return it to the Goddess, whatever that was. And, what's more, he really thought Tacita had it. Jed also realized that, in spite of Karnik's long explanation, Tacita still didn't know what he was talking about.

Reluctantly, feeling very ill-used and miffed, Jed rejoined prisoner and interrogator at the bed.

"Are you sure you don't know what this Eye thing is, Miss Grantham?" He tried to keep his voice from revealing his grumpiness.

She shook her head, as puzzled as he. "No. I have no idea."

"Perhaps my employer is mistaken, Miss Grantham," Karnik offered hopefully. "Perhaps you are not after all the possessor of the Eye."

"Brilliant deduction," Jed grumbled. Tacita kicked him. He frowned at her.

"It won't do any good to frighten him again," she hissed.

Jed allowed as to how she was right. He didn't like allowing it.

"Besides, somebody other than Mr. Karnik apparently believes I have this Eye thing, too, whatever it is. If he went to all the trouble of sending Mr. Karnik after me, he's not likely to give up now." Another thought occurred to her and she drew Jed away from the bed. "Do you suppose this man is in cahoots with that awful Mr. Picinisco, Mr. Hardcastle?"

The thought had already occurred to Jed. He shook his head, not because he doubted it but because he didn't know. Then he shrugged. Then, when Tacita looked like she was about to kick him again, he said, "Damned if I know. Shouldn't think Pinkersnicky had enough money to hire anybody, not even this damned little poop."

Turning abruptly toward the bed again, Tacita huffed, "I do wish you would cease your terrible swearing, Mr. Hardcastle."

Jed frowned after her for a moment, as annoyed with himself for forgetting his manners and swearing as at her admonition. He rejoined her and decided to glare at Karnik for a while since he still felt like glaring.

"And you still want us to believe that this whatever-his-name-is fellow is the one who hired you?" Karnik had insisted from the beginning that he was employed by a person named Avinash Agrawal, but Jed wasn't sure he believed him since Tacita had never heard of Agrawal. He had to acknowledge, however, that the little crook seemed to be so scared by this time, he probably wouldn't withhold any information that might help his cause. The knowledge only frustrated Jed more, mostly because he wanted Tacita's Uncle Luther to be the author of their problems and prove that Jed had been right.

"I don't think we're going to get any more information out of him, Mr. Hardcastle," Tacita said thoughtfully.

His eyes eloquent with hope, fear, and pain, Karnik nodded energetically. "I know no more, Miss Grantham. Not a thing. Nothing. There is nothing regarding this endeavor that you do not now know. My bank of knowledge has been completely exhausted and now resides in your own revered pockets. Truly." He spread his hands out in a beseeching gesture.

Jed had never cared for fancy talk. "Shut your blamed mouth," he advised Karnik now. Tacita kicked him again.

After another several minutes, during which he exchanged many more hot words with Tacita than with Karnik, Jed agreed to hog-tie the villain and take him to the train's engineer. He wasn't gentle about it, and he viewed Karnik's sigh of relief when he left him to the engineer's tender mercies with satisfaction.

As he stomped back to Tacita's stateroom, Jed was still mad. Shoot, he hated it when people interfered while he was executing his duties. Besides, although he disliked admitting that his pride was involved and he wanted to look good in Tacita's eyes, it was the truth. Therefore, he especially resented her interference. He was the strong one here; she was supposed to be relying on him, dadblast it. Maybe he'd been a little rough on Karnik, but he was tired, blast it, and needed a nap.

He got it at last, curled up against the wall of Tacita's stateroom. Tacita had one more demand to make upon him before she let him sleep.

"Here, Mr. Hardcastle, cover yourself with my bathrobe. You're apt to catch a chill otherwise."

Jed looked at her bathrobe as if he feared it might smother him. "I don't need your bathrobe. I never get sick."

"Don't be ridiculous. It's chilly in the train, and you're as susceptible to chills as anybody else on earth."

He heaved an exasperated sigh. "I won't get cold. Shoot, I've slept out under the stars in the dead of winter. This is a train, for Pete's sake."

Tacita tapped her foot and held out her bathrobe. "It's cold on this train and I refuse to allow you to act like a baby for the sake of your image. Now, take this bathrobe and use it to cover yourself up, Mr. Hardcastle, or I shall keep talking and not let you rest."

Jed snatched the robe from her fingers, feeling abused. Tacita smiled sweetly at his compliance. "That's a good boy," she murmured, making him harrumph harder.

"I still think covering up's stupid." Actually, he thought it was a sissy thing to do. It was a good thing nobody from his other life was here to see him.

As his eyelids drooped lower over his gritty eyes, however, Jed had to admit this was a cozy way to nap, with his huge shoulders swaddled in her little robe. And it was kind of nice of Tacita to make such a fuss over his welfare, too. Shoot, he hadn't been fussed over by a female for years. Not even his mother bothered anymore, and he was pretty sure Miss Amalie

Crunch would laugh if anybody suggested Jed would appreciate such a thing.

He barely noticed Tacita bustling about, cleaning up her bloodstained bedclothes and tidying things. He drifted off to sleep with the faint sweet smell of her perfume soothing his senses, and happy images of them making beautiful love together floating in and out of his brain. A second or so before his brain shut down and sleep claimed him, he wondered why Tacita Grantham cared if he was comfortable.

# *Chapter Twelve*

If Rosamunda never saw the inside of a saddle-bag again in this lifetime, it would be too soon for her. With her hind feet buried in soft rabbit fur and her front paws balancing on the sides of the stiff leather bag, she glared at the passing scenery and resented every "Oooh" and "Aaah" her mistress uttered over the stupid wildflowers growing alongside the trail and the equally stupid sky spread overhead. If anybody'd release her from this awful leather-and-rabbit-fur prison, Rosamunda'd show them what she thought of those stupid flowers.

Since she wasn't allowed to dig up the flowers or water them, Rosamunda spent her time wishing Tacita, for all her virtues, hadn't decided to breed Rosamunda to Prince Albert. Rosamunda would almost rather remain single and childless than endure any more of this obnoxious journey with the obnoxious Jedediah Hardcastle.

At least the train had been comfortable. This packsaddle-overland nonsense was more than any Yorkshire terrier should be asked to endure. Particularly a Yorkshire terrier of Rosamunda's superb breeding.

Bah! She couldn't stand it! She didn't care how much danger Jed Hardcastle believed they'd be in if they remained on the train all the way to San Francisco. For her money, Rosamunda would far rather perish in the comfort of a railway carriage than in this wretched saddlebag strapped to the side of a smelly old horse.

The monster and Mistress had hired the horses, some mules, and a small pack wagon in a place that didn't even deserve the appellation "village." They'd debarked one stop before the train was to have reached Santa Fe, and were now making their way to Denver—another heathen city in the heathen West, Rosamunda presumed. From Denver, Jed said, they'd be able to hire a stagecoach to carry them the rest of the way to San Francisco.

Whatever a stagecoach was. It sounded mighty sinister to Rosamunda.

She sniffed, inhaling a snootful of dust that made her sneeze. Her resentment against Jed edged up another notch or two. Although she knew nothing about stagecoaches, she expected their trip from Denver wouldn't be very restful. At least she wouldn't have to endure this horrid saddlebag anymore. Tacita, who generally had her priorities straight except in certain circumstances, would probably hold Rosamunda on her lap once they boarded the stagecoach. That was something to look forward to. Rosamunda could hardly wait to get to Denver.

With one last, hot scowl at Jed's enormous back—and it was a sin for anything to be as big as that monster's back, too—Rosamunda lowered herself into the saddlebag. She dug furiously at the rabbit fur for several seconds, more to indicate her displeasure in this latest twist in her fortunes than to build a nest. Then she turned around thrice, subsided into a little ball, and closed her eyes, praying for sleep.

Let these benighted human beings find their own way to San Francisco, if that's the way they were going to be about it. They'd receive no further help from Rosamunda.

Tacita stared at Jed's broad back. They were alone together again. She and Jed and the vast American frontier. Well, and Rosamunda, but the Yorkie hardly counted, since she was so small and all.

Traveling over hundreds of miles with no company other than Jed's was a thrilling prospect for Tacita. While on the train, she'd enjoyed such luxuries as baths and decent food, but she discovered herself missing their cozy chats by the campfire. Although she'd tried her best to disguise it, she hadn't been disappointed when Jed suggested traversing the rest of the way to San Francisco by some means other than rail.

"This Agrawal character, whoever he is, obviously knows your route, Miss Grantham," he'd told her when they left the train right before it reached Santa Fe. "And if that man you saw on the other train last night really was your uncle, he does, too."

209

"I refuse to believe Uncle Luther has anything to do with this strange series of events, Mr. Hardcastle."

He'd looked particularly impressive when he'd lifted an eyebrow and stared down at her. His expression let her know he thought she was being foolish, if not downright stupid, and it aggravated her almost as much as his assertion that her uncle could be somehow involved in these criminal activities. Still, his ironically lifted brow had reminded her forcefully of a character in her favorite novel.

For just a moment, he'd looked exactly as she'd always pictured Prince Michael's dashing friend, Rupert Hentzau, in *Prisoner of Zenda*. Only much, much bigger. And, it must be acknowledged, of a finer character. Tacita was certain Jed Hardcastle wouldn't betray her, or leap into the castle moat and swim to safety, abandoning her to her fate, should things take a dangerous turn.

No. Jedediah Hardcastle would protect her. Tacita knew it, and her heart thrummed a thrilling rhythm in her breast. She'd never had anybody make it his business to protect her before. Actually, she'd never had anybody pay any attention at all to her before.

She decided not to think about that right now.

She did, however, discover an almost ungovernable itch to have Jed pay attention to her some more. After a moment's thought, she decided she had nothing to lose by speaking to him. He might not appreciate her insinuating herself into his silence, but Jed Hardcastle wouldn't run out on her just because she was tedious.

\*    \*    \*

"Mr. Hardcastle?"

Jed had harbored a faint hope that he'd be able to forget that he and Tacita were alone again. He'd hunched himself in his saddle and done everything he could think of to become one with nature. That's what he'd always done before; or at least that's the impression he'd tried to give to all his other clients. And it hadn't been difficult, mostly because he preferred the silence of the land to the inane chitchat indulged in by most of the back-easterners he'd met in his life.

At Tacita's question, however, he realized how silly he'd been. There was no way on earth he could forget Tacita Grantham rode with him. And that there was probably not another human being within a fifty-mile radius of them. And what he'd like to do with her out here in the quiet. Or anywhere else, for that matter. Not even the devil-tongued terrier was in evidence to torment him at the moment. For several miles, she'd hung out of her fancy saddlebag and glared daggers at Jed, but she'd given it up at last.

As soon as Tacita's sweet voice caressed his ears, he felt like groaning.

Instead, he growled, "Yeah?"

"Er, how long did you say it will it take us to get to Denver?"

Frowning slightly—he hadn't meant to sound so gruff—he said, "About a week or so."

She cleared her throat, and Jed realized she was feeling a little shy. Probably because he hadn't been very polite in his response, a fact his mother would deplore. He could almost hear her lecture on courtesy as he rode, in fact.

He tried again. "I expect it won't take us more

than a week or so, Miss Grantham. The accommodations along the stage route won't be this rough, although they won't be near as comfortable as they were on the train."

"Oh, I don't mind the roughness," Tacita said quickly.

Hearing sincerity in her voice, Jed glanced over his shoulder, nonplussed. "You don't?" He regretted that he hadn't hidden his incredulity better when he saw her pretty eyebrows draw together.

"You needn't look so surprised, Mr. Hardcastle. Just because I'd never been exposed to camping out before we undertook this journey doesn't of necessity mean I can't learn."

"No, ma'am. I reckon that's true."

Warming to her subject, Tacita added, "Nor does it mean I can't enjoy the experience. I find I rather appreciate life in the wild and nature in all her untamed glory."

Rosamunda snorted, sending a few strands of rabbit fluff sailing out of her saddlebag. They wafted away on a breeze.

Tacita gave an indignant sniff, sending a tremendous urge shooting through Jed. He wanted to snatch her off her saddle and into his arms. Good gravy, he thought glumly, he had it bad.

"In fact, I think I've done rather well on our journey thus far."

Suppressing his urges, Jed murmured, "Yes, ma'am. You have. You've done mighty well." There. That had been polite, hadn't it? Besides, it was more or less the truth. He hoped it would make up for his earlier shortness of manner.

"I have? Do you really think so?"

She sounded so amazed and so pleased by his

offhand compliment, that Jed's sympathies were stirred. An urge to prop up Tacita's self-regard swelled in his large chest. This woman needed her confidence bolstered. He expected that parents who found a body tedious as a child might leave anyone feeling insecure and unsure of herself. He'd heard female children were particularly vulnerable to slights, perceived or real.

Jed knew for a fact that when anybody told him he was a nuisance when he was a boy, he used to figure he was just doing his job. From what Tacita had said about her childhood, if anybody had told her she was a nuisance when she was a girl, she'd have figured she was being bad. He knew it was silly of him to want to undo in a couple of months a lifetime's worth of bad feelings about herself, but he also guessed he wouldn't lose anything by trying.

"Yes, ma'am," he continued, feeling quite noble about his mission. "You've held up pretty well on this trip so far. For a female."

"Thank you."

She didn't sound as appreciative as Jed might have wished, and he figured maybe she was still feeling shy. Because he was in an expansive mood this fine morning and had finally had a good rest, he decided it wouldn't hurt to elaborate.

"Yes'm. When we first met up in Powder Gulch and I got a gander at you and your fancy clothes and your dog and all, I figured you for one of them—those—worthless, snobby city females who'd screech and scream every time you saw a snake or sat on a rock of something."

"Really?"

"And when I saw how you pampered that dog

213

of yours, I pretty much figured you were like a lady I met up with once in Houston. She weighed around three hundred pounds and carried a French poodle with her everywhere. Called it Fifi, and fed the stupid thing better than her servants."

"Servants?" She must have swallowed wrong, because the word came out sort of strangled.

"Had a whole house full of 'em," Jed continued. "Hell, I figure if she'd done a third of the work she had those poor people do for her, she'd'a lost a hundred pounds easy. Nothin' like settin' around for gettin' fat, my ma always says."

"Does she?" Jed heard her suck in a big breath. "And you thought I was like that lady?"

"Yup. Then, on the first day, when you insisted on using that stupid sidesaddle, I knew it. Hell—er—shoot, I expected I'd be having to sling you over my shoulder and carry you most of the way to San Francisco."

"Indeed?"

"Yup. But then you surprised me and agreed to ride astride. Reckon the insides of your thighs must have been pretty chapped by that time, but you never moaned about 'em." He chuckled, then realized Tacita, being a proper lady and from the city and all, would probably frown upon him talking about her thighs. He cleared his throat. "Er, anyway, I thought it was mighty bold of you to agree to ride astride, ma'am."

"I see. Well, now, isn't that interesting?"

Jed couldn't account for the way her words seemed to have gone cold. To the best of his recollection, he hadn't ever said so many nice things about anybody in one conversation be-

214

fore. Especially not a female. He gave a mental shrug and decided being so extravagant with his praise felt kind of good. Anyway, she could use it. Might bolster her confidence and make the rest of their journey less burdensome to her if she knew he approved of her performance so far.

"Shoot, ma'am, all in all, I reckon you've held up better'n most of the men I've guided. After all, the most we ever generally face on one of my guided trips is a few buffalo, a deer or an antelope, or bad water. Maybe a mountain lion or a bear. I've never encountered an Indian or a crazy Gypsy drummer or a gun-totin' bandit before I met up with you."

She was silent for the longest time. Jed figured she was embarrassed about having been honored with such an array of accolades. He hardly blamed her. If all those compliments had been aimed at him, he'd be blushing from the glory of it.

Tacita bowed her head and stared at her fingers, which had tightened over her saddle horn. She didn't know whether to scream or cry. Or be flattered. Since her teeth were clenched up hard enough to bite through barbed wire, she supposed she couldn't do any of those things until she calmed down a trifle.

"Anyway, I think you've done real well, Miss Grantham. Real well."

At last prying her teeth apart, Tacita opened her mouth. Her intention was to say "Thank you." What came out was, "Please call me Tacita, Mr. Hardcastle."

Immediately, heat infused her cheeks, and she knew she'd turned red. Of course, since she'd been out in the elements for so long and her face was now as brown as a berry and freckled to boot, she didn't suppose Jed would be able to tell. Nonetheless, she turned her head away so he couldn't see. Rosamunda took that opportunity to utter a ferocious growl, so Tacita bowed over the saddlebag and began to fuss with her.

Silence greeted her utterance, and Tacita wondered if Jed was as astonished by it as she was. She heard him clear his throat again.

"Er—you want me to call you by your first name, ma'am?"

He sounded uncertain, and Tacita's embarrassment grew. Along with embarrassment, a sense of ill-usage blossomed. Imagine, him comparing her to a three-hundred-pound female with a poodle named Fifi! Why, she didn't weigh more than ninety-five pounds, if that, and anybody who'd compare so superior a Yorkshire terrier as Rosamunda to a French poodle was unfit to own a dog!

She snapped, "Yes. Unless that offends your ideals of Western masculinity, Mr. Hardcastle."

After she heard the sarcasm in her voice, she expected him to bridle and the conversation to degenerate into one of the verbal battles they'd been waging ever since they left Powder Gulch. She was, therefore, surprised when he said, "Well, then, ma'am, thank you kindly. And I'd take it as a real honor if you'd call me Jed."

At once her indignation evaporated. Why, he sounded quite diffident. Tacita was charmed.

"Thank you, Jed. I'd be pleased to call you by your Christian name."

For some unaccountable reason, Tacita felt inordinately pleased with herself as the mules clopped her and Jed and Rosamunda along the mountainous trail on their way to Denver.

It was because of her parents, of course. Jed had known it for some time now. They'd left her all alone to the mercies of hired help and she'd never learned to appreciate herself. That's why she doted on that fat-assed terrier of hers and had no self-confidence. It was 'cause she didn't realize she could give her affection to a human being who would value it.

A vague itch he'd been nursing along for many a day now began to solidify in Jed's breast. He knew it wasn't a good thing, but he couldn't help but wish Tacita could lavish some of her affection on him. The at-first-tentative wish had grown over the days until it could now be classified as a full-fledged longing.

His longing had not abated when they camped that night. In fact, it had become stronger and more fully defined as the day progressed.

This was terrible. He was promised to Miss Amalie Crunch. He had no business harboring lustful thoughts about Miss Tacita Grantham. Honor, right, suitability, prudence, rectitude, propriety: All of those virtues and more dictated that he redeem his word and marry Amalie Crunch. Nowhere in the entire gamut of human principles was one that forgave a man for jilting a woman to whom one was practically betrothed in order to take up with a female after whom one merely lusted.

Unfortunately, Jed couldn't seem to fight his attraction any longer. Not only that, but he'd come to the dismal conclusion that mere lust wasn't his primary problem. Hell, he'd conquered physical desire before.

No. His problem, as he saw it, looked to be dangerously close to love. His mind tiptoed around the word cautiously, eyeing it askance from different angles and hoping it would turn out to be something else; something not so frightening.

It didn't work. No matter how he looked at it, the result was the same. He—God save him— loved Tacita Grantham. He loved a pampered, rich city woman who didn't know beans about the West and who was engaged to marry somebody else. He sighed, hoping he'd get over it before he made a fool of himself.

Tacita dismounted that evening feeling as stiff as if she'd never been on a horse before. She wanted to rub her sore bottom, but since Jed was right there watching her she didn't. Then she had the perfectly sinful thought that she'd like him to rub her bottom for her.

Oh, dear. This was terrible. After having deliberated all day long, ever since she'd asked Jed to call her by her first name, Tacita had come to some uneasy conclusions.

For years, she had whiled away idle moments in the contemplation of how it would feel to be loved. Although she would never allow herself to believe that her parents didn't love her—they were, after all, her parents—she had come to the realization long since that the kind of love her parents had for her wasn't the most comforting in the world. Her parents' love for her wasn't the kind that invited a person to unburden herself of her problems, or the kind that kissed skinned knees and made them better.

When Tacita had had problems with teachers, she never talked to her parents about them. She talked to Mrs. Wilkins, the housekeeper, if she talked to anybody at all.

When Billy Jones had called her a pumpkin head, she hadn't cried and told her mama about it. No. Tacita had merely figured Billy was right, since she'd never been given reason to believe he wasn't. In fact, when Mrs. Wilkins assured her she was no such thing, she wasn't quite sure whether to believe her or Billy Jones. After all, Billy Jones's parents hadn't gone away and left him to the tender mercies of a housekeeper. Only the parents of pumpkin heads did that.

When Tacita thought about being loved, the kind of love she'd received as a child was not the kind she craved.

No. If Tacita were ever to be loved, she'd want a gentleman to admire her not merely for her physical attributes, which, she admitted without vanity, were fairly good. She'd want more than that. She'd want his attention and his affection, too.

She'd want him to consider her a worthwhile person and one to whom he felt drawn to spend his time. She'd want him to enjoy chatting with her on chilly evenings by the fireplace, and to enjoy being with her at other times as well. Over breakfast, for example. Or whilst riding on horseback through the wilderness.

Tacita knew these reflections were silly. For years, she'd been keenly aware of her own dullness. She knew she was too uninteresting to attract the kind of attention she longed for from a gentleman.

For some days, however, she'd been uncomfortably aware that she regarded Jed in a light that was about as far removed from her initial dislike as it was possible to get. Today, for the first time, she admitted that she regarded him in exactly the way she'd want to be regarded by a person who loved her.

Her stomach tipped upside down when she realized she'd fallen in love with Jedediah Hardcastle. Head over heels. Which was bad enough. The most depressing part, though, was that she knew he could never return her regard.

After all, Jed was a man who had conquered the wilderness. He was at home in the wild and woolly West. He could handle a gun and defeat evil villains, yet she felt sure he would also feel at home in fancy drawing rooms, as well. After all, he'd been quite adept at life on the train. And his grammar, except when he was trying to prove himself rugged, was quite good. Yes, indeed. Jed Hardcastle was a fascinating man who'd lived a fascinating life. He needed a woman as fascinating as himself. No matter how hard she tried, Tacita couldn't feature Jed being happy with a boring woman.

She dug Rosamunda out of the saddlebag and hugged her tightly as she limped, stiff-legged, over to the campfire Jed had started.

"You all right, ma'am? Tacita?"

Her heart went slushy at the way he said her name. He sounded tentative, as if he wasn't really sure he should be using it. How genteel he was, in his rough-hewn way. She smiled at him, tenderness filling her from her toes to her ears.

"I shall be, thank you, Jed. I'm a little stiff tonight."

"Reckon you are, ma'am. We had a long, hard day."

"It seemed particularly hard after the luxuries of the train, I suppose."

"I reckon."

Since she was too sore to sit, Tacita stood braced against a tall tree and stroked Rosamunda while she watched Jed preparing their campsite. Oh, but he was magnificent. The perfect man. Kind, compassionate, talented, competent. She didn't know a single other man who could do all the things Jed could do. The only men she knew back home were accountants and bankers and other kinds of stuffy businessmen, who were at home in the city, but who would be dismal failures out here in the wilderness.

Not Jed. Why, Jed could draw comfort from the wilderness and earn money at the same time. Plus, he cared for his family and spoke of them with great affection.

She didn't know another man who talked with such respect and fondness about his mother, father, and siblings. Recalling various dealings with her family's retained assistants back home, she decided most of them, in fact, seemed to forget they had families unless reminded.

She was sure Jed would treat a wife with the same esteem and affection as he did his parents and siblings. Why, if he were to carry Tacita off to his home in Busted Flush, Texas, she would be the happiest woman in the world.

How foolish she was being! As if a man with such a large, interesting life could ever look upon her with anything but ennui.

221

Although he did say he admired the way she was holding up on their trip. Tacita contemplated Jed's words, which earlier in the day had irritated her. Now she held them close to her heart, a tiny beam of light in an otherwise shadowy landscape.

Then she contemplated Jed. A fantastic notion entered her head and she blinked, wondering if the strangeness of her circumstances had sent her over the edge of reason and into insanity.

"Good heavens!"

Jed looked up from the pot he was stirring over the fire. "Beg pardon, ma'am? Er—Tacita?"

But Tacita was too stunned by her idea to form words just yet. She shook her head, hoping Jed wouldn't press her to explain or repeat herself. Of course, he didn't. The taciturnity that alternately pleased and annoyed her led him to turn back to his task after he realized she didn't need him.

Of course, he'd never love her. That was a given. But the notion that had just burst fullblown into Tacita's mind took root and began to grow. It grew like a weed, too, and uprooted all her prior proper notions and tossed them aside like chaff in a strong wind.

Would Jed be willing to make love to her? To allow her to pretend, for however long it took them to finish their journey, that she *could* be loved? To pretend that a man *might* find her interesting enough to bed, if she didn't expect him to tolerate her insipidity on a more permanent basis?

And how on earth did one go about asking a person such a shocking question? All through dinner, Tacita's mind roiled with the problem.

To Jed's few questions, she returned monosyllabic answers, until Jed finally shrugged and subsided into his more familiar silence.

When they'd consumed their one-pot meal and cleaned up the utensils, Tacita was still lost in contemplation. Tonight, for the first time, she didn't join Jed at the campfire. Rather, she spread out her bedroll, made her customary bed for Rosamunda beside her head, changed into her flannel nightgown behind a boulder, and slipped between the blankets in silence. She still hadn't solved her problem when her brain, tired of pondering the dilemma, shut down and she went to sleep.

They got off to an early start the next day, and Tacita seemed awful quiet. In fact, she didn't say more than three or four words to Jed as they continued their journey. When she was silent during the long morning hours, Jed thought she was merely tired from the journey. As the day progressed and she remained mute, he began to worry. Tacita Grantham and quiet didn't go together. Unlike Jed himself, Tacita seemed to find silence uncomfortable. Until today. Today, quiet seemed to engulf them until it made him as nervous as a frog on a frying pan.

She didn't say more than three words when they stopped for their midday meal. She didn't speak at all after they resumed their travels. Every now and then Jed would ask a question. More often than not, she didn't seem to hear him.

Along about five in the afternoon, her silence was beginning to plague him and his nerves had started to crackle like dry twigs in a flame. Every minute or so, he shot a look over his shoulder, trying to decide if Tacita looked ill. Each time he did so, he saw her gazing idly at the landscape. Her expression didn't look idle. It looked intense. He'd never seen such an expression on her face before and a nasty feeling began to gnaw at his innards.

His mother had told him more than once that when people got sick, they didn't act like themselves. Their behavior was apt to undergo a change, and this change was apt to manifest itself in the form of lassitude or unusual quiet. Jed's heart lurched painfully. He'd seldom encountered Tacita and silence in the same place at the same time before. No. A silent Tacita Grantham was a Tacita Grantham definitely different from the normal one.

Licking lips that had suddenly gone dry, he finally decided to take the bull by the horns. "You feeling all right, ma'am—Tacita?"

"Hmmm?"

Tacita's head jerked up so quickly, Jed feared she'd get a crick. He winced in sympathy. "You all right? You're pretty quiet. You sure you're feeling well?"

The dreadful thought occurred to him that Tacita had been stricken with some kind of camp fever. He'd heard awful stories about camp fever wiping out entire wagon trains during the great migration across the very plains over which he and Tacita now traveled. Granted, they'd only been on the trail for a couple of days this time and it was only the two of them, but she was no bigger than a minute. He knew she was fragile, no matter what she wanted him to believe and no matter how well she'd held up so far.

"I'm fine, thank you, Jed."

She gave him a smile sweet enough to frost a cake. Jed blinked, enchanted, and stared at her for several moments until he recollected his purpose. Then he shook his head and muttered, "Good. That's good."

He'd never received a smile exactly like the one she'd just given him. It worried him more even than he'd been worried before. Tacita Grantham didn't like him. She hadn't liked him from the very beginning of their trip together, back in Powder Gulch. Plus, she was going to marry that sissy Englishman. She shouldn't be giving him such warm, sugary smiles.

She must have a fever. Jed could think of nothing else that would account for her smile and her silence. Damn, he'd known she was too delicate to withstand the rigors of this trip. He never should have brought her. He should have turned her down in Powder Gulch. Of course, she'd just have hired somebody else—somebody less competent than Jed—if he had. But no. Jed could have figured out some way to prevent her from attempting this foolish trip. Hell, he should have gone to San Francisco and carted that damned Englishman back to Powder Gulch. He hadn't, and now Tacita was sick.

He looked around, spied a nice stand of trees beside a bubbling brook running through a serene meadow, and abruptly reined in his horse. "Better make camp now," he said, his voice brusque.

Tacita looked surprised. "But it's full summer, Jed. There's still hours of daylight left. Don't you want to keep traveling as long as we have light?"

He didn't want to upset her, so he didn't voice his worries. Trying to keep his tone light, he said, "Reckon it'd be good to rest the animals early today, ma'am. We're still holding to our schedule pretty well."

Shrugging, Tacita said, "All right. You're the boss."

He was the boss? Criminy, this was worse than Jed had thought. She was obviously sick. Whatever it was looked like it was pretty bad, too. She never simply obeyed him without an argument. Oh, Lord. His stomach began to cramp up with worry.

Quickly, he led them into the meadow and over to the brook. Then he slid from his horse and hurried to her side. "Here, Tacita, let me help you."

He hadn't needed to help her dismount for quite a while. Tacita looked at him as if he'd lost his mind. And maybe he had. All Jed knew for sure was that he felt compelled to take care of her in her hour of distress and, with luck, nurse her back to health. He hoped to heaven she wasn't too far gone already. He wasn't sure he could stand it if she died on him. Hell, he'd just admitted he loved her. It wouldn't be fair of God to take her away now, before he got over it.

She didn't weigh much more than a feather, even holding onto that blasted dog of hers. Rosamunda uttered a low growl. For once Jed was too worried to growl back.

"Thank you," Tacita said, sounding shy.

He set her under a tree as gently as he could, being careful not to jostle her poor aching joints, and tucked a blanket around her. "You just sit right down here, ma'am, whilst I brew up some tea I keep for the purpose in my saddlebags."

He rushed over to his equipment and didn't see Tacita's astonished expression.

"You brought tea with you?" She scrambled up, thrusting the blanket aside, and followed him.

Looking down and finding her beside him, Jed felt a rush of frustration. Drat it, it was just like her not to act like an invalid's supposed to act when he needed to doctor her! Maybe the fever was making her irrational. How could he tell? She was always irrational. Oh, Lord, this was awful.

"Get back to your seat and wrap that blanket around you. I'll bring it to you."

"I didn't know you had any tea. Please let me help you. I've been dying for a cup of tea."

When she said "dying," a spear of panic thrust itself through Jed's heart. Oh, sweet Lord have mercy, what if she was? "I'll get it. Just you go sit down now." His voice was sharp.

"Well, really! I don't want to sit. I've been sitting all day long. I don't know why you're being so mean this evening, Jed. I'm only trying to help."

"I don't want your help!" Anxiety made his voice rise. He was almost hollering when he added, "I want you to sit yourself down under that tree and wait for me to get this tea brewed up."

She gave a sniff he'd heard before, one that told him she was getting testy. Well, Jed was sorry if he'd riled her, but he'd rather have her riled than sick. Or dead. By this time, he was sure she was not merely ill, but on her way to the great hereafter. Fear made his hands tremble.

"Well, we guess we can tell when we're not wanted!" Tacita huffed back to the tree and snatched the blanket up from the ground. Glaring at Jed, she wrapped it around her shoulders. Rosamunda snarled at him.

He regretted having made her feel bad, but panic was ruling him now. He didn't dare voice his worries aloud, for fear of scaring her. As quickly as possible, he got water from the stream, boiled it up, and dumped in the special willow bark-and-herb mixture his mother always made him bring with him on these trips, just in case. This was the first time he'd ever had occasion to use it. The knowledge made his terror surge higher.

Oh, God; oh, God. This was awful. He'd just realized he'd fallen in love with the woman, and now she was sickening up and about to expire on him. His hands still shook when he stirred the mixture and boiled it for three and a half minutes, counting precisely 210 seconds, as his ma had told him to do. He had to force his mind not to wander at about the hundred-and-twentieth second because he was so scared.

When the brew had finally steeped enough and he'd poured out a steaming cupful, Jed was almost quaking with fear for Tacita. The mixture stunk something awful, but he didn't care. He had to get it down her before the fever got a death grip on her. She was so delicate, so tiny. Jed knew she couldn't last. Not for long. Not with a fever that high. Not with her having been sick for a day and a half already.

What was wrong with him that he hadn't no-

ticed sooner? And why hadn't she said something? He'd have wrung his hands if he hadn't
needed them to carry the cup to Tacita.

"Here, ma'am. Drink this." His voice wobbled.

"What is it?"

"It's good for you. Just drink it."

"But what is it?"

She wrinkled up her nose. Her beautiful little
nose, freckled now after having been exposed to
the sun. Jed's eyes stung.

"It's tea, ma'am. It's good for you."

Tacita took the proffered cup and sniffed its
contents. "Phew. It doesn't smell like any tea I've
ever drunk before."

Since he didn't have to worry about holding
anything anymore, Jed gripped his hands together to stop them from shaking. "It's special,"
he said.

He might have appreciated the look she gave
him if he wasn't so terrified for her health. She
made a face that could have won a prize back
home in the "Silly Face Contest" they ran during
the Busted Flush annual harvest fair. This evening, he barely noticed.

"Where is it from? I've had tea from India and
China, but never any that smelled like this."

"My ma makes it." Oh, God, why didn't she
drink it? Jed was in a perfect state now.

"Really?" She sniffed it again, as if she hoped
it would smell better this time. It didn't, and she
sat up and sighed.

"You like tea, don't you?" Jed asked encour-
agingly. "It's good for you."

"Thank you very much, Jed, but I think I'd prefer to wait until we get to San Francisco before

229

I drink any tea. I do think it was very kind of you to brew this up for me, though."

Why was she always so damned balky? Jed wanted to shake her. Instead he fell onto his knees beside her and grabbed the cup before she could dump it out.

"Here. Let me help you."

"Thank you, but I'd rather—" Her face registered a moment of absolute shock when he grabbed her.

Jed didn't wait to hear what she'd rather. Seizing her by the shoulders, he tilted her head back and lifted the cup to her lips. Rosamunda yipped viciously once and attacked his trouser cuff. Jed hardly noticed since he was occupied in getting tea down Tacita's throat.

It wasn't easy. She struggled like a wildcat and came up spluttering, but he succeeded at last and felt good about it. He'd managed to tip most of the smelly brew down her gullet without spilling more than a quarter or so of it over the two of them. He hoped she'd swallowed enough to do her some good.

Relieved and proud of himself, he sat back on his heels and realized Rosamunda was trying to gnaw his leg off. Grabbing her by the ruff, he said, "Quit it." He didn't bother to look at her, nor did he shake her, but kept his eyes on her mistress. His concern for Tacita was so great, he didn't even holler at the nasty little rat.

Tears poured down Tacita's cheeks, and she couldn't talk for choking, but she snatched Rosamunda back and hugged her. Jed hoped that was a sign she was still well enough to want to cuddle her dog and not a sign that she was on her last gasp and wanted the animal to comfort her as she slipped the bonds of life.

He wanted to hold her so bad, he ached. He didn't dare because she was so fragile and he feared for her ribs. Instead, he wrapped his arms across his chest, hugging himself to keep from shaking. Oh, poor Tacita! The poor thing. The poor beautiful, darling thing. Jed had never known anyone to be so sick and not ask for help. He almost felt like crying himself when he considered the probable reasons for Tacita's reticence.

She didn't think he'd care. She was so sure nobody gave a damn about her—except for that stupid dog of hers—that she'd kept her illness and misery to herself. Hadn't said a single word about her fever. She could have died on the trail and he wouldn't have noticed until she slipped from the saddle and fell off her horse. He couldn't remember the last time he'd felt so guilty about anything.

Shakily, he asked, "You all right now?" He stood before her, hugging himself harder, praying she wouldn't die. She couldn't die. He loved her.

For the longest time Tacita could only cough and choke and wonder why Jed Hardcastle, who had actually seemed to be tolerating her fairly well up till now, had tried to poison her. He'd been crude about it, too. In most of the novels she'd read, the villains generally tried to murder their victims unobtrusively. Jed had actually grabbed her and dumped the poison down her throat, without the least pretense of subtlety.

All in all, she decided that if he wanted to kill

her she'd as soon he just break her neck or something. He was certainly big enough to do it, and she was pretty sure it would be a less painful way to go. If she wasn't so furious with him, her feelings would be hurt.

When she could finally gather breath enough to speak, she hacked out, "What in the name of heaven did you do that for?"

Tears still streamed from her eyes; Tacita didn't know whether they were left over from having almost strangled on that vile-tasting "tea" of his or from grief that he obviously hated her after all.

"Are you all right?"

Over her own wildly careening emotions, Tacita heard the strain in his voice. He must really be bored with her if he was as concerned about the outcome of his attempt on her life as his tone indicated.

Tacita grabbed a handkerchief out of her pocket and began mopping her face. Rosamunda, the darling, was trying to comfort her. She gasped, "No thanks to you, I expect I'll last until the poison begins to work."

And what would happen to Rosamunda after she was gone? Now that she could breathe again, Tacita was able to think about her pet. Good heavens, Jed couldn't have gone into some kind of vile partnership with that horrid Mr. Picinisco, could he? She hugged Rosamunda more closely and stared, wild-eyed, up at him.

"Poison? What poison?" He still looked worried. He even sounded worried.

How contemptible of him to pretend innocence! Tacita scrunched back against the tree, sat up straighter, and scrambled for her shredded composure. If she was destined to die, she at least wanted to do it with dignity.

"Don't be coy with me, Mr. Hardcastle," she said in a hard, sarcastic voice. "I know what you're up to."

"Are you still feverish, ma'am?"

His pretense sickened her. "Stop it! I can't imagine anyone being so vile as to murder someone just to get at her dog!"

"Huh?"

"I know you tried to poison me with that evil tea of yours. Well, you may be able to kill my body, but you can't kill my spirit!" Even though she was trying to be strong, Tacita began to weep again, thinking about what would undoubtedly happen to Rosamunda after her demise.

Jed's eyes widened. He looked even more frightened. "Oh, Lord," he whispered. "Oh, Lord, it's worse than I thought. She's delirious."

"Stop it! Stop pretending innocence, you murderer. I know you want me out of the way so you can sell my darling Rosamunda!"

All at once Jed straightened. He unclasped his hands. He stared. "Huh?"

"I know everything. You can stop acting now." With an indignant sniffle, she added, "You're a terrible actor."

Jed leaned closer. Tacita shrank back. He reached out and pressed a hand against her forehead, as if testing for fever. Tacita stopped Rosamunda from attacking his hand and then wondered why she'd bothered.

"You don't feel hot," he said, sounding bemused.

Tacita tossed her head and huffed indignantly. "Of course, I don't feel hot. Not unless the poison you shoved down my throat gives you a fever before it kills you."

Straightening up again, Jed put his hands on his hips and considered her. She wished she didn't still find him so attractive. She must have a weak character, indeed, if she could find her own murderer attractive right after he'd tried to kill her. It was a lowering reflection, although she guessed it wouldn't plague her for long. She wondered when the poison would begin to take effect and hoped it wouldn't hurt when it did.

"You mean you weren't sick?"

His voice sounded funny. Tacita glared at him. "What on earth are you talking about?" The disagreeable aroma of the awful mixture he'd poured down her throat still lingered in the air, probably because he'd spilled a lot of it on her shirtwaist. Tacita hoped to heaven it would wash out. Then her heart squeezed when she realized she'd never know if it did or not because she'd be dead.

"B-but I thought you were sick."

Eyeing him sharply, Tacita didn't say anything for a moment. She examined his expression and his posture and had to admit that he looked genuinely worried.

Cautiously, she asked, "Whatever do you mean?"

He cleared his throat. "I—I thought you were sick, ma'am."

"You thought I was sick?"

He nodded.

She still didn't trust him. Oh, he looked worried—even frightened—but she didn't believe it. Why on earth would he think she was sick? Even if he did think that, why would he be frightened? It certainly couldn't be for her welfare. In her entire life, nobody had ever worried about her welfare. The fact no longer bothered her much; Tacita was accustomed to the world's indifference.

"And that's why you poisoned me?"

Perhaps this was some sort of bizarre Western custom: to kill the ill and weak so as to prevent them from delaying the wagon train or something. Not that they were on a wagon train. Not that Jed had any reason other than Tacita to go to San Francisco. At least, no reason she knew about. She still didn't believe him.

This time he shook his head. "I didn't poison you, ma'am."

Tacita sniffed indignantly. "Oh, come now, Mr. Hardcastle. You can't really expect to fool me. I was here, remember? It was down my throat that you poured that vile liquid."

"That was my ma's special tea, ma'am."

She gave him an acid smile. "Of course it was."

She almost shrieked in alarm when he fell to his knees in front of her.

"It was, ma'am! Honest. My ma makes it special out of willow bark and other stuff she grows in her garden back home in Busted Flush. It's powerful."

"It certainly is."

"No. I mean it's powerful medicine."

With a thought to the dime novels she'd read, Tacita said tartly, "You sound like an Indian, Mr. Hardcastle."

"It cures fever."

Her brows drew together. "I can believe it. No self-respecting fever would be caught dead in

235

the same body with that awful tea of yours."

"Don't say that!"

Her brows shot up again. "Don't say what?"

"Dead. Don't say that. It—it scares me."

She didn't respond at once, but continued watching Jed suspiciously. Taking note of his expression, she did have to grant that he looked sincere. Of course, she supposed most of the best confidence men in the world looked sincere or they wouldn't be successful.

"I thought you were sick, ma'am. Tacita. I—I got scared. That's why I made up my ma's special tea. I've never had to use it before."

"I'm sure your prior customers are grateful."

He didn't seem to notice her sarcasm. "I just got real scared when I thought you were sick, ma'am. I didn't say anything about it, because I didn't want you to worry."

Frowning, Tacita watched him carefully for some minutes, silent.

If what he said was true, Tacita had to acknowledge that his motives were pure. Even sweet. Imagine him not wanting to worry her by voicing his suspicions that she was ill. Giving another thought to her life before Jed, she decided she didn't quite believe him yet. After all, nobody else had ever cared if she were ill or not. It would be imprudent of her to allow her heart to accept what it wanted to hear when indications pointed elsewhere. She most assuredly wasn't sick. Tacita never got sick.

"What on earth made you think I was ill?"

He spread his hands out in a helpless gesture. "You were so quiet. I never heard you be so quiet before." Bowing his head, he whispered, "I was sure you were fevered and going to die. It scared me."

"You thought I was sick because I was quiet?"

His eyes still aimed at the ground, Jed nodded. "I ain't—I never saw you be quiet before. I thought for sure you was—were sick. My ma says people get quiet when they're in the grip of fever."

Tacita wasn't sure what to make of Jed's confession. After mulling it over for a second or two, she decided she wasn't flattered. "Are you saying that I'm usually garrulous, Mr. Hardcastle? That I rattle on?"

His nod came immediately. He lifted his head and smiled at her hopefully, as if he were glad she understood now.

"Yes'm. That's it, all right. You gen'ly rattle on until my ears ache. When you was so quiet yesterday I didn't think anything of it. When you were still quiet today, I was sure you were sick. It scared the pants off me, ma'am."

Tacita hardly noticed his indelicate phrasing, which, under normal circumstances, would have offended her. She was already offended.

"Why, of all the nerve! You actually made me drink that horrid stuff because I was being quiet?"

"Yes'm."

Incensed now, she continued, "Well, I like that! You thought I was sick, when for the last two days I've been wracking my brain trying to think how on earth to ask you to make love to me!"

As soon as the words left her lips, Tacita blushed.

Jed was so shocked, he fell over.

Rosamunda barked violently.

# Chapter Thirteen

"You—you"—Jed stared at her—"you what?" He sat in the dirt, bracing himself on his hands to keep from tumbling over backward. His eyes had gone as round as billiard balls.

Tacita wished fervently that she'd not been mistaken in believing him. She'd rather die an agonizing death by poison than face Jedediah Hardcastle after having made such a scandalous confession.

"Nothing," she mumbled.

Rosamunda was barking so savagely that Tacita couldn't even hear herself. She knew good and well Jed couldn't hear her. If only the silly dog had decided to bark a few seconds earlier. Feeling guilty about her unkind thought, Tacita hugged Rosamunda and muttered, "Hush, darling," without much conviction.

To Jed she said, "Nothing," more loudly.

He shook his head hard, reminding Tacita of Rosamunda after her bath. "It wasn't nothing. It was something." His voice was more gravelly than usual.

Tacita averted her head, annoyed. She wished Rosamunda would be quiet. She also wished Jed would stop staring at her in that unseemly manner. Not that it was any more unseemly than her own declaration had been.

But that was the whole point. A true gentleman would pretend he hadn't heard her. She sniffed and for the first time wished Jed bore more resemblance to some of the stuffy businessmen she'd known back home in Galveston. The ones who never talked about their families or paid any attention to her.

"What did you say, ma'am?" He cleared his throat. "Er, that is, would you mind repeating what you just said?"

Oh, this was simply impossible. Feeling sorely put upon, Tacita snapped, "I *said*, I was quiet because I was trying to think of a way to ask you to make love to me."

There! Let him chew on that for a while!

"You—you want me to make love to you?"

He still sounded punchy. Tacita wanted to punch him. She glared at him instead. "*Yes!* Yes, yes, yes! Are you happy now?"

He didn't answer for the longest time. Tacita continued to scowl, wishing he'd say something. Or that the world would open up and swallow her.

Nothing so convenient happened, of course. Jed stared at her as if one of them had lost his or her mind until she wanted to shriek.

Then, all at once, he shoved himself up from the ground.

"Wait there."

And with those two curt words, he turned. As Tacita watched, dismayed, he took off toward the stream and vanished into the trees growing along its bank.

Her lips trembled and she wondered when she'd ever learn to keep her foolish mouth shut.

The train that had been specially commissioned by Avinash Agrawal arrived in Santa Fe in time to meet the train Tacita Grantham and Jed Hardcastle were supposed to be on. When the train arrived, however, neither Tacita nor Jed got off of it. Instead, the two had disembarked at the prior train station, after having been burgled by an Indian man named Virendra Karnik.

The porter who gave Agrawal and Luther the information chuckled. "Yes, sir! That little dog of hers liked to chew the bandit's ears off first, too."

Agrawal managed to pry Virendra Karnik out of the engineer's hands, giving that phlegmatic individual a plausible story about how Karnik was a relative of Agrawal's and had slipped away from his erstwhile keeper.

"Alas, my cousin is unwell, my good sir. Indeed, we try to prevent him from appearing in public, as he is prone to outbursts." Agrawal's eyes glittered. Karnik shivered as if he were standing in an arctic breeze.

"That what his problem is?" The engineer chewed on a straw and eyed Karnik unemotionally. "Figgered it was something like that."

Agrawal's smile would have made Luther quake if his brain wasn't so numbed with alcohol. "Indeed, sir," Agrawal said. "My poor cousin comes from a family of lunatics."

The engineer only nodded and accepted the cash Agrawal offered as a bribe. He tipped his striped cap, and Agrawal led Karnik away. Luther left, too, flanked by a couple of Agrawal's burly bodyguards.

It certainly hadn't been difficult to convince the engineer Karnik was a maniac. Luther knew that by this time, it wouldn't be difficult to convince someone he was insane, either, if anybody cared to try.

Agrawal had conversed with several porters before they discovered that Tacita and Jed intended to travel by packhorse and mule to Denver. From there, they were going to book stage passage to San Francisco. Agrawal sent a telegraph message to one of his innumerable hirelings, this one in Denver. Luther wasn't sure what the message said, but he presumed the stagecoach wouldn't make its trip to San Francisco unmolested.

After he took care of business at the train station, Agrawal questioned Karnik.

Karnik squeaked, "Goddess preserve me, Master, I have failed you."

Avinash Agrawal looked down his imperious nose at Karnik, who trembled before him.

Luther Adams Williamson watched. The three of them and two of Agrawal's ever-present henchmen were seated in a room in Santa Fe, in a hotel not far from the train station. Luther was so used to being terrified by this time that he didn't even bother to be disappointed that Karnik, too, had failed to secure the Delhi Hahm-Ahn-Der Eye. He did sigh, however, and take another sip of his beer.

Obviously, Luther decided, he was cursed. Whoever the Goddess was from whom that bedamned Eye had been stolen had cursed him. He never used to believe in those Oriental curses, but he did now.

"It was the dog, sahib," Karnik said, casting a beseeching glance at Luther. "The vicious dog almost tore me to shreds."

Luther shook his head, recalling Farley Boskins's story.

"I understand the dog is very small, my friend." Agrawal's silky voice sent a chill up Luther's spine.

It apparently had the same effect on Karnik, because he shivered. "It has the soul of a devil."

Although, he didn't say so, Luther didn't guess he'd argue the point. Rosamunda had thwarted Luther often enough for him to have formed the same opinion, although he'd never thought to express it exactly that way.

"A very small devil." Agrawal's left eyebrow lifted.

Until he met Agrawal, Luther had never seen anybody who had such precise control over his eyebrows. Everything about Agrawal was precise, a fact Luther had begun to find disturbing even before they left El Paso.

"How large would you say the animal is, my friend?"

It took Luther a moment to realize Agrawal was speaking to him. He swallowed his beer quickly and focused his attention on the suave Indian. His focus wasn't the best these days, fuzzed as it was in a froth of beer foam, but he did his best.

"It weighs about five pounds." Luther was rather proud that he didn't slur.

"It's not only the dog!" Karnik had started to wring his hands, but stopped when the wringing aggravated his wounds. "It's that man, too. That Mr. Hardcastle whom you hired." He cast Luther an accusing look, as if to let him know he should have hired a less competent guide. Luther couldn't find it in his heart to blame him. "Mr. Hardcastle is not a small fellow. He is a very large fellow. A giant, Master. And he has brains, too, may the Goddess grant us mercy. A giant and a little devil, alas, conspired to prevent me from carrying out my mission."

"We are no longer in India, my friend," Agrawal said dryly. "I don't think Americans believe in giants and devils. Or goddesses, either."

Luther chuckled, surprising himself.

Karnik blinked. "Oh."

As for Luther, he believed in devils. He believed he was in the presence of one right this very minute, in fact. He eyed Agrawal through bloodshot eyes and attempted to remember when he'd stopped trying to figure out how to escape. He wasn't sure. He only knew that there was no escape from this Indian devil and that if the wretched Eye couldn't be found, he was a dead man.

The thought hardly bothered him any longer. He swallowed another mouthful of beer to keep it that way.

For the longest time, Tacita sat still under her tree and tried not to give in to tears. At first, she wasn't sure Jed hadn't poisoned her, no matter what he said. A nasty taste lingered on her tongue. She considered getting up and trying to find something minty to get rid of it, but couldn't seem to find enough energy within herself to do so. In the space of a heartbeat—in the second in which Jed had turned and left her, in fact—her spirits had fallen into a bleak depression.

The day was still light, although shadows lengthened along the edges of the clearing and the sky was beginning to take on the pinks and oranges of sunset. The entire episode of Jed's attempted poisoning and her ultimate, embarrassing confession hadn't taken more than thirty-five or forty minutes. By Tacita's reckoning, it was probably only five-thirty or six o'clock. She could have taken out her watch and looked, but she lacked the spirit. If she'd been in a better mood, she might have appreciated the play of light and shadows as they crept across the grass in the rustic glen and turned the grass from emerald silk to deep jade velvet.

She was still sitting there, feeling wretched, when she heard a rustle in the bushes.

"It's probably a bear, Rosamunda."

Rosamunda had calmed down as soon as Jed left the campsite. Now she licked Tacita's hand, a comfort-giving gesture Tacita appreciated very much.

"Thank you, darling."

She looked toward the bushes, wondering if she should stand and meet her fate bravely or sit here in a miserable heap and let fate find her. Then she decided she didn't care. Let the bear gnaw her to death sitting down. She didn't have enthusiasm enough to fight. She didn't have enthusiasm for anything. Not even the thought of Rosamunda and Prince Albert's children could lift her spirits.

Shutting her eyes, she hoped the bear wouldn't take too long dispatching her. She might be depressed, but she didn't relish dying slowly and in great pain.

The first thing Jed did when he got to the stream was throw cold water over his face. Then he washed out his ears. Sitting back carefully, he tested them.

Nope. They still worked.

She must have said what he'd heard. Heard twice, because she'd repeated it.

He sat on the riverbank, absolutely still, for what seemed like an hour or two, although he knew it wasn't. He tried to make sense of things. Ultimately, he gave up. There was no making sense of this.

Tacita wanted him to make love to her. Tacita Grantham wanted *him*, Jedediah Hardcastle, to make love to *her*.

There was no fathoming women, he reckoned, although this latest confirmation of their unfathomability surpassed him completely. Why on earth a tiny, beautiful, precious gem of a female like Tacita Grantham would want an ugly, hairy fellow like him pawing her outstripped his understanding.

He'd been too stunned to ask her to explain herself. Now he supposed it was too late.

Then, in a fit of determination, he decided that wasn't true.

"No." He said the word aloud to make himself believe it. "It isn't too late."

He had to know what on earth she'd meant. She couldn't possibly have meant what he'd heard. She must have been using some kind of mysterious city-speech that he didn't understand.

He stood, knowing he was wrong in having left Tacita alone for so long. He was her guide and guard, after all. Anything might happen to her out here in this perilous territory, from wild animals to wild people to poisoned plants.

Shaking his head, he decided that was another thing he'd like to understand. Had she really thought he'd try to poison her? Taking out the bar of soap his ma had told him always to keep handy, Jed finished washing himself in the stream.

He did a thorough job of it. After all, if she'd meant what he thought he'd heard her say, he didn't want to be smelly when they made love beside the fire. The thought sent a strong surge of lust through him. It lodged in his sex and made walking back to the clearing difficult.

Tentatively stepping into the glen, Jed saw Tacita stiffen and look at him. Her eyes were as big as huckleberry muffins and as blue as the sky. Luggett Lake had nothing on her eyes when it came to blue.

Holding his hat before him in a gesture that would have made his parents proud and also served to hide his indelicate condition, he slowly made his way to Tacita. Rosamunda, he noticed, bristled immediately and began to growl low in her throat, low being a relative term. If ever God had created a soprano animal, that idiot dog was it.

Tacita didn't rise to greet him. She stared at him almost sullenly. He couldn't tell if she was angry or embarrassed.

"Er, ma'am?"

She couldn't hold his gaze. "What?"

Jed licked his lips nervously. "Um. I, ah, wondered if you'd mind explaining something to me."

He was going about this all wrong; he knew it. Shoot. Even though his carnal experience was rather large, his understanding of females was limited. Up till now, Jed would have told anybody who asked that there were two kinds of women. There were good women, like his mama, sisters, aunts, cousins, and Miss Amalie Crunch; and there were bad women, like whores and divorcées.

Tacita Grantham had tossed his notions up into the air like so many dandelion puffs, and the wind had scattered them away. Up until several minutes ago, he would have categorized Tacita as belonging to the first group. In fact, he still did. That's what was confusing him so badly.

"What?" She still wouldn't look at him.

"Um . . ." He had to lick his lips again, and swallow. "Um, why do you want me to make love to you?"

Now she looked at him, balefully. "Well, why do you think?" She sounded resentful and not a little pugnacious.

"I don't know," he said simply, because it was the truth.

Tacita glared daggers at him for several moments. Then, her voice too loud, she said, "I wanted the experience, Mr. Hardcastle. I wanted to experience lovemaking for once in my life. Do you understand now?"

Her cheeks sported twin banners of red, as if she were either angry or mortified. Or both.

Jed swallowed and forged onward, truth and the sincere desire for knowledge propelling him. "Er, well, ma'am, no. I'm not sure I do understand."

She gave an enormous huff. "Oh, for heaven's sake!"

Feeling almost desperate, Jed said, "Don't you want to save yourself for your husband, ma'am?"

He straightened all at once, the awful thought having struck him that Tacita wasn't as innocent as he'd believed her to be. Jehosephat, what if she frolicked with every frontier guide she met up with? He'd heard some city women were peculiar that way and had always been disappointed not to have encountered one.

Immediately, he shook his head to dislodge the thought. He might not know what had prompted this strange start of hers, but he knew, deep down in his guts, that Tacita was still innocent. No man had sullied her; he'd swear to it. She meant what she said about being inexperienced.

"I don't have a husband!"

He saw her lips tremble and felt terrible. He wasn't sure he could stand it if she cried. "But, ma'am, that's why we're going to San Francisco, isn't it? So's you can marry up with that Mr. Jeeves fellow?"

"Reeve," she said. "Edgar Jevington Reeve.

And—and I don't know if I'll be marrying him or not."

"But you might be."

She lowered her head and looked even more resentful. "I suppose I might be."

"Don't you want to save yourself for him?"

Her head snapped up. "No! No, I don't want to save myself for Edgar! There. Are you happy now?"

Scratching his head, befuddled, Jed said, "No."

Tacita huffed again. Then she said, "Edgar's— different."

"Different?"

"Oh, for heaven's sake!" She cast her glance into the trees in what looked like a perfect fever of frustration. "Yes! He's different!"

"Different how?"

Scowling at him, she said, "He's—he's different from you."

Different from him. Jed ruminated on that that one for a moment. Different. How was Jeeves different from Jed?

Well, Jed was an American and Jeeves was an Englishman. Intuitively, Jed knew that wasn't the correct answer and ruminated some more.

Jed was a rugged frontiersman and the Englishman was a sissy with a sissy's dog.

All at once he jerked to attention. Good Lord! That must be it! His shock was profound and the emotions in his large breast flashed hot and cold.

"Shoot, ma'am, do you mean Jeeves is one of them—those fairy fellows?" Poor Tacita! Forced into a union with a man who wasn't even a man.

Jed's compassionate nature thrummed, and his heart filled with sympathy.

Tacita's brows drew together, not in anger but in puzzlement. Fairy fellows? What on earth was the man talking about? Casting him a peek from under her lashes, she decided, whatever it was, it had touched Jed's heart somehow. She decided to play the only card she'd been dealt that wasn't completely humiliating.

Trying hard to look sad, she nodded and murmured thinly, "Yes. That's it all right."

He sank to the earth beside her. Rosamunda lunged, but Tacita caught her and held her in check.

"Oh, ma'am. Oh, Tacita. I'm so sorry. But why would you marry a man like that?" His voice held some powerful emotion. Tacita had the oddest feeling it was distaste. Coupled with empathy.

Hmmm. Why would she marry a man like that? Tacita, her nerves strung taut already, had a hard time thinking of a good reason. This was especially true since she didn't know what it was she was making an excuse for. She also felt vaguely guilty about poor Edgar who was, as far as she knew, a perfectly decent man. She decided to use an old but time-honored justification.

"My—my parents wished it."

"They wanted you to marry a pansy?"

Pansy? Fairy? What on earth did those words have to do with Edgar Jevington Reeve? She nodded because she figured she'd better.

"Good God! I've never heard of such a thing."

He sounded shocked. Tacita murmured, "Perhaps things are different in the big city, Jed."

Shaking his head, he growled, "They must be."

He seemed to have thrown off his shock at her initial request. His amazement over her possible marriage to Edgar (poor Edgar; she hoped she hadn't maligned him too terribly) still seemed strong, however. Tacita decided it was time to press her advantage.

"So will you make love to me, Jed? I'd truly appreciate it." She'd treasure the experience for the rest of her life, in fact, but she didn't want him to know that. Her unrequited love for him seemed slightly pathetic to her. She was sure other women didn't have to beg men to bed them. Other women's love didn't languish unrequited.

He stared at her for long enough for her to begin to squirm. Good heavens, did he consider the prospect of making love to her that revolting?

"Yes."

His answer came quickly and explosively, startling Tacita into a little jump. Rosamunda took the opportunity to snap at Jed, but Tacita caught her before she connected.

Jed licked his lips and looked strangely vulnerable. She felt a tremendous urge to cuddle him. How curious.

He repeated, "Yes."

Although her heart thundered almost painfully, Tacita couldn't suppress her triumph. "Thank you, Jed! Oh, thank you!"

Jed's own heart crinkled up around the edges. Poor Tacita. His ill-will toward her deceased parents had grown to full-fledged antagonism by this time. He couldn't understand people like that. First they ignore her, and then they decide they want her to marry one of those unnatural fairy fellows.

Not that Jed disliked Jeeves on that account; hell, Jed was a tolerant sort. He'd met a couple of perfectly decent fairies in his life. But they hadn't been destined to marry the woman Jed himself loved. He thought such a marriage would be a travesty. Actually, in Tacita's case, he considered it a downright tragedy.

Yet Tacita—sweet, obedient Tacita—was willing to marry Jeeves because it would have made her parents happy. It made him mad, is what it did. Jed hardly blamed her for wanting to experience real love with a real man once in her life before she got herself shackled forever to a pansy.

"I'll be gentle, Tacita," he said.

Her radiant smile washed him in heat. He felt weak with love for her; weak and really, really lusty.

"Thank you, Jed."

"I—I'll try not to hurt you."

"Thank you."

She still held the rat, which had been growling in a menacing manner during their entire conversation. When Jed reached for Tacita, intending merely to press her soft cheek with his palm to show her how gentle he could be in spite of his great size, the animal lunged. Breaking free from Tacita's grip, she sank her tiny fangs into Jed's hand.

"Oh, Jed, I'm so sorry."

Rosamunda heard Tacita's apology and resented it. She had never been so offended in her entire life.

They had imprisoned her. Her! Rosamunda!
They'd thrust her into the slammer for trying to
protect her mistress from Tacita's own obvious
insanity and that ghastly monster, Jed Hardcastle.

What an undignified fate to befall a noble Yorkie.

She lay curled up on her bed of rabbit fur inside the saddlebag, nursing her shattered sensibilities. No light seeped into her jail. Mistress
and Monster had seen to that when they
strapped the bag shut.

Feeling very sorry for herself, Rosamunda
would have cried if Yorkshire terriers did such
things.

While Tacita gave herself an icy bath in the
stream, Jed went about the prosaic task of fixing
dinner. Tacita had originally hoped he'd just get
on with the business of lovemaking without further delay, but Rosamunda had put an effective
end to those vain hopes. Tacita guessed she just
wasn't created to live romantically.

After they'd secured the dog, Tacita realized
how hungry she was. She was willing to over-
look her own hunger in order to learn about the
mysteries of love, but when she heard Jed's own
large tummy growl, she decided amour would
have to wait.

It was probably better this way. At least now
she wouldn't have to worry about smelling like
that horrible tea and her own perspiration when
they consummated their love. Rather, her love.

She sighed deeply and closed her eyes, con-
juring images of Jed falling onto his knees before her and declaring his undying adoration.

The splash of icy water when she wrung her washcloth over her leg brought reality back with jolt.

"Don't be stupid, Tacita Grantham," she advised herself firmly. "He'll never love you. Besides, even if he did, he's too honorable to declare himself."

Tacita had never given much thought to Jed's honor before now. She had to admit, though, that he was every bit as noble and estimable as any of the heroes she'd read about in novels. Indeed, he epitomized the ideals of the chivalrous Western man exalted in those books—which was one of the reasons she'd fallen madly in love with him in the first place, although it rather annoyed her now.

He'd never renounce his engagement to that horrible Crunch woman. Tacita knew it. He was too noble. Too chivalrous. Too—too—well, he was simply too something, and she knew that whatever it was, it would prevent his ever acknowledging his love for her.

Not that he had any. Tacita harbored no illusions about herself. She knew she was too boring for words and entirely too tiresome for Jed.

Sighing again, she allowed herself a little smile. It hardly mattered any longer. Boring or not, she was going to get at least some of her deepest yearnings satisfied tonight. And she could pretend there was more to the act than that. She was good at that. She'd been pretending all her life.

If Jed didn't possess such a practical nature, he'd have gladly foregone supper for the more urgent desires of his heart and body. He wanted to make love to Tacita so much, his whole large frame was tight with lust and longing.

He knew better, though. He might put on an act for his clients, wearing buckskins and a taciturn mien like an actor wore makeup, but Jed never let himself forget the real perils extant in his chosen arena. Out here on the frontier a body had to keep his strength up, and strength required food.

Besides, his baser nature reminded him, he could perform better if he wasn't hungry. And he aimed to give Tacita the finest performance of his entire life tonight. Another shot of desire surged through him at the thought.

He ate quickly.

So did Tacita.

For the first time in her life, Rosamunda refused her dinner.

"Are you comfortable, Tacita?" Jed's voice was unsteady.

"Yes, thank you." So was Tacita's.

She was stiff as a board. So was Jed, although only one part of him was stiff. The rest of him felt almost unreal, as though his sex occupied the body of another man entirely.

He was also so excited at the prospect before him that he feared for his endurance, so he decided to think about his family. That had always worked before when he was afraid overpowering desire might make him finish before his partner. It worked this time, too. There was just something about remembering his uproarious siblings, cousins, aunts, and uncles that took the edge off of carnal excitement.

"Um, would you like me to join you now?" he

asked, striving to conceal his eagerness.

"Yes, thank you."

Her voice still shook, and he felt a pang of empathy. Poor Tacita, reduced to seeking physical pleasure from a rough frontier guide because she was doomed to marry a pansy. Even if she did care for Jeeves, marriage to a man who fancied men would be one sadly skimpy in the physical pleasure department. Well, he'd do his best for her tonight.

"Move over, then, and I'll get under the blanket with you."

She scooched over so far, Jed worried about her slipping off the pad he'd made and ending up on the dirt. Quickly, he shucked off his shirt, trousers, and drawers, scrambled under the covers, and caught her around the waist so she wouldn't slide out from under the blanket. He'd made up this bed specially, using both of their rigs and creating a larger surface for them to lie on.

Her heavy flannel nightgown covered her from neck to toe, and the material was too thick to be revealing. Nevertheless, when Jed felt her tiny waist under the fabric, his sex pulsed a strong response. It was so strong, in fact, that panic smote him. She was so small. And he was so big. Glory, he hoped he wouldn't rip her apart.

"I'll try to be gentle," he whispered for the seventy-fifth time. Actually, it was more of a croak. He was so scared.

"I know you will," she whispered back, surprising him.

Her trust humbled him. This whole experience humbled him, in fact. Imagine, a beautiful, delicate flower like Tacita Grantham choosing him to indoctrinate her into the pleasures of the flesh. The notion was daunting and Jed decided he'd better not think about it. It was one thing to try to keep his urges under control until she'd been satisfied. It would be an entirely different thing to have those urges crushed completely.

Well, he was under the covers now and guessed he'd better do something. Tacita had gone rigid at his touch and now lay on her back again, as motionless as a corpse. Jed reckoned it was now or never. Striving to appear unrushed, he leaned over and gently nuzzled her neck. His lips met flannel, but he didn't guess he should complain. His manly parts were back to near busting again.

"I'll try not to hurt you, Tacita, but I reckon it always hurts a lady the first time."

"Yes. Yes, I understand."

"I'll do my best, though. Honest, I will."

"I know you will, Jed."

He nuzzled her again, aiming higher this time and finding the warm skin on her neck. This was better. He kissed her throat gently, gently, relishing the warmth of her flesh and praying he wouldn't get too excited and disgrace himself.

"I—I'll try to be gentle," seeped from his lips.

Suddenly, she cried, "Oh, I know you will. You're the most gentle, wonderful man I've ever met!"

And she threw herself into Jed's arms, nightie and all, nearly astonishing him out of his wits.

Fortunately, most of his wits were visiting elsewhere this evening, and Jed recovered in an instant. Still reeling from her passionate response to his initial fumbling overture, he kissed her on the mouth.

She didn't know anything about kissing. She kept her lips puckered up as tight as Jed's Aunt Minnie when he had to kiss her on Christmas Eve. Tacita's lips were prepared for a duty kiss. Jed knew it was up to him to teach her the difference between duty and pleasure, and he decided to do it without words since she always argued with him.

He kept his lips deliberately soft, skimming her rigid mouth over and over, undermining her fear with tender, warm caresses. It wasn't long before her pucker eased. With a little sigh, her lips parted. He explored her mouth gently, tenderly, finding delight in tasting her.

Tacita didn't taste like any of the other women he'd had. She was a delicacy, like the sweetened whipped cream his ma slopped over gingerbread. She was gingery, too, his little Tacita. Sweet and spicy. He felt light-headed, nearly drowning in delight.

While his lips and tongue taught hers what to do, his big hands loosened their grip on her waist. He was pretty sure she wasn't going to slide out from under the covers now. Tentatively, he began to explore her body. He wanted to feel her skin, but didn't suppose he'd better push his luck for a while.

"Oh, Jed," she whispered, the words warm on his neck. They feathered over his bare shoulder, sent hot shivers through his body, and almost made him forget his promise to be gentle.

He reached for the hem of her nightie, hoping she wouldn't object. She didn't, and when he found one little foot and began to massage it, her mew of pleasure was music to his ears. Since that had worked so well, he started a slow exploration up her leg.

She was exquisite in every detail, and about half the size of most of the women Jed had known. Used to buxom, meaty frontier females, Jed used special care with Tacita. He didn't rush; his hands studied every dip, mound, and plane on her body as carefully as if he were conducting topographical research.

Soon he was dazed with wonder and hunger. "You're so beautiful," he told her more than once, meaning it, although what he wanted to say was, "I love you." He didn't dare, some fragment of sanity preventing him from exposing himself to her ridicule. But he said it in his heart, and meant it.

Her skin was as soft and smooth as a baby's. He feared his calluses would hurt her, but her tiny, breathy moans didn't sound like those of a woman in pain. Every now and then he'd whisper a query about her state of well-being. Each time she assured him, in gesture or speech, of her willingness to continue. Which was a good thing. Jed wasn't sure what he'd do if she got scared and made him stop. He'd never forced a woman in his life and wouldn't now, although he suspected forbearance might kill him in this instance.

Fortunately, they both lived. Taking the most exquisite care of his life, Jed coaxed Tacita into a mindless, writhing state of fulfillment. Her reaction was music to his ears. He'd have loved to watch, but settled for tactile understanding of the magic his hands and fingers wrought, as he didn't dare lower the blanket far enough for the stars and campfire to illuminate the two of them. He knew Tacita would be scared if she saw him because he was so big.

Then it was his turn. Ready to burst already, he thrust home, capturing Tacita's surprised cry with his lips. By this time, he was so overwrought that his fourth or fifth thrust carried him beyond sanity and into the most awesome delight he'd ever experienced in his life.

# Chapter Fourteen

Tacita lay for a long time, stunned by what she'd experienced. She hugged Jed's big body tightly to hers, wishing she never had to let him go, even if he was heavy on her.

How perfectly amazing the act of love could be. Even though she'd longed to experience it, Tacita hadn't realized the full magnificence of it. And its magnificence wasn't confined only to the physical sensations, which were, admittedly, interesting and—well—fulfilling.

For Tacita's money, however, the intense intimacy engendered during the act was the primary point of appeal in what she and Jed had just done—were still doing, for that matter. She'd never felt so close to another person in her life. All things considered, that made sense. How much closer could a body get to another body than this? She'd longed for closeness for such a

261

long time. Thanks to Jed, she'd now experienced it, if only briefly. With a deep sigh, she wished it could continue.

"Are you all right, Tacita?"

Jed's voice drifted, muffled, into her right ear, and she realized his nose was buried in her hair. He was panting as if he'd just run a long race, too, and Tacita guessed it wasn't only she who'd been moved by the experience they'd just shared. A tiny smile curled her lips when she considered that she, Tacita Grantham, a woman so boring even her parents couldn't bear to be around her, had reduced this great, strapping man to a state of exhaustion. Even a tedious woman had some power, she decided, and held the knowledge close to her heart, very much as she held Jed.

She had to clear her throat before she could get her voice to work. "Yes. Yes, I'm fine, thank you." That sounded inadequate, so she tacked on, "And you?"

She felt a sense of loss when he pushed himself up from her body. They were both drenched in perspiration. Since the blankets covered them up entirely, the weather in their woolen cocoon felt rather muggy.

"Fine. I'm fine," he said, sounding unsteady. He rolled to her side, much to Tacita's disappointment. She'd felt so protected with him on top of her, so cherished somehow, even though she knew the feeling to be an illusion.

When Jed pushed the blanket back, Tacita immediately saw another blanket, one crafted of black velvet and diamondlike stars, spread overhead. The scene was magnificent, and she drew

in a deep breath. What a perfect night in which
to learn the glories of love.

"Are you sure?" Jed asked quietly. He traced
her cheek and chin with a big finger.

When she turned her head, she found him
propped up on one elbow, watching her with unmistakable concern. How truly nice he was!

She smiled. "I'm sure, Jed. Thank you."

"Thank you, Tacita. I—I—"

She saw him swallow. He looked almost shy,
as though whatever he wanted to say was embarrassing to him somehow. It was unlike Jed
to be unsure of himself, and Tacita mentally
braced herself. She hoped he wasn't going to say
something prosaic and dash the sweet spell that
had woven itself around them in the night.

Reaching out, she began to trace his chin. He
rubbed his cheek against her fingers, as if he
took as much pleasure in her touch as she did
his.

"I hope I did all right," he said. Then he
seemed to be annoyed with himself.

Although she wasn't sure what etiquette prevailed in this instance, she sensed that Jed
needed her reassurance.

"You did very well, Jed. Wonderfully well." At
least Tacita thought so. Of course, she had nothing by which to compare Jed's performance, but
she couldn't imagine another man taking so
much care about introducing her to the wonders
of love.

"I—um—never felt anything so good, ma'am."

His voice sounded funny. Tacita got the feeling he felt silly, but his admission thrilled her,
even if she didn't quite believe him. After all, he
was a vastly experienced man and she a mere

novice; he was undoubtedly just being kind. Still, love swelled in her heart.

"I never did, either, Jed."

It was the truth. Granted, when he'd thrust into her it had hurt, but the preliminaries had been perfectly wonderful. Tacita hadn't ever felt the complete, all-consuming pleasure that Jed had made her feel. And she hardly hurt at all anymore.

"I didn't hurt you?"

Oh, how sweet! He was worried about her. Tacita heard it clearly in his voice. Deciding honesty would serve her well since he knew more than she did about lovemaking and would probably not believe her if she lied, she said, "Well, only a little."

His head dropped to the hollow between her neck and shoulder, and Tacita found herself petting him. She heard him whisper, "Thank God. I was so afraid I'd hurt you," and she thought that was sweet, too.

"No, you didn't hurt me, Jed. You were very gentle. Very kind."

He proceeded to deposit tiny kisses on her neck and shoulders until Tacita thought she'd die with longing—not for more lovemaking, but for love.

Jed wrapped her in his strong arms after a little while, and she subsided into them with a sigh. Curling onto her side, she allowed herself the liberty of stroking his broad chest as they lay there in the dark. Her last conscious thought was of how splendid this felt, to be out here in the wilderness under the stars, with Jed Hardcastle hugging her and the big, ugly world far, far away.

* * *

Rosamunda's feelings had not softened when Tacita and Jed stirred the next morning. Her dignity had suffered an almost unendurable outrage, and she was still bitter. She did not, however, refuse her breakfast. After all, a human being, even so superior, albeit misguided, a one as her mistress, was only worth so much. Rosamunda wasn't about to allow herself to fall into a decline just because Tacita was a fool.

Imagine, succumbing to the lures of the overgrown beast, Jedediah Hardcastle! Rosamunda fully intended to become a bride someday. As soon, in fact, as she got to San Francisco. She, however, knew enough at least to keep her proportions straight.

Prince Albert would suit her admirably. *He* wasn't as big as a house. No. Prince Albert was a champion Yorkshire terrier just like Rosamunda, and he would be only a tiny bit bigger than she, if he was any bigger at all, for heaven's sake. The thinking processes of human beings were totally incomprehensible to her—*if* they possessed thinking processes. Rosamunda had begun to harbor serious doubts on the matter.

"There, my darling," Tacita said when she unstrapped the saddlebag and scooped Rosamunda out. "Is my sweet precious darling Rosie-posie all right this morning?"

*Rosie-posie?* Rosamunda stared as Mistress lifted her into the air. Rosie-posie? Good grief! Had it really come to this?

"There, darling," Tacita said, fluffing Rosamunda's fur with her nose and chin. "Everything will be fine now. Darling Rosamunda, you're still my best friend, you know. Is everything all better now?"

All better? With Mistress having sunk to calling her *Rosie-posie*? It was bad enough when she'd made Rosamunda give up her rightful place on her pillow beside Mistress's head to that lout, Jed Hardcastle. Now Mistress was calling her by a name no self-respecting Yorkshire terrier would come with fifty yards of. Rosamunda gave an indignant snort and looked pointedly away from Tacita. Her show of resentment earned her an enthusiastic hug, which alarmed her.

Then she took a good look at Tacita and realized her mistress was in the throes of some exalted emotion and wasn't paying any attention to her at all. Rosamunda glanced sharply at Jed and found him staring at Tacita, his eyes hot with longing. Why, he looked like a lovesick coonhound Rosamunda had met once back home in Galveston. It wasn't a pretty sight, even on the coonhound. On Jed Hardcastle, it was downright ludicrous.

It did, however, give Rosamunda pause. Good heavens, were these two benighted humans actually in love with each other? She'd heard such things sometimes happened among humans, although she'd always assumed her mistress would be immune to such nonsense, as she was generally a most superlative example of the species. Rosamunda decided to keep a close eye on these two.

By the time they'd packed up to resume their journey to Denver, she had come to a most unwelcome conclusion.

Leaving Rosie-posie aside for a moment—if

such a thing was possible—"love," whatever it was, had gored both Mistress and Monster with its long, deadly horns. What a pickle.

As he loaded the mules, Jed decided that if he'd known before now how painful love would be, he'd have tried harder to avoid it. Not, of course, that he'd have had much luck, he guessed. It had attacked him behind his back when he wasn't paying attention, like the low-down sneaky demon it was. It hadn't even given Jed a chance to come up with an evasive maneuver, which was just the sort of thing a body could expect from a devil or an illness. He'd been stricken with influenza once when he was a lad, and it had snuck up on him just like this.

Glumly, he decided there was no hope for it; he was well and truly caught in the clutches of love. His buddies back home would laugh if they knew. Casting another surreptitious glance at Tacita, he decided maybe they wouldn't after all. It was far more likely that they'd be jealous.

At least they would be if she could ever belong to Jed.

But no. He yanked on the strap, making the mule glower at him and utter a short bray.

"Sorry," he murmured, loosening the strap.

Tacita couldn't be his. She was destined for that ridiculous, dog-loving, unnatural Englishman. He wished Edgar Jevington Reeve would go down with the boat on the way over from England. That would solve Jed's problems. Tacita might have him then, since he was the one who'd taken her purity. He didn't expect she'd marry him otherwise.

The specter of Miss Amalie Crunch rose before him, almost as large as Miss Amalie Crunch herself, and Jed groaned.

"Are you all right, Jed?" Tacita asked sweetly.

He smiled at her, thinking how wonderful she was. Even if she did talk a lot and liked to argue a bit too much to please him, and was a little overfond of that idiotic dog of hers.

"I'm fine, thanks."

"I thought maybe you'd hurt yourself. You made that funny noise."

He sighed. "No. I'm fine."

"I'm glad."

She gave him the most beautiful smile he'd ever received from a woman. It was almost, but not quite, enough to banish Amalie's apparition. Jed couldn't think of anything big enough to do that.

So that was all he'd ever have from Tacita Grantham: those stolen moments last night under the stars. Well, under the blanket under the stars. Maybe, if he was very lucky, she might allow him to touch her again. He didn't dare hope very hard, for fear his shattered dreams would shatter him.

Lord, Lord, why couldn't he have fallen in love with a woman he could have? Why couldn't he be in love with Amalie? Amalie was a nice girl. She was a real nice girl. In his inner vision, Amalie grinned, reminding him strongly of a Halloween jack-o'-lantern.

He quickly thrust aside the unworthy hope that maybe Amalie'd fall off a rock and cease to be a burden to him. Hell, even if Amalie wasn't back home in Busted Flush, waiting for him, Tacita Grantham still wouldn't want him. He knew it, and the knowledge made him sad. He wondered if his heart would hurt forever or if it would heal someday. Either way, he didn't expect he'd ever fall in love again.

His spirits alternating between heaviness and elation, Jed doggedly continued his task. He didn't know why he loved Tacita, didn't know why he couldn't love Amalie. He didn't understand any of it.

Work was something he understood, so he worked.

Tacita had never felt so marvelous in her life. Overnight, her turbulent imaginings had settled, and this morning she decided to continue pretending Jed loved her until they reached San Francisco. She was pretty sure she'd fall apart then, but didn't care to have the awareness of their ultimate, separate destinies make her miserable until she no longer had a choice. In San Francisco, she would cry. Until then, she would be happy.

Tacita carefully folded the blankets they'd used for their tryst last night. She could smell their love on them, and see faint traces of rustiness, where she'd bled slightly. If she were home, she'd preserve this evidence of her first experience into the realm of physical love. She had no means by which to do so out here on the trail, but she'd remember this morning's sights and scents forever.

When she handed the blankets to Jed, her gaze caught his, and they stared into each other's eyes for what seemed like hours. The perfect moment was only broken when Rosamunda started barking. Glancing over, Tacita saw her beloved pet squared off as if she meant to attack something, her hackles risen, her teeth bared. Rosamunda's testiness seemed general this morning. When Tacita scanned the campsite, she saw nobody else within snarling range. Poor Rosamunda. Tacita guessed she felt left out.

Jed caught fish for breakfast, coated them in cornmeal, and fried them over the campfire that he'd earlier coaxed to life with dry twigs. Tacita marveled anew at his powerful frontier wisdom. A dime novelist would have a field day with Jed Hardcastle.

"I've never tasted anything so good in my life, Jed."

"Thank you."

"This fish is delicious."

"Well, reckon fish is better when it's caught and cooked fresh."

"I imagine you're right. What kind is it?"

Jed frowned at his tin plate. "Perch? Pike? One of them—those, I reckon."

"Well, it's wonderful."

"Yeah. Reckon it's pretty good."

Even his natural taciturnity thrilled her. Tacita sighed, knowing she had it bad and wishing it could continue. If she'd known how delicious love could be, she'd not have resisted so hard when she felt herself falling in love with Jed.

Pulling fish bones from between her teeth, she wished a convenient lightning strike would eliminate her rival. Perhaps if Miss Amalie Crunch were dead, Jed would marry her. After all, he was an honorable man. Wouldn't an honorable man wish to wed a woman whose virginity he'd taken? It took a moment, but eventually her conscience smote her for thinking such an un-Christian thing about Miss Crunch.

Anyway, as she glanced at Jed she knew she wouldn't want him to marry her simply because he'd bedded her. No. Tacita wanted the impossible. She wanted his love.

The trail to Denver was well-used, well-marked, and fairly good. They met several other travelers on this leg of their journey, unlike their trek through New Mexico Territory. Always, Jed led the way and allowed Tacita to speak to strangers only after he'd ascertained they were no threat to their little party. Tacita was enchanted by this further show of protectiveness and pretended it was for her alone and that he wouldn't protect another client with such diligence.

She knew she was only putting off the inevitable, but that was all right. A few more weeks of bliss might make up for the rest of her lifetime spent alone and unloved.

Except, of course, for her beloved Rosamunda. Tacita peered into the saddlebag she'd prepared for her darling before they'd begun their long journey, and smiled. Rosamunda looked up at her with such confidence. It made Tacita's heart sing to know Rosamunda trusted her so implicitly.

She and Jed made love often as they covered the long miles to Denver. At first, he'd seemed reluctant, and Tacita believed he didn't want to bed her again. She'd even gone so far as to ask him, risking rejection. If he told her he never wanted to touch her again, she'd be humiliated, but at least her belief in herself as unworthy would be verified once and for all. She'd never harbor idle hopes again.

"Not want to?"

He'd sounded as astonished as he'd looked. Taking note of his eyebrows, arched like twin horseshoes over his gorgeous brown eyes, Tacita took heart. Unwilling to succumb to mistaken assumptions, she nodded, reserving her opinion.

"Yes. I shall understand if you don't want to— to make love again." She'd used the term guardedly, since what they'd done the prior night undoubtedly bore no resemblance to love in Jed's mind. She couldn't think of another term for it, though, being a proper young woman and unversed in the vocabulary of sexual congress.

"Not *want* to?" he said again.

And again she nodded. "Yes. It's all right, Jed. I certainly don't wish to force you to do anything you don't want to do."

"Not *want* to?" he said yet a third time.

This time, Tacita's patience frayed. After all, it had taken all of her courage to ask him the first time. "Yes!" she snapped. "For heaven's sake, stop looking at me like that!"

Jed's mouth closed with a clink of teeth, although his eyebrows remained arched into their expression of astonishment. Tacita wondered if he considered her question so outrageous, so utterly revolting, that he could find no words with which to express his repugnance. The idea made heat spread across the back of her neck and creep into her cheeks. She turned away, unable to watch him any longer.

"I—I'm sorry, Tacita." His voice was very soft and unusually full of feeling.

She sniffed.

"I'd like nothing better than to make love to

you again, ma'am. Tacita. I—I didn't think you'd want to."

She turned around again. "Really?"

Apparently finding words difficult, Jed took refuge in a nod.

"You mean it?"

He nodded once more.

Her smile broke free of her trepidation. "Oh, I'm so *awfully* glad!"

Rosamunda snarled once and then desisted, turning her back on them and hunkering down on her bed. She didn't even acknowledge Tacita's fond goodnight.

Jed made her feel even better that night. If asked before it happened, Tacita would have declared such a thing to be impossible.

It was incredible how gentle those big hands of his could be, though. They brought every single inch of her body to life. Tacita realized, in fact, that she'd barely been alive until Jed stroked her into awareness. It was as if her body had been slumbering until he awakened it.

After she reached her shuddering release and welcomed Jed into her body with open arms and a loving heart, she admitted to herself, silently, that it would be difficult to continue life Jed-less. He had come to mean so much to her in such a short period of time, the thought of resuming her life with only Rosamunda to love filled her with sadness.

Even before she'd cajoled him into making love with her, she'd loved him. Now she considered the moment of their parting with dread. Renewing her vow not to think about it, she revived her pretense and welcomed it with pleasure. Un-

til they got to San Francisco, Jed Hardcastle
loved her, and that was that.

She went to sleep that night with Jed in her
arms and a body tingling with newly discovered
pleasures.

Luther Adams Williamson, Avinash Agrawal,
Farley Boskins, and Virendra Karnik sat in the
largest of the suite of rooms Agrawal had hired
at the fanciest hotel in Santa Fe. Agrawal's ever-
present henchmen stood guard at the door, their
faces impassive, their white costumes and turbans concealing deadly weapons and giving Luther the impression of evil angels. The
henchmen were unnecessary. He decided not to
tell Agrawal so, but the truth was, Luther possessed neither the moral backbone nor the bold-
ness to attempt an escape. At the moment,
moreover, he wasn't sure he could even stand.

Agrawal stroked his upper lip and gazed dis-
passionately at Luther, as though he were studying a fairly dull passage in a boring book. Luther
tried to keep him in focus, but wasn't altogether
successful. He sipped steadily on his beer as the
only way to keep panic from consuming him.

Farley Boskins and Virendra Karnik sat
nearby, discussing politics. Luther's fuddled
mind couldn't follow their conversation. It was
having enough trouble concentrating on Agrawal. Besides, every time a snippet of their dis-
cussion penetrated Luther's alcohol-soaked
brain, words like "tyranny" and "Kali" and
"plumbing" struck him as extremely odd. When
he tried, Luther didn't have the wit to sort them
out, so he quit trying.

Every now and then a flicker of hope would

remind him that all wasn't lost yet. The flicker was becoming dimmer as the days passed and the Eye remained with Tacita. Maybe whoever Agrawal had hired to hold up the stage from Denver would be successful, but Luther had been foiled too neatly too often lately to hope very hard.

"So you believe Miss Grantham will take up residence at the Palace when she arrives in San Francisco, Mr. Williamson?"

Agrawal's suave voice oiled its way through the beery puddles in Luther's head and settled slowly into comprehensible language. He nodded once, then stopped when his head swam.

"Yesh," he said and frowned. That didn't sound right, so he tried again. "Yes." There. That was better. Making a gigantic effort he added, "She always stays at the best hotels." She might as well, he added silently; after all, she had all the money in the world.

"Then I believe we should remove ourselves to San Francisco with dispatch."

Luther stared hard at Agrawal's lips, hoping to use what was left of his senses to decipher meaning in the Indian's clipped words. After a moment or two, he succeeded.

"Yesh. Yesh, that's prolly besht."

Agrawal frowned. "Perhaps it would be better if you were not to drink so much, my friend."

Luther's heart stumbled over a beat, not being quick enough by this time to skip. "No," he said, and shook his head even though the motion made unpleasant waves crash through it. "No. Need it. Doctor's orders."

Agrawal's left eyebrow lifted. "Truly?"

After attempting a nod, Luther hunched over

and hugged his beer mug to his chest. It was all he had left.

"Ah, well, then, I shan't chide you. I suppose it doesn't matter."

That's exactly what Luther was afraid of.

Tacita was a little surprised to discover how bustling a metropolis Denver was. She'd expected a rowdy, dusty, rutted boom town with little beauty and few amenities. What she found was that Denver was indeed rowdy, quite dusty, and entirely too rutted. The boom, however, had settled into a rather more steady rumble of commerce in precious ores, with long-established businesses rumbling right alongside it in supporting positions. And is was lovely, too, in spots.

The opera house, in fact, was beautiful, and it wasn't the only nice-looking building to catch her eye. She gazed with rapt interest at the swarms of citizens thronging the streets. Why, the place looked quite urbane.

"My goodness, it's such a big city."

"Yup. It's big all right." Jed didn't sound pleased.

"You don't like it?"

Jed was leading the mules and baggage wagon through the crowded streets, hunched over his saddle, staring straight ahead. Tacita rode her little mare next to him. He wore a scowl on his face, but his expression softened when he turned to look at her.

"I'm not real fond of big cities, Tacita."

"Oh." Tacita considered his words as she looked around. This seemed to be an exciting place, but she guessed she could understand

Jed's distaste. Denver did not appear to be a very peaceful town. If all she'd read about it was true, it wasn't nearly as peaceful as Galveston, which had been civilized for fifty years or more before Denver had begun to sprout up around the mines, and Galveston wasn't especially peaceful.

"You prefer the quiet of a small town?"

He looked at her for a long time before he said, "Reckon that's it."

"I see." Tilting her head as she mulled the matter over, she said, "I've never lived in a small town myself."

"Figured as much."

Now he sounded morose. Tacita could think of nothing to account for his tone. Before she could take exception or ask him about it, he interrupted her thoughts.

"You ever think about trying to live in a small town, ma'am?"

"Why, I've never considered it before."

"Didn't think so." His shoulders slumped a little more.

"It must be pleasant to know all your neighbors, though."

"It's pretty fair."

"I imagine it's especially agreeable if you have relatives there," she offered, considering how satisfying it would be to be surrounded by a large, affectionate family like Jed's. One would certainly never be lonely, even if one were relatively boring by nature.

"Even if you don't," he said, and she had to scramble to remember what she'd said that he was responding to. When she did, she was stricken by how logical his assertion was.

"Of course. I do believe you're right. Why, if

one has no family, one would still know everyone in a small town and, therefore, have friends and companions. I know that in Galveston, most of the people I had communication with were connected to my parents' business enterprises in one way or another. Since my school days were spent in a boarding school in New York, I didn't have very many friends in Galveston. It's surprising how anonymous a large city can be."

"Wouldn't know."

Tacita's heart trilled a beat at his terse response. He was so rugged. So matter-of-fact. So to-the-point. So—so Western, somehow. He didn't waste breath in idle chitchat.

"Well, it is, I can tell you that," she said.

He grunted.

When they were on the trail, Jed was able to fool himself into thinking that maybe, if he tried really, really hard, he could win Tacita Grantham's love. As they traveled farther into the lively city of Denver, the disparity between their backgrounds thrust itself into his mind like a headache. There was no way on earth she'd ever give up her big-city connections and go for a small-town hick like him.

No. She was a city woman and she needed a city fellow. Somebody with polish and sophistication; somebody who knew which fork to use when and didn't have to think before he used good grammar. Somebody who could carry on conversations about nothing with people he'd never met before. Jed guessed grudgingly that even a pansy Englishman would probably have more in common with Tacita Grantham than he did.

He remained grim as he purchased tickets on the next stage to San Francisco and hired a carrier to transport the bulk of Tacita's belongings, since they wouldn't fit on the stage.

Of course, he wasn't *that* much of a hick. After all, he did have a university degree. Granted, it wasn't from Yale or Harvard or one of those fancy Eastern universities. Still, it was a degree and he reckoned he could use it somewhere besides Busted Flush. Maybe she'd want him if he agreed to give up his life in Busted Flush and move to Galveston.

The notion no sooner appeared than Jed began to experience a queasy feeling deep down in his guts, and he knew he was only kidding himself. Spending long enough at Texas U. to get a degree had almost killed him, because of all the people there. Even for the sake of securing Tacita, he wasn't sure he could survive indefinitely in a city the size of Galveston. If the crowds didn't drive him berserk, the weather would. Jed was used to the dry, open plains around Busted Flush. Humidity and hurricanes were a couple of things he'd just as soon avoid if he could.

No. It didn't seem likely that he'd have Tacita Grantham on a permanent basis. He'd just have to make do with the time they had together, and pray he'd get over her in time to make a decent, if lukewarm, husband for Miss Amalie Crunch.

Not having had much practice in pretending, Jed's spirits didn't rise appreciably. He trudged up the stairs of the fancy hotel Tacita insisted they stay in as though he bore the weight of the world on his shoulders.

\*    \*    \*

Rosamunda inspected the hotel room closely, sniffing into every corner, scratching the flocked wallpaper, visiting under the bed, investigating the gilt claw feet on the chairs and table, and taking a tentative nip at the draperies. At last she decided the room would do. It wasn't up to her standards, but it was far superior to any of the other accommodations she'd been subjected to recently.

Tacita placed a plush velvet cushion from the sofa on the floor for her. After giving her mistress a baleful stare, which Tacita completely ignored, Rosamunda lifted her dainty paws and climbed onto the cushion.

Imagine, having to give up her rightful place in her mistress's bed in order to accommodate that oaf, Jed Hardcastle. Rosamunda's sense of correctness in the universe had suffered many blows lately, including Tacita having taken to calling her by a silly diminutive, but this last was the most severe. Rosamunda had always slept with her mistress.

She felt exceedingly ill-used when she turned around thrice, dug madly at the velvet fabric for several seconds, and sank into a furry curl of resentment on the cushion.

# *Chapter Fifteen*

Jed took Tacita to the opera that night. He didn't know what possessed him to ask her, but something did, she accepted, so here they were, looking like underdressed chickens in a flock of peacocks.

"Shoot, I didn't know folks dressed so fancy to hear a bunch of people sing," he murmured as he escorted Tacita to her seat. Before they'd arrived at the opera house, he'd thought her gown must be the fanciest he'd ever seen. He realized his mistake as soon as the cab disgorged them amid a sea of men in long tails and beaver hats and ladies trussed up like geese with whalebone and decorated in ruffles, diamonds, and furs.

"Yes, we do seem to be a bit less elaborately clad than the rest of these people," Tacita said, apparently unaffected by the matter. "But it was so lovely of you to ask me, and it's such a pleasure to go to such a function, that I don't mind."

Her smile was so warm, so lovely, so affectionate, that Jed guessed he didn't mind either. Mind? Hell, he'd have been willing to show up at this shindig buck naked if she asked him to. That damned pansy Englishman had better appreciate what he was getting in Tacita Grantham, is all Jed had to say about it, or he'd have to answer to Jed Hardcastle.

The folks in Denver didn't seem to mind their less-than-magnificent state of dress. After the first act, Jed figured it was because their senses had been blunted by exposure to the screechy warbles emanating from the stage.

Then, during the second act, his own sensibilities were scandalized when several ladies in pink tights pranced out onto the stage. Shoot, he hadn't seen meat that rare since he'd visited a saloon in Kansas City in '89. The pigeons in the K.C. coop had been displaying their wares for purchase. These birds only seemed to have been stuck in the middle of the opera in order to titillate the audience. As far as Jed was concerned, the former performance was more honest than the latter.

"Don't be silly, Jed," Tacita purred into his ear when he voiced his outrage during an interval. "That's only the dance. There's always a ballet in the middle of an opera."

"It's immoral."

"It's not immoral. It's art."

"It's art for a female to strip herself naked and prance around in front of five hundred people?"

"For heaven's sake, Jed! Those women weren't

282

naked. They were in costumes, and they were performing a ballet."

"Like hell." He folded his arms over his chest and glared at the drawn curtains sheltering his eyes from the licentious display that had lately cavorted across the stage.

"You're being silly." Tacita's tone suggested his attitude peeved her, too.

"You think I'm being silly? What if I told you I've seen women dressed just like that, singing and dancing in front of a bunch of drunkards in saloons? Would you call that silly?"

"Of course not!" Tacita began to fan herself, and Jed noticed her cheeks had gone pink. He was still mad and didn't care if he'd offended her.

"What's the difference between this and that?"

"It's entirely different! Those females who dance in saloons are—are not ladies."

"And these are?"

"Well—well, yes, they are. They're in the chorus and undoubtedly studying to become lead singers one day."

"Lead singers, my ass."

"Jed!"

"They're hoping some rich silver millionaire in the audience will spot 'em and offer 'em a position in his bedroom, is what they're doing."

"*Jed!*"

"Bet I'm right." He nodded with mulish satisfaction.

"You are not." Tacita's fan sped up and she sounded really cross. "Why, I went to the opera all the time while I was going to school in New York City. If there was anything scandalous about it, Miss Featherstone would never have taken us there."

Jed fumed for a moment, trying to organize his thoughts.

"Well, all I can say is that if you ever stripped naked and frolicked out onto a stage like that, I'd throw a blanket over you and haul you home quicker'n you could spit."

A small pause met his vehement declaration. Then Tacita said, "You would?" in a very small voice.

"Damned right I would."

"Oh, Jed, that's the sweetest thing anybody's ever said to me in my whole life!"

As Jed turned to stare at her in astonishment, Tacita latched onto his arm, leaned against him, and sighed. He patted her hand because he couldn't help it, but he knew he'd never understand females if he lived to be a hundred.

Tacita had relished love under the stars. She was nearly overwhelmed by the bliss of love on a feather mattress. This was particularly so because both she and Jed had bathed before the opera, in real tubs, with hot water and fragrant soap. Tacita had even had the foresight to purchase some lavender-scented lotion in the hotel's gift shop.

Although it was late by the time they returned from the opera, and their dispute over the relative morality of opera dancers remained unresolved, it didn't take much time for Tacita to persuade Jed that she needed to use more lotion.

"My skin has become so dry on the trail, Jed. It feels like sandpaper."

"Sandpaper?"

She nodded and stepped out of her chemise. His eyes bugged for a moment. Then he grabbed the jar of lotion, licked his lips, and gestured to the bed. "Here," he said, his voice shaky, "I'll do it."

Tacita obliged happily.

He seemed to take great delight in smoothing the lotion over her body after she climbed onto the bed.

"I've never felt skin like yours, Tacita. It's not like sandpaper. It's as smooth as silk."

"Really? Even after so long on the trail out in the sun and wind?"

"Yup." Jed's voice sounded gravelly. Tacita was beginning to recognize that quality in his voice as betokening great emotion. She sighed happily and wiggled on the sheets, eliciting a choked growl from him.

"Thank you," she said, thinking she'd never received such a pretty compliment from a man before. Or anybody else, either, for that matter.

Gooseflesh rose on her when she felt his lips caress the path his hands had just smoothed over with lotion. She closed her eyes, thinking that even if she had a lifetime with Jed, she'd never get used to these delicious attentions he lavished upon her. The fact that she didn't have a lifetime with him, but only another month or so of hard traveling, made her appreciate them all the more. Perhaps other women received these favors with complacence. Tacita's affectionate heart had never felt the joy of reciprocation, and it didn't.

"This lotion was a good idea," Jed spread his gentle words across her shoulders along with the soothing balm. "It feels real good."

"Mmmmm." Almost beyond words by this time, Tacita managed to turn over and whispered, "Spread some on my front, Jed."

She saw him gulp twice before her eyelids fluttered shut again. Then she felt his big hands massaging lotion into her tummy and breasts, her calves and thighs. Heat seemed to radiate from his fingers until Tacita feared she might ignite into an inferno of sensation right here, on the bed, in the Silver Baron Hotel in Denver, Colorado.

Jed had taught her how to feel these things. Jed had opened her to the magnificence of life. Before she met him, she'd been insulated, isolated from the world of sensation by fear and the conviction of her own lusterless personality. But Jed had been willing to ignore her imperfections. He'd taught her that even so flawed a specimen of womanhood as Tacita Grantham could experience the joys of passion. Oh, how she loved him!

Because she feared the only words she knew to express her feelings would have disgusted Jed, Tacita lifted her arms.

Jed fell into her arms eagerly. He wished he were more loquacious by nature. He longed to tell Tacita how she made him feel. When he was with her, he was a giant, a hero, the ruler in his own universe. With her, he could conquer worlds. Before he met Tacita, he was a rough frontier guide. Now he was a king. No. Better than a king; he was a magician.

It was he who had unearthed the fire in her; he who had stoked the fire until she felt, for the first time Jed was sure, the fullness of her delight. He'd have bet anything that until he bedded her, she didn't know she possessed such passion.

Recalling that it had been she who initiated this evening's joy, Jed's heart felt full. *I love you,* whispered through his mind. Only by great force of will did he keep the words from slipping through his lips.

When Jed handed Tacita into the stage the next morning, he knew this was to be the last leg of their journey. This was the final phase. Before long, they would be in San Francisco, California, and he'd be headed back to Busted Flush, Texas. Alone.

The thought subdued him. He managed a nod for the other passengers, but his heart wasn't in it. In fact, he'd have a real struggle to keep his heart patched together and in one piece until they arrived in San Francisco and it broke for the last time.

*Pretend,* he commanded himself. *Pretend.* Even if he didn't have any practice in deceiving himself, he'd be a damned fool if he allowed his ultimate fate to make his last, pitifully few days with Tacita miserable.

*You're already a fool, Jed Hardcastle,* his brain sang mockingly. He told his brain to be quiet.

Rosamunda eyed the preacher seated across from Tacita on the stagecoach and knew something about him was amiss, although she couldn't put her paw on what it was.

There was something about his eyes, she thought. They were too cunning to belong to a man of God.

Or maybe it was his mouth. It smiled, but the

rest of his face didn't mean it. There were lines around his mouth that hadn't been created by prior smiles; Rosamunda would bet her jeweled collar on it, if Yorkies did such idiotic things as lay wagers.

His hands were dirty; maybe that was it. Dirt lodged under his fingernails and in the creases around his wrists. In Rosamunda's experience, preachers were a tidy lot. They read, prayed, and yakked for a living, and didn't have much reason to dirty their hands. She couldn't feature the hands of this stranger pressed together in an aspect of prayer. And before she'd allow him to wave them above her head in a blessing, Rosamunda'd sure want to check to make sure they didn't hold anything unsavory.

Maybe it was that turned-around collar of his. It seemed to be chafing his neck, as if it were too tight or he wasn't used to wearing it. By Rosamunda's reckoning, this man would be more than thirty in human years. That was plenty old enough to have become accustomed to the trappings of his profession.

He was wearing boots, too, and they were scuffed and dirty and looked like riding boots. Did preachers ride horses? Rosamunda had never heard about it if they did. Of course out here, she supposed with a sniff, anything was possible. Even if they did, though, nobody had cause to wear riding boots on the stage. Even Jed Hardcastle had abandoned his riding boots for a slightly more civilized pair of shoes. Although, it must be acknowledged, nothing about Jed Hardcastle was very civilized. Whatever Jed's shortcomings, there was no reason Rosamunda could think of for a minister to be wearing riding boots at all. And if he did, he'd surely take time to shine them up before he undertook a long trip in a stage-coach.

Before she could figure it out, the man smiled at Tacita and offered her a pleasant, "Good morning, ma'am."

Tacita, who didn't possess a fraction of a Yorkshire terrier's instincts about such things, smiled back and returned his "Good morning" with one of her own. To Rosamunda's disgust, she compounded her lack of perception by continuing on in a friendly voice, "Lovely day to begin a journey, isn't it?"

"Indeed it is, ma'am." The man's expression turned pious. "The Lord has provided us with splendid weather, hasn't He?"

When she heard the man's patent hypocrisy, Rosamunda snarled softly.

Tacita said with a happy sigh, "He certainly has."

Jed climbed into the stage. He looked at the so-called preacher and said, "Howdy," a deplorable word and one Rosamunda hoped she'd never hear again after she got to San Francisco. The preacher "Howdied" back. Rosamunda lifted a brow and cast him a withering look. He didn't notice, which figured. Human beings were so obtuse.

She and her mistress shared the coach with the phony preacher and a fat woman carrying a wicker basket. They all had to scrunch over in their seats because Jed took up so much space. Rosamunda chalked up another transgression against him. He'd accumulated so many by this time they'd be heavier than Rosamunda if anybody cared to weigh them. Renewed indignation over the insults she'd been forced to endure recently made her dig at her mistress's skirt for a second.

"Rosamunda! Here, darling, don't claw my gown."

"Cute little thing," the preacher—or whatever he was—said.

He reached out to chuck Rosamunda under the chin, a human affront that never failed to offend her. She was about to bite his fingers to let him know in no uncertain terms exactly what she thought of strangers who mauled her, when an idea struck her.

There was no telling exactly what this man's game was, but Rosamunda knew he wasn't what he claimed to be. She also decided it would behoove her to discover his purpose and nullify it, should it turn out to be dangerous to her or to Tacita. The perils the two of them had already suffered on this ill-fated trip made Rosamunda view with caution anything that didn't fit comfortably into the natural order of things.

Glaring resentfully at Jed, Rosamunda decided she'd better do it, anyway. Although it galled her to admit it, occasionally Jedediah Hardcastle had demonstrated a grasp of situations that seemed to elude her mistress. It was undoubtedly due to some kind of instinctive, involuntary animal quirk in his nature, since he didn't otherwise possess wit enough to recognize enemies. He had, however, determined that man on the train was Mr. Cesare. Jed must possess some innate sense, like a coonhound's snout, that helped him in his line of work.

At present, however, Jed Hardcastle was as useless as Mistress in these matters. Rosamunda glanced at him once and then looked away again, disgusted. It appeared to her as if Jed were so besotted with Mistress, he wouldn't notice anything unusual about their traveling companion if he pulled out a gun and shot them all.

Their safety was up to her, then. So be it. Rosamunda was up to the challenge.

"My goodness!"

Jed had been staring gloomily out the window at Denver as the stagecoach rambled through its streets, calculating how many days it would be before he'd have to bid Tacita a final farewell. At her exclamation, he turned, wondering what had prompted it. What he saw surprised him, too. His mouth dropped open in awe, in fact.

"I've never seen her do something like that before in my life." Tacita's voice was hushed, as if she'd just witnessed a holy miracle.

Jed closed his mouth. "Me, neither." He rubbed his eyes to clear them of impediments. When he opened them again, he guessed they'd been clear all along, because the scene hadn't changed. Rosamunda still sat on the fake preacher's lap, and it looked like she aimed to curl up there and take a snooze.

"I guess she knows a good man when she sees one," Tacita continued, causing Jed's gaze to veer from the astonishing sight across the aisle and focus on her.

Good man? Jed opened his mouth again, then decided not to bother. Hell, it was no skin off his teeth if this fellow wanted to dress up like a parson and if Tacita wanted to believe him. Out in this neck of the woods, people did all sorts of things to escape their pasts. Or their presents, if need be. He didn't suppose Tacita had to know that, since she wasn't going to be tarrying here long.

His innards gave a hard spasm at the thought, and he told himself to stop thinking about when they would part. Such thoughts did no good, wouldn't alter the future, and only made him feel bad.

Gunpowder! Rosamunda sniffed again to be sure. Yes. It was there all right: gunpowder on the fake preacher's fingers. Humph. The last she'd heard, human preachers didn't have much to do with guns, fools that they were. If Rosamunda ran things, she'd take all the guns away from bad human beings and give them to the good ones, because they were the only ones fit to use them. Humans, of course, had the whole thing backward.

Well, it's just a good thing she'd decided to follow this course of action, then. Rosamunda, unlike other people she could mention, recognized a possible danger when she saw it. She also knew what to do about one when she was sitting on its lap. So she proceeded to do it.

Since humans were the way they were, nobody on the stagecoach thought anything about it when she began to burrow under the parson's coat. Well, perhaps Mistress noticed, because she uttered another exclamation of surprise, but Rosamunda paid her no heed. She went about her business, knowing she was the only sentient creature anywhere around who realized the job had to be done.

The parson himself had gone to sleep, and was snoring loud enough to rattle the windows on the stagecoach. Not that it would have mattered, since Rosamunda knew how to be silent when she needed to be, and how to insinuate herself into the smallest coat pocket without the pocket's owner knowing anything about it. She'd have made a good pickpocket if she'd been a human, although humans tended to frown upon pickpockets—which just went to show what kind of sense they had.

"Is Rosie sick, do you suppose, Tacita?"

Tacita eyed Rosamunda's feathery stump of a tail with misgiving. At the moment, it was sticking out from underneath the preacher's coattail. "I'm not sure. She seemed perfectly well this morning."

"Well, I don't know if she's sick or not, but I sure never saw her take to anybody before."

"I never did, either. My goodness."

Jed shook his head and repeated, "Never saw her take to anybody before." Although he supposed it would figure that she'd take up with a fraud if she took up with anybody. If he recalled correctly, she'd seemed kind of fond of that Pickywhisky fellow after she got through gnawing on him. Of course, Pinkywinsky had had meat on him, and Rosamunda was the piggiest dog Jed had ever seen in his life. Maybe this preacher carried some jerky around in his pocket. He spared Tacita his unflattering conclusion.

He saw her gaze at Rosamunda's tail, a fond smile on her lips, and a curl of jealousy snaked its way through his middle. It figured Tacita would take a fancy to a parson, too. Even a fake one.

She had no qualms about naked ladies dancing in the opera, and didn't see anything wrong with people pretending to be ministers of God. Some city girls had their priorities all tumbled around, is all he had to say about it. To make himself feel better, he gave the pretend preacher a good, snarling glare. He got a thundering snore in return, and didn't feel any better at all.

Disgusted by everything, Jed decided to ignore the whole lot of them. With an unhappy grunt, he pulled his hat down to cover his eyes, folded his arms over his chest, leaned against the side of the coach, and tried to sleep. The coach springs being what they were and the road being what it was, his attempt met with uneven success.

Rosamunda hoped Mistress would appreciate this. As she spat a hunk of leather into the space between the coach seat and the door, she decided she probably wouldn't if life continued upon the course it had begun several weeks ago. Which was a lowering reflection, and one Rosamunda had best not contemplate if she expected to save them all from this villain's fell purpose.

Well, it didn't matter. Rosamunda knew where her duty lay, even if this sorry assortment of human beings didn't. Perhaps her valor would cause Mistress to realize how far she had strayed from goodness and right.

Peeking out from the preacher's deep pocket into which she'd nibbled herself, the sight that greeted her eyes caused her to reassess her prior hope. Mistress and Jed were staring into each other's eyes as if they were the only two people in the universe.

Rosamunda dove back into the pocket, almost glad to have it to hide in.

Four strong horses pulled the Butterfield stagecoach across the country at an alarming speed. It wasn't quite as alarming as that achieved by the train, and the road the stage traveled was much bumpier than the tracks the train rode upon. They still made pretty good time, though, although Tacita wasn't sure her bottom would survive the trip.

Every several miles the driver would pull into a stage stop. Immediately men would rush out, unharness the sweaty team, harness up another one, and they'd be off again. Only occasionally were passengers allowed to climb down, shake the kinks out of their aching limbs, and use the necessaries or grab a cup of incredibly bad coffee. She and Jed generally tried to take a few steps out of doors just to keep their circulation going.

The preacher never debarked at the stage stops. He merely woke with a start, then smiled benevolently and said that he'd use the time to meditate and read passages from his Bible. Unless Tacita insisted, Rosamunda stayed on the stagecoach with him.

There was very little time to see the sights at these stops. Not that they were worth seeing, being primarily visions of trash that had accumulated around the various stops. Tacita sniffed at the third of these unsightly mounds and decided it would be a good thing for the Wild West if women ever began settling out here.

Tacita was no fool; she knew as well as anyone that trash had to be dumped somewhere. If women had a hand in things, however, it would be dumped into pits dug especially to accommodate it. No longer would men be allowed to pile their old smelly bottles and tin cans in the backs of wagons, drive them outside of town and leave them in unsightly heaps for the elements to corrode.

Heaven alone knew when such a softening feminine influence would make its presence felt out here, though. The only woman Tacita had seen so far was the fat, friendly passenger on the stagecoach. The remaining citizens out here along their route seemed to be men. And rough-looking men, at that.

She didn't fear them, though, because she had Jed to guard her. With a happy sigh, she snuggled against him. It was dark now, but the stagecoach continued to rattle them through the night. This trip might have been romantic if they'd been alone. Or if the road weren't so rough.

Rosamunda continued to sit with the minister, which was strange behavior on her part, but Tacita didn't begrudge her a friendly lap. The poor darling. She'd been ousted from her place of honor in Tacita's bed, and that must have been a blow. Tacita knew also that, while she still loved Rosamunda dearly, another love now filled her heart. She squeezed the muscled arm filling her hands and rubbed her cheek against it. Jed squeezed her back, and she knew a moment of ecstasy. If only it could continue.

She frowned out the window and commanded

herself to stop thinking in terms of eventuality. What mattered was the present, and Tacita had to keep that in mind or she'd enter San Francisco in tears.

# *Chapter Sixteen*

It must have been nearing three in the morning when a strange thing happened.

Exhaustion had finally claimed Tacita, in spite of the uncomfortable ride. She had been napping on and off for two or three hours, although her sleep was unrestful, being interrupted every few minutes when the stage jogged over a big rut or bump in the road. Jed's comforting arm warmed her, and his chest served as her pillow. Rosamunda had finally abandoned the preacher and climbed back onto her lap, and Tacita was surprised by how glad she was to have her back.

Her hand rested on Rosamunda's soft fur when a loud clatter and assorted yells jerked her awake. She recognized the racket as indicating the coach's entry into a stage stop and sat up, rubbing her eyes. Then, without thinking, she yawned.

Almost immediately, she perceived the impropriety of her action. "Oh, my goodness. I beg your pardon. How dreadfully rude of me."

"It's all right, Tacita. Nobody can see you. It's still nighttime."

Tacita recognized the grin in Jed's voice as the one he used when she was being big-cityish. Although she was excessively sore and sleepy, she didn't take umbrage. Rather, she smiled at him. At least, she hoped it was him. The atmosphere was so dim both inside and out, she couldn't tell for sure.

Soon the door opened, and faint lantern light filtered into the coach.

"If'n you folks want to get down and stretch, we'll be here for about fifteen minutes. There's sandwiches and coffee inside, if y'all want."

"Thanks. Reckon I will step down for a minute or two. Want a cup of coffee, Tacita?"

"Yes. Thank you. That sounds like a good idea." She frowned. "If I can get my lower limbs to work, I might even enjoy a brisk walk."

Tacita was certain, too, that Rosamunda would appreciate the opportunity to do her doggie duty. She didn't say so aloud, as it would have been inappropriate to do so. A sandwich didn't sound like a bad idea either, although she doubted that it would taste very good if her experience with prior stage-stop sandwiches was anything by which to judge.

As they'd been doing since they entered the stage in Denver, she and Jed allowed the fat lady to climb down from the stage first. They would have done this for courtesy's sake, even if the preacher traveling with them hadn't made a point of mentioning its propriety at their first stop. Tacita thought that was nice of him.

After the fat woman had chuffed and grunted her way off the stage, Jed whispered, "You all right, Tacita? Do you need me to help you?"

"Thank you, Jed. That's very sweet of you, but I think I can manage." She gently set Rosamunda on the seat next to her and began to test her own legs and back for cricks.

All at once the preacher made a lunge for the door. Tacita had been about to stand, but he knocked her back into Jed's lap.

Startled, she cried, "What on earth . . . ?"

"Shut the hell up," the preacher snarled, barring the door and shocking Tacita greatly.

She saw his eyes glittering in a strange way. In fact, his whole manner seemed to have undergone a sudden, inexplicable change. He looked quite mean all at once. She didn't understand, although his peremptory command offended her. Then she had the frightening thought that perhaps the stagecoach was under attack by wild Indians or stage robbers.

"Oh, dear. Is something wrong?" She leaped up again and glanced quickly toward the door.

Jed grunted and grabbed her around the waist, hauling her back into his arms. "Better be quiet," he whispered.

That offended her, too. "What do you mean, be quiet? I want to know what's going on."

"I'll tell you what's going on," the preacher said in an ugly, growly voice. He reached for the door handle with one hand, as if he planned to yank the door shut, and dug into his coat with the other.

It had just occurred to Tacita that the preacher was behaving in a most incongruous

300

manner when she saw his eyes, which had narrowed into two ill-natured slits, pop open wide. He whuffed out a startled, "Huh?"

And then he wasn't there anymore. They heard a loud thump and a grunt from the ground outside the coach, but he had disappeared.

"Good heavens, Jed. What on earth was that all about?"

"I don't know." Jed's voice sounded as bemused as she felt. "But I bet it's nothing good. I think our friend the preacher isn't what he pretended to be." He stood and leaned out the door.

"Did he just fall out of the coach?"

"Yup." And then Jed stepped off the stage, too.

Provoked that he should abandon her at such a time, Tacita snatched Rosamunda off the seat next to her, uttered an indignant "Humph," and stepped to the door to peer out.

"My goodness."

At the foot of the steps the driver had set out for their convenience, she saw the preacher sprawled. His eyes were closed and he appeared to be sleeping. Which was silly, as she understood at once. He must have knocked himself out when he fell out the door, poor thing.

By the dim light of two lanterns hanging from hooks on the coach, Tacita noticed that his trousers had slipped down and bunched up around his knees, too. She pressed a hand to her cheek in empathetic embarrassment.

Then she noticed his gunbelt. It had apparently been hidden underneath his coat, but it had slipped down with his trousers and now lay beside his knees. How strange. Tacita didn't know ministers carried firearms. The practice must be confined to the West.

Jed picked the gunbelt up even as she watched and removed a gun from its holster. Tacita could plainly discern that the belt had been cut through next to its buckle. Or, rather, it seemed to have been chewed. Oh, dear.

It looked as though the poor man had lost all of his buttons, too, because his coat gaped open, exposing his shirt and knit underdrawers. Tacita closed her eyes, shocked at being exposed to such sights, her recent experiences with Jed and those nearly naked opera ladies notwithstanding.

Jed stood up again, holding out the gunbelt, and peered up at her. "Looks like your dog's been busy, ma'am."

As he bent to investigate the parson's pockets, Tacita stared down at Rosamunda. Rosamunda looked up at her, a satisfied expression on her face.

"My goodness, Rosamunda, did you chew that poor man's clothes off?"

Rosamunda snorted. If Tacita didn't know better, she'd think she was cross.

"Rosie did a good job of it, Tacita. If she hadn't chewed through this fellow's belt and pockets and gnawed off all his buttons, he'd probably have held us up." Jed stared down at the sprawled figure. He looked vaguely astounded.

"Held us up?" Tacita hurried down the steps to get a better look at the parson, studiously avoiding the view of his underwear. "Why would he want to hold us up? What reason would he have to delay our trip?"

"I didn't mean he wanted to delay us." This time Jed sounded exasperated.

302

Tacita didn't understand. "But you just said—"

"I said he wanted to hold us up. Hold up. At gunpoint. He wanted to rob us."

"Rob us?" Tacita stared at the scene, bewildered. Other men had dashed up to Jed and the fallen parson, all talking at once, barking out questions and answering them in the same breath. Neither questions nor answers made sense to Tacita.

Suddenly she heard somebody say, "The *dog* did it?" And he started to laugh, huge guffaws that bludgeoned Tacita's nerves. Anger flared in her bosom and she turned toward the offending party, keeping Rosamunda close to her chest in case any of these uncivilized men offered to punish her dog.

"Stop laughing this instant! Help this poor man, if you please." She ceased her indignant tirade as things began to settle into place in her mind. Merciful heavens, how embarrassing this was going to be.

Taking a deep breath, she said, "Apparently, my dog has injured this poor minister in some way. I didn't realize what she was doing at the time."

"Me, neither," said Jed. He sounded amused. Tacita didn't think it was funny.

"She done good, all right," another man said. He was the one who had been laughing. Tacita looked at him, irritated both by his grammar and by his sentiments. She wasn't sure she'd ever understand Western sensibilities. These men found the most outrageous things amusing.

She said, "Well, she didn't mean to."

Jed, still squatting next to the parson, grinned

# Emma Craig

up at her. "Sure she did." He cast Rosamunda a look of outright approval. "Maybe old Rosie's not completely worthless after all."

Rosamunda lifted her lip in a sneer.

"Oh!" Tacita stamped her foot, something she hadn't done in years. "How can you be so callous? Help that poor man!"

"I'll help him, all right," Jed muttered.

"Here. I'll help, too," another man offered. "O'Casey's gone to wire the sheriff in Boulder. We can tie him up and keep him in the station house in the mean time."

"Tie him up? Sheriff? What on earth are you talking about?" Tacita looked at the group of men gathered around the preacher, whose eyelids were beginning to flutter. She wished somebody would pull up his trousers. The poor man would be mortified when he came to and found them bunched up around his knees.

"Why, ma'am, don't you know who this here feller is?"

The question came from a beefy fellow with a scraggy beard. She hesitated, then said, "Er, I don't believe we were ever properly introduced. He's a minister of the Gospel, though." A glance around the semicircle of rough-looking men, all grinning, made her reassess her answer. "Isn't he?"

A roar of laughter greeted her timid addendum. Even Jed was smiling when he detached the ever-present rope from his belt and laced it around the parson's hands and tied them together. As he did the same with the man's feet, he said, "Nope."

Tacita said, "Nope?"

The bearded man said, "Parson? Hell, ma'am,

this here som'bitch is Stagecoach Willy."

"Stagecoach Willy?" What an odd name. Tacita had never heard the surname Willy before. Or of the first name Stagecoach, for that matter. Most of the ministers she'd met in her day had been blessed with more dignified names than that. On the other hand, she was beginning to get the feeling that perhaps the man had duped them into thinking he was a preacher. Such a deception seemed dreadfully unethical to her.

"Do you mean to tell me this man is not a minister?"

Her question precipitated another round of laughter, which didn't sit well with her.

"Tacita, apparently this fellow's been robbing stagecoaches for years along this route. He's no more a parson than I am."

"Oh."

Tacita stared down at the man. Then she stared at Rosamunda, who peered back mildly.

Then she saw the fat lady, hanging back at the edge of the group of men, and decided it was time for her to get a sandwich. Carefully, she picked her way through the throng to the fat woman.

"I do declare," said the woman, "have you ever heard the like?"

"No, I certainly haven't," Tacita declared, meaning it.

The fat woman, whose name, she told Tacita, was Gloria Withers, continued to chatter her excitement as they entered the stage stop to purchase a sandwich. Tacita bought one for Rosamunda, too, and fed it to her outside.

"What an adorable little dog, Miss Grantham. What kind is she?"

"Rosamunda is a Yorkshire terrier, Miss Withers."

"She must be a very intelligent dog, to have seen through that terrible man's disguise and recognize a criminal."

"Yes," Tacita said mechanically. Then she took herself to task. "Yes," she repeated with more enthusiasm. "Indeed, she is very intelligent. Why, Rosamunda is a direct descendent of the great Huddersfield Ben himself."

"My goodness," said Miss Withers, sounding suitably impressed.

Now how on earth, Tacita asked herself, could Rosamunda have known that alleged preacher was an outlaw? No answer occurred to her.

"I don't know how she knew," Jed said when she asked him. "But I'll bet you anything that man was hired by your uncle."

Tacita didn't speak to him for a good hour.

Ah. This was better.

Rosamunda curled up on the coach seat where Stagecoach Willy had sat, on a cushion the stagecoach driver had given her. He'd done so because he appreciated her efforts on behalf of the Butterfield line. He'd told her so himself. Rosamunda had thanked him in her usual gracious way. Her tummy was pleasantly full of the beef she'd eaten out of her sandwich and the cheese the other men had offered her in thanks for doing such a good job in helping them nab the desperate criminal, Stagecoach Willy. She considered both cushion and treats merely her due. As she saw it, they were the least those humans could have done.

"Do you really think she knew, Jed?"

Rosamunda saw him shrug and decided he'd never amount to anything.

"Well, he fooled me."

Rosamunda lifted a brow and peeked at Mistress from across the aisle. Mistress had very few failings, all things considered, but she certainly had a knack for misjudging people.

First Jedediah Hardcastle and then Stagecoach Willy. Rosamunda wondered if there were some way to educate humans, and then decided the task, even if it could be performed, was too daunting for her to attempt.

She dozed off.

Cesare Cacciatore Picinisco had seldom felt so ill-used. First Jedediah Hardcastle thwarted him in his attempt to steal that ridiculously expensive dog. Then Farley Boskins beat him up. Then Virendra Karnik foiled his attempt to snatch the dog from the railway car.

He'd even shaved off his beautiful beard, discarded his colorful clothes, and stashed his wagon in Alamogordo, of all heathen places. And all of those sacrifices, so far, had gone for naught.

Well, he wouldn't allow the gods to impede his progress any longer. He was going to get that dog if he had to go to the ends of the earth to do it. Which, he decided grimly, was about the size of it.

"They went to San Francisco?" he asked the clerk behind the registration counter at the Silver Baron Hotel in Denver. He hoped he'd heard wrong. His ears hadn't worked right since that dog had gotten hold of them.

"That's what she told me," the clerk said, dashing Picinisco's hopes.

"But that's the end of the world."

The clerk grinned. "Reckon it about is, all right."

Picinisco frowned at the man, finding nothing in this situation worthy of mirth.

"Do you know how they planned to travel to San Francisco?"

The clerk shrugged. "Butterfield Stagecoach, I think."

The stagecoach. Well, Picinisco's finances couldn't stand the expense of purchasing passage all the way from Denver to San Francisco by stagecoach. It had taken almost everything he had to get to Denver. With a discouraged sigh, he decided it was time to perpetrate another robbery.

Agrawal's face lost its expression of impassivity for the first time since Luther'd gone into business with him—the more fool he—in Galveston several months before. It wasn't a pretty sight. Luther slugged down an entire glass of beer without taking a breath.

"He failed." The telegraph in Agrawal's fingers shook. His eyes glowed like hot coals.

"Who failed?"

Agrawal's stare bored into Luther like a drill and he knew he shouldn't have asked.

"The man I hired to interrupt their stagecoach journey from Denver to San Francisco.

"Oh." Luther couldn't hold Agrawal's implacable gaze. His own staggered away. "Too bad."

"Isn't it?"

The way Agrawal asked the question, and the

smile with which he asked it, penetrated the alcohol-slush in Luther's head unpleasantly. Luther had a very bad feeling about it.

The remainder of Tacita and Jed's journey to San Francisco was accomplished without further delays, barring those necessitated by a flood in Utah and a broken axle outside of Carson City. They both considered these occurrences acts of God and merely incidental to their expedition. No other villain after Stagecoach Willy threatened them.

Jed hoped this was an indication that her uncle had given up attempting to obtain whatever it was he was after. He didn't give his hope much weight. He did, however, pray fervently that the sissy Jeeves would be able to protect Tacita from whatever evil seemed to be following her. The thought gave him a prolonged case of indigestion. Unless that was caused by the lousy food they had to eat along the stage route.

Tacita uttered suitable ohs and ahs about the scenery they passed through. In truth, the setting was grand. However, although she tried very hard to concentrate on the trees and mountains, rocks and fauna along their way, her mind was more often occupied by the wretchedness of her situation.

Oh, she knew she should appreciate Jed during the short time she had left with him and leave tomorrow's worries until tomorrow. She'd been trying to do so ever since their first night together out under the stars, in the middle of the immense American frontier. Being a mere human, she was unsuccessful more often than not. As the stagecoach continued its obstinate progress and San Francisco got ever closer, the less successful she became.

More than once she even pondered the wisdom of asking Jed to marry her. Since he'd bedded her, he'd probably feel honor bound to do so should she ask. Her pride rebelled, though, and she couldn't bring herself to pop the question.

Even if he could be brought to sacrifice his principles and break his engagement with Miss Amalie Crunch, Tacita knew it was the gentleman's business to propose, not the lady's. She'd embarrassed herself enough by asking him to make love with her in the first place. She wouldn't complete her humiliation by asking him to become her husband.

Anyway, Jed needed a suitable wife. Not her, a woman with no more idea about how to survive in the rugged West than Rosamunda. Although, she couldn't help adding in her own defense, she'd done remarkably well thus far. So had Rosamunda.

Besides, if he cared for her enough—if he loved her—he *would* ask her, Amalie Crunch or no Amalie Crunch.

He didn't, and Tacita's heart ached painfully.

As the coach rattled its relentless way through the towering redwood forests in the northern part of California and neared San Francisco, Jed's heart and mind both were turbulent. Guilt gnawed at his guts and a sense of impending loss ate at the rest of him.

He'd taken Tacita Grantham's purity, thereby violating his own code of honor and his almost-engagement to Miss Amalie Crunch. And once they arrived in San Francisco, Tacita would expect him to go on about his business as if she meant nothing to him, just as he meant nothing to her. But she didn't mean nothing to him. She meant more to him than life itself.

Time after time, he almost abandoned his principles and his pride and begged her to marry him. He was even willing to endure the censure of his family, knowing he'd be breaking both a promise and Miss Amalie Crunch's heart, in order to have Tacita. The knowledge that she was engaged to that dratted Jeeves fellow stopped him every time.

Jeeves could offer Tacita everything she wanted, barring protection, although Jed supposed his money could buy that well enough. Jeeves could offer her world travel and a fancy home in England and all the damned Yorkshire terriers she could ever want. Jed could offer her a pretty nice home in Busted Flush, Texas, and a bunch of horses. And his love. And, he guessed, he wouldn't even object too strenuously if she wanted another one of those damned rat-assed terriers. It was a puny bargain, and he knew she'd never go for it.

# *Chapter Seventeen*

Rosamunda had her back feet propped on Tacita's knees. Her front paws rested on the windowsill of the stagecoach, and her head hung out as far as Tacita would let it. She looked around eagerly, sniffing furiously, her eyes bright with interest.

So this was San Francisco. Interesting place. It smelled of salt water and creosote, fish guts and chopped liver, incense and roasting meat, poverty and wealth, and thousands of humans and horses and cats and dogs. Somewhere in this milling throng was Rosamunda's one true love, Prince Albert.

As her little tail wagged back and forth like a crazed pendulum, Rosamunda could hardly wait to meet him.

\*　　\*　　\*

The stagecoach rumbled to a noisy stop, and what looked like a hundred men ran out to take care of the horses and baggage. Urchins crowded around the coach, hoping for tips if they helped passengers to their final destinations. City noises, dust, and odors swelled up around them.

Jed cleared his throat. "Reckon we're here at last."

"Yes." Tacita cleared her throat, too. "Yes, I guess we are."

"I'll see you to the Palace."

"Thank you."

He hesitated, then asked, "Is there anything else I can do for you? Anything at all?"

She hesitated, too. "No. No, I don't believe so."

They looked into each other's eyes for several moments. Tacita said, "Thank you."

After another few moments, Jed said, "You're welcome."

Rosamunda growled impatiently.

Jed said, "I'll get your suitcases and hire a wagon to take your other stuff to the hotel."

"Thank you."

They hardly spoke after they boarded the cab that would transport them to the Palace. Jed looked out of a window on one side of the cab and Tacita looked out of a window on the other.

Rosamunda shared the window with Tacita. Her tail wagged up a storm.

Although Tacita had been in several large cities, including some in the eastern United States and Europe, she had never seen anything like San Francisco. Rough-looking characters who seemed like something out of the Gold Rush days shared the sidewalks with men in fancy suits who might have appeared more at home in New York City. Chinese boys rushed here and there, pigtails flying out behind them, with buckets suspended on long poles balanced on their shoulders. Other lads, dressed in knickerbockers and soft caps, darted up and down the streets, carrying messages or selling newspapers. Shrill cries went up from street vendors. A cable car clanged and pelted down a tall hill in front of their cab. To Tacita's surprise, the horse pulling their cab didn't so much as flinch at the racket.

Many downtown buildings were draped with red, white, and blue bunting, in anticipation of the city's Fourth of July celebrations, Tacita supposed. She wondered what today's date was. They'd planned their trip so that she'd arrive in San Francisco sometime before the middle of July. She presumed Jed, who was so utterly competent in every regard, had adhered to the schedule.

Excitement filled the atmosphere as effectively as the city's famous fog, and hammered for entry in Tacita's heart. Her heart, however, brimmed too full of sorrow to allow room for excitement. Or anything else. She and Jed would part as soon as they got to the Palace. She hoped she wouldn't burst into tears and embarrass them both.

And then they were there.

"I'll help you down," Jed said.

"Thank you."

Rosamunda gave a shrill bark of excitement.

The Palace was about as grand a hotel as Tacita had ever seen. Plush carpets muffled

314

their footsteps and gilt trappings caught their eye.

Trudging next to her, Jed looked as stoical as any man Tacita had ever seen. If he possessed any emotions, they were so well hidden that she couldn't see them. She wondered if their impending parting would wound him at all, or if his heart was as hard as his outer demeanor. She didn't think he possessed a hard heart, but she wasn't sure of anything anymore.

"Do you suppose that fellow's here already?"

His question interrupted the dismal flow of her thoughts and she jerked, squeezing Rosamunda and making her yip. "Who? Edgar? I don't know. What—what's the date? Do you know?"

"It's the first of July."

Right on time. Tacita had known how it would be. She smiled faintly, recalling her first meeting with Jed Hardcastle and how she'd mistrusted him. Now she'd gladly offer him her life. In fact, she'd do it in a minute if he had any use for it, which he didn't.

She felt her smile tremble on her lips, and pinched them together so they wouldn't tilt into a sob and give her away. "I expect he's already here. I believe his ship was to dock sometime near the end of June."

Jed nodded. They had reached the registration desk. Tacita stepped forward, knowing she had to take over now; her days of relying on Jed to take care of things were gone, never to be recaptured.

The clerk behind the counter smiled at her in a superior way, as if to let her know that, while he was here to serve, he was doing so in an establishment known to play host only to the rich and famous and that she'd better belong to that group or she'd soon feel his contempt. Tacita was familiar with that smile. She gave the clerk one of her own, which was geared to let him know she understood his message and, what's more, she could buy him and a dozen just like him.

The clerk understood, too, and his attitude immediately became ingratiating. He even rubbed his hands together, sending thoughts of Uriah Heep darting about in Tacita's brain. For the first time in her memory the little game, which she used to play without so much as a thought, struck her as ridiculous. Of course, she'd become used to the rugged Western honesty displayed by Jed Hardcastle. He didn't have any use for silly games like this one. She played it with the clerk now, though, since she didn't perceive an alternative.

"My name is Tacita Grantham. I believe you are holding a suite of rooms for me?"

She saw Jed glance at her quickly and knew he hadn't heard her sound like this since they first met in Powder Gulch. She smiled at him to let him know her tone was only for the hotel clerk.

"Yes, ma'am, Miss Grantham," the clerk said. "Indeed we are. Allow me to get a bellman for you."

"Thank you."

Tacita, Jed, and Rosamunda stood before a pile of luggage while Tacita gave directions to a harried-looking bellman. All of a sudden Rosamunda began barking in a manner that sounded hysterical to Jed. He glowered down at her because he was in a really bad mood.

Tacita, on the other hand, who must have known her dog's barks better than he did, said, "Oh, my goodness, darling, do you see someone you know?"

Allowing himself one brief, incredulous look at Tacita, Jed turned toward the elaborate front door of the lobby. What he saw made him frown.

It was Jeeves. Jed would recognize the prissy sissy anywhere, even if he weren't hauling another Yorkshire terrier behind him on a fancy braided leash, and even if Tacita hadn't whispered "Edgar," to confirm his knowledge. The damned pansy looked like he ought to be wearing a monocle. So did his damned dog.

Because he felt so rotten, he growled, "It's your intended, Tacita."

"Yes," she said. "I see." She didn't sound as happy as Jed would have expected her to sound.

Rosie, he noticed, acted like she was about to swoon from ecstasy. It figured. He wished he could kick something. Preferably Rosie, although the Englishman would do in a pinch.

Tacita lifted a hand. "Edgar?" She said it too softly and the pansy didn't notice her, but continued to mince his way across the lobby to the registration desk. Jed glowered menacingly at his back, which did every bit as much good as Tacita's greeting.

She spoke a little louder then. Jed got the curious feeling she didn't really want Jeeves to hear her. Wishful thinking, he decided contemptuously, and told himself to get used to it. Tacita belonged to Jeeves now, and that was that. His stomach heaved.

"Edgar! Prince Albert!"

The fairy heard her that time. He had just turned with his royally named dog, and had just smiled, when a shrill cry from Tacita pierced Jed's eardrums. Irritated, he turned to scowl at her, only to find her gaze glued to the front door again. He spun around, hoping whatever had captured her attention was something he could kill, preferably with his bare hands.

It was Farley Boskins. And Stagecoach Willy, whom somebody must have bailed out rather more quickly than Jed considered seemly. And Virendra Karnik. And another Indian fellow Jed hadn't ever seen before. And a man with bushy muttonchops who started walking rather unsteadily away from the group until Boskins caught him by a coattail and dragged him back in line.

Two tall, burly men, swaddled in strange white cotton clothes and turbans, walked several paces behind the others. Even though Jed couldn't see a single weapon between them, he had a feeling these two could be really dangerous.

"Uncle Luther?" Tacita stared uncertainly at the group of men, then turned to look up at Jed, her wide blue eyes making him want to kiss her—which didn't surprise him any, as he always wanted to kiss her. She said, "It's my Uncle Luther," in a very doubtful voice.

"The drunkard?" he asked, just to be sure, although he didn't figure the unknown Indian could be her uncle.

"He's not a drunkard!"

Although Jed lifted a skeptical brow, he didn't

argue. Nor could he figure out what was going on.

Tacita took a hesitant step forward. Jed got the strong impression that she didn't know why these men were here, any more than he did.

"Miss Grantham?"

The high-pitched, rather nasal question startled both Jed and Tacita into turning toward the registration desk again. Rosamunda began straining on her leash, her toenails digging fluffs of carpeting into tiny balls under her feet.

"Edgar?" Tacita took a step toward her intended bridegroom, then stopped and looked at her uncle and his entourage once more. She took a step toward them, too. "Uncle Luther?"

"Tash," fell out of Luther's mouth. Jed's nose wrinkled up in distaste. He'd never been fond of drunks, and was surprised to find one in Tacita's family.

"Miss Grantham?" the unknown Indian said, making both Jed's and Tacita's attention veer in his direction.

"Tacita?" Edgar said again.

"Ha!" said Farley Boskins

"Miss Grantham?" the Indian said at the same time.

"Mr. Hardcastle," Karnik murmured, looking as though he'd rather be hiding in a corner.

"Tash," Uncle Luther repeated.

"Huh," Stagecoach Willy muttered.

Rosamunda yipped.

Prince Albert answered.

Jed held up his hands. He hated confusion. "Let's all be quiet for a minute."

Nobody complied until he bellowed his request a second time. Then noise ceased all over the hotel. Prince Albert squatted and peed on the lobby carpet. Rosamunda flattened herself out on the floor and squeaked. A group of businessmen turned to look at Jed. A bellboy dropped a piece of luggage. Uncle Luther fell to his knees. Even the registration desk clerk stopped speaking in mid-sentence and ducked behind the counter. Crystal tassels on the chandelier above their head tinkled into the silence.

A little embarrassed, Jed decided he might as well continue what he'd started. While Farley Boskins helped Luther Adams Williamson to his feet, he growled, "All right. One at a time." He turned and pointed at Luther. "Are you Tacita—er—Miss Grantham's uncle?"

Luther nodded, a gesture that made him list to starboard. Fortunately, Farley Boskins still held onto his arm. Jed eyed Boskins next, not kindly.

"I know who you are, even though I don't know what the hell you're doing here." His gaze fastened on Karnik. "And you."

Karnik, quaking a little, nodded. "Yes, sahib." He still looked like he wished he were elsewhere.

Jed's gaze fastened on Stagecoach Willy. "How'd you get out so fast?"

Stagecoach Willy shrugged.

"Who are you?"

Jed's peremptory question had been asked of the unknown Indian, who had seemed to be quietly assessing Jed through the prior commotion. He smiled now.

"I, dear sir, am Avinash Agrawal, at your service." He gave an elaborate bow.

Jed was not charmed. "Don't reckon I can use your services, Mr. Agrawal. And I sure as the devil aren't your dear sir. Just tell me who the hell you are and what the hell you're doing here." Tacita yanked on his sleeve. He wasn't inclined to feel charitable or to modify his language today, however, so he ignored her.

"Ah, my dear friend—"

"As to that, I don't reckon I'm your friend, either, dear or otherwise," Jed barked, cranky as all get out.

Agrawal bowed slightly, as if acknowledging the appropriateness of Jed's mood, as well as his words. "As you say, sir."

Edgar Jevington Reeve, evidently fascinated by the motley assortment of humanity gathered in the Palace's lobby, moved closer to the action. Rosamunda greeted Prince Albert with ecstatic yaps. Prince Albert reciprocated. Jed glared at all three of them. Only Edgar seemed intimidated.

"So, Mr. Agrawal, who the hell are you and why the hell are you here with all these other people? You the one who hired 'em all to follow us? What'd you aim to do? Kill us? What for?"

"Oh, no, no, no, my dear fellow. Nothing so crude."

Jed snorted. Luther, unable to stand perfectly still, veered to one side and Boskins yanked him back again. Jed bunched his hands into fists.

Agrawal, taking note of Jed's fists, sped up his recitation. "You see, sir, Miss Grantham's uncle, Mr. Williamson"—he nodded at Luther, who blinked back fuzzily—"has assured us that Miss Grantham is in possession of the Delhi Hahm-Ahn-Der Eye."

Tacita and Jed exchanged a glance. Jed muttered darkly, "That damned eye again."

321

Tacita said nothing. She looked terribly confused.

"It is imperative that the Eye be returned to the Great Goddess in Delhi. Otherwise, immense misfortune will befall my people."

Jed offered a grunt. Encouraged by his show of interest, Agrawal went on. "Therefore, I made arrangements with Luther Adams Williamson. He in turn hired several of these people to fetch the Eye and bring it to me. I, in return, shall replace it in its rightful place, in the shrine of the Great Goddess in the Temple of Hahm, in Delhi."

"Well now, isn't that just dandy." Offering the assembled men a good glare each, Jed said, "I don't know what the hell you're talking about." He turned to Tacita. "Do you know what the hell he's talking about?"

Apparently too surprised by this turn of events to take exception to his language, Tacita only shook her head, bemused, and said, "No. No, I have no idea."

"Y'neck. It'sh 'round y'neck."

Everybody looked at Luther. He looked back, his unfocused stare creating the impression that he was watching a rather dull play while his mind dwelt on other matters.

Agrawal smiled. Jed didn't like his smile one little bit. He snarled, "What the hell's he talking about?"

"Ah, my dear fr—er—Mr. Hardcastle. I fear Miss Grantham's uncle is under the weather."

"Under the table's more like it," grumbled Jed.

"Perhaps." Agrawal inclined his head. "At any rate, he has assured me that Miss Grantham is in possession of the Eye. As a matter of fact, I have already paid him a good deal of money to get the Eye back."

"You paid Uncle Luther to get something from me?" Tacita sounded flabbergasted.

"Told you so."

She turned to look up at Jed, frowning, obviously unhappy to have had his suspicions confirmed.

"But what is it? What is this Eye, Uncle Luther? What on earth do I have that you need? I don't have any idea what this Eye is. Oh, this is so frustrating!" Tacita stamped her foot again, surprising herself more than anybody else.

"You got it." Luther nodded too emphatically for his state of balance. Again, Farley Boskins steadied him.

Tacita was almost in tears when she asked her uncle, "But why couldn't you just ask me, Uncle Luther? You know I'd give you anything if you needed it."

This time he shook his head, which didn't do any more for his balance than his nod had. "No, y'wouldn't."

"Yes, I would."

"No, y'wouldn't."

"Yes, I would! I would, too!"

Another shake sent Luther careening into a potted plant. He sat heavily on the lip of the enormous pot. "M'brother-in-law gave it t'you," he said as if that would explain his behavior.

Tacita glowered at her uncle. "I do believe Jed is right. I think you *are* inebriated."

"Told you so," Jed mumbled again. Tacita ignored him.

Uncle Luther shrugged.

"But I still don't know what you're talking

about." Tacita started tapping her foot. "What is this Eye everybody keeps talking about?"

"Ah, my dear child, it is a—"

Tacita whirled around so fast, Agrawal's words failed him. "I didn't ask you! And I am *not* your dear child!"

"Just so," Agrawal said, and swallowed. His henchmen had each taken a step forward, but he shooed them back again.

Jed smiled his approval at her. So did Rosamunda.

Returning her attention to Luther, Tacita planted her fists on her hips and resumed glaring at him. She also resumed tapping her foot. "Well, Uncle Luther? What is this Eye?"

"Em'rald," Luther said, struggling with the word. "Em'rald. Round y'neck."

"An emerald around my neck?" Her glare didn't waver. "An emerald around my neck that my father gave me?"

Luther nodded. He had to clutch at the pot to keep from sliding into the soil holding the plant in place.

Suddenly Tacita's foot stopped tapping. Her hands fell to her sides. Her eyes opened wide. She said, "Oh!"

Everybody stared at her. She said, "Oh," again.

Then, with all eyes upon her, she lifted her hands to the lace on her high collar, reached inside her gown, and seemed to grope for something.

"Do you mean this?"

Her fingers reappeared, dangling a thin gold chain. Suspended from the chain a large, glittering emerald winked at them, its facets catching light from the gas lamps in the lobby. Jed remembered that emerald well because it had rested between Tacita's breasts when they'd made love. He eyed it with longing until a loud gasp made him jerk his attention away from it.

The gasp was so loud because it had issued from several throats at once. In fact, everybody present—except Luther, who was too tipsy, and Jed, who was too unhappy—had gasped at the sight of the emerald.

"Is this it?" Tacita asked again.

Luther nodded.

Agrawal stepped forward. Tacita closed her hand over the emerald and flung him a hot look. He stopped short and inhaled a sharp breath.

"You just wait a minute," Tacita commanded.

Agrawal murmured, "As you wish, miss." With a wave, he halted his henchmen, who had stepped forward also.

"Now," Tacita said firmly. "I plan to get to the bottom of this. Jed—that is, Mr. Hardcastle and I have been plagued by people following us and bothering us and trying to snatch my dog and all sorts of things, and I don't appreciate it one bit." She glowered at everybody to let them know she meant business.

"I want to know once and for all: Was all that harassment perpetrated for the purpose of securing *this* emerald, given to me by my own beloved father right before he and my mother left for their last trip to India?" She paused to take a deep breath. "Is *this* the wretched Ham-and-Rye you keep blathering on about?"

In a dramatic gesture, Tacita held up the emerald, which twinkled like a bright green star as it twirled from her fingers. Another gasp went up.

Uncle Luther said, "Yesh." He sounded utterly miserable.

Agrawal took another step forward. He took a jeweler's glass from his left front pocket, lifted it to his right eye, and peered at the emerald dangling from its chain in Tacita's hand.

Agrawal took a step back. He replaced his jeweler's glass.

He said, "No."

Luther said, his voice squeaking, "Yesh. Yesh. That'sh it."

Agrawal gave Luther a look filled with disgust. If Luther hadn't been trying to crawl his way out of the potted plant, he might have been affected by it. "It musht be it. I shwear thatsh the one."

Agrawal shrugged. "There is a vague resemblance, but this is definitely not the Delhi Hahm-Ahn-Der Eye. Don't be absurd, man."

The advice, though sound, came several months too late. Tacita spoke severely to her uncle. "This is certainly not any goddess's eye, Uncle Luther."

Luther stammered feebly, "It'sh—it'sh not? Are you absho—absho—are you absholuley sure?"

Tacita frowned at her uncle. "My father and mother bought this emerald for me in Bombay, and had the setting made specially. They told me so. It's the sweetest thing they ever did for me." She went on. "The person they bought it from was a reputable jeweler. This emerald never once resided in a religious artifact. You know my parents would never deal in such stolen icons, and they hated the practice of robbing treasure from temples. You should be ashamed of yourself!"

For the space of several heartbeats, utter silence settled over the lobby of the Palace Hotel in San Francisco.

Then a high-pitched, keening wail slid from between Luther Adams Williamson's lips. He fell backward into the potted plant.

Farley Boskins said, "son-of-a-bitch."

Virendra Karnik said, "Oh, my goodness gracious."

Stagecoach Willy said, "Damn!"

Tacita, shocked to her toes, clamped her hand over the emerald to stop it from bouncing against her bosom, and staggered back several steps.

Edgar Jevington Reeve, still standing apart from the jumble of men and Tacita, said, "Really, Miss Grantham, what is all this about?"

Rosamunda barked.

Prince Albert whined.

Avinash Agrawal's air of suavity deteriorated into a grumpy pout. "This stone bears not the least resemblance to the Great Delhi Hahm-Ahn-Der Eye." He sounded disgusted.

All hell broke loose.

Three unhappy villains lunged for Luther, who struggled vainly among the palm fronds. Clods of dirt flew out of the pot and landed on the lobby carpet. The registration clerk, eyeing them with horror, leapt over the counter and raced toward the fracas.

"Stop! Stop! You're dirtying the carpet!"

Jed, who had been watching the whole scene with displeasure, decided enough was enough. Drawing his gun from his waistband, he fired it once, into the soil of another potted plant.

The entire lobby froze into a tableau of absolute rigidity. For a moment, it was as if a god of winter had touched them all with his icy finger and paralyzed them into place. Not a creature stirred.

Except one.

From a corner of the lobby, where he'd been crouched, watching everything with intense interest, Cesare Cacciatore Picinisco stirred.

While everybody stood stock-still, motionless with shock, he crept toward Rosamunda. And Prince Albert.

# *Chapter Eighteen*

"All right, everybody shut up right now!"

Jed's words were superfluous at this point, since he'd already scared all persons present speechless. He swept the assembled group with a militant eye.

For his money, he'd as soon shot somebody as not, but since nobody moved he guessed he couldn't. Damn. All morning long he'd been itching to hurt something because he was in such a bad mood. It galled him to keep having his murderous impulses thwarted in this way. Every now and then, civilization really got on Jed's nerves.

After making sure they all knew he was only sparing them because he had to and not because he wanted to, Jed stuffed his gun away again. Then he pinned a glare on Luther, who trembled on the floor next to the potted plant, having been hauled roughly out of it by Farley Boskins.

Jed nudged Luther's toe with his boot. He wasn't gentle about it. Luther shrank back. Sneering at this further show of Luther's cowardice, Jed jerked his head toward him and said, "You. Tell your story."

"I—I—I—" Luther's wild-eyed gaze steadied after several panicky moments and fastened on Tacita. "I'm sorry, Tash—Tass."

"For what?"

Jed's gaze shot to Tacita's face. He'd never heard her sound so implacable before. She looked implacable, too, and he silently applauded her for it. He'd feared she might take pity on this miserable excuse for a man just because he was her uncle.

Luther's glance wobbled and fell. "I'm sh-sorry for trying to sell your em'rald to thish man." He made a vague gesture in the approximate direction of Avinash Agrawal.

A moment of silence stretched between them. Then Tacita said, "You should be sorry, Uncle Luther."

Fat tears leaked from Luther's eyes. Jed didn't feel sorry for him. Neither, apparently, did Tacita. She didn't even bother trying to comfort him, but turned her attention to Agrawal.

"And you," she said. "Who are you and what is this Eye that's so important?"

"Avinash Agrawal, at your service, miss."

"Don't make me laugh!"

Tacita sounded altogether revolted by Agrawal's facade of servility. Jed grinned. He was so proud of her. God, he loved her.

"Ahem. Yes, well, perhaps not at your service. I beg your pardon."

"Oh, stop waffling around and get on with it!"

Agrawal looked peeved. "Yes, ma'am. At any rate, your uncle, Mr. Williamson, agreed to secure for me—for an exceedingly large sum of money, I might add—the Delhi Hahm-Ahn-Der Eye, which, as I have already explained, was stolen from the shrine of the Great Goddess in Delhi. Mr. Williamson assured me that you were in possession of the Eye."

Luther began to weep harder.

Tacita said, "Well, he was wrong, wasn't he?"

Agrawal grimaced. "Yes. So it would seem."

"So, I guess you can go away now and continue your search elsewhere, can't you?" Tacita's eyes narrowed. It looked to Jed as though she were daring Agrawal to dispute her assessment of the situation.

She noticed the appraising glance Agrawal gave her uncle and added, "And you will not hurt Uncle Luther, either." She shot Luther a withering look. "*I'll* take care of *him*."

After a moment or two, during which Agrawal seemed to be evaluating Tacita, Luther, Jed, and his own henchmen, Agrawal bowed. "Yes, miss, I believe you will. I shall depart then."

"Not so fast," Jed cut in, usurping Tacita's thunder, which made her frown. "You and the rest of your lot caused us a whole lot of trouble, Mr. Agrawal, and put us in danger more than once. Now, I think the law'd be interested in you."

Out came his gun again. This time, he aimed first at Agrawal's henchmen, since he respected them more than any of these other fellows. "Drop 'em," he barked in a voice that had been known to make vicious Texas outlaws quake.

It worked on Agrawal's henchmen, too. One of them dropped a large curved knife he'd pulled from a hidden scabbard. It made a soft thud on the hotel lobby's carpet. His fellow lackey did likewise.

Jed directed his next question to the hotel clerk, who had picked himself up by this time and now stood, gaping, along with all the other people in the lobby who weren't directly involved in the altercation. "Got someplace to store this sorry lot?"

"Yes, sir!" The clerk snapped to attention, clearly pleased to have been asked to participate. "Right here, sir!"

So Jed herded his diverse flock into the room the clerk indicated, and locked the door. He was somewhat uncertain about Luther's fate among all these men who'd been led on by him, then decided he didn't care. Neither, evidently, did Tacita, who muttered several scathing epithets to her uncle as he was being ushered into the room. Luther only hung his head in apparent shame. The useful emotion had attacked him a good deal too late, in Jed's estimation.

The clerk secured a bellman and Jed gave him some money and a few concise instructions. He had just seen the bellman out the front door, intending to wait for the police before he unlocked the door to the makeshift prison, when a shriek startled him nearly out of his wits. Which wasn't too difficult a task at present.

The clerk clapped his hands over his ears and uttered, "Holy moley."

Jed didn't bother speaking. He saw Tacita, hands pressed to her flaming cheeks, an anguished expression on her face, and all thought of anything but her safety deserted him. He began rushing to her side when another voice lifted into the lobby atmosphere, ululating a tenor counterpart to Tacita's shrill soprano. Jed winced inside, but didn't stop. Tacita needed him, and he was hers to command, screaming British pansies or no British screaming pansies.

This was it as far as Rosamunda was concerned. She had already taken more nonsense in a few short weeks than any self-respecting Yorkshire terrier—and Rosamunda didn't know any other kind—should be expected to endure in lifetime. She'd been carted from the semicivilized city of Galveston, Texas, to Powder Gulch in the overtly uncivilized New Mexico Territory, to Denver in the questionable Colorado Territory, to San Francisco, California. She'd been mauled and kidnapped and disparaged and virtually abandoned by Mistress, only to be kidnapped again and by the very same scoundrel who'd done it the first time, what's more.

The dastardly Mr. Cesare had snatched her and Prince Albert right up from the lobby floor while nobody was looking. Which just went to demonstrate yet again the abysmal priorities displayed by human beings who ought to know better. Now, as if they were twin sacks of flour instead of championship Yorkshire terriers, Mr. Cesare was loping off with her under one arm and Prince Albert under another.

Well, Rosamunda was through with Mr. Cesare. She was through with Tacita and Jed. In fact, she was through with all of them. No longer would Rosamunda, descendant of the great

Huddersfield Ben himself, rely upon the tender mercies of the humans who were supposed to be her protectors.

Because she was so small, it was difficult for her to wriggle herself forward to view Prince Albert over Picinisco's paunch, but she managed. She noted with satisfaction that Prince Albert had conceived of the same idea. *This* was a Yorkshire terrier she would be proud to have father her children. They exchanged a meaningful glance.

Then, to the sounds of the hot pursuit Jed and Tacita were undertaking behind them and Edgar Jevington Reeve's pitiful cries, and working together as a precisely synchronized team, they attacked.

Jed watched Rosamunda with an abiding sense of appreciation. Old Rosie might be a pain in the ass, she might attack the wrong people nine-tenths of the time, and she might hate his own personal guts, but by God, there was no way on this earth Jed could fail to respect her resolution. If he wasn't so busy, he'd have applauded.

As two sets of doggy teeth set to work on him, Picinisco's screams of pain and terror blended with the chaotic sounds already echoing throughout the Palace Hotel's plush lobby. Jed saw one Yorkie balancing on his shoulder and chewing on his earlobe and another solidly gnawing its way though his arm and grinned, silently congratulating Rosamunda and Prince Albert for their attention to detail.

Right before he struck, Jed shouted, "Jump, Rosie!" Then he launched himself into a tackle that had felled galloping cows back home in

Busted Flush during their annual branding roundup. Picinisco crashed to the floor, his chin skidding on the lobby carpet. His shriek bounced off the walls.

With a skill honed over years of hard practice, Jed snatched the rope from his belt and had the villain's feet and hands tied before the average person could blink twice. Leaping back from his fallen foe, he thrust his arms in the air, as if to show a judge he'd completed his task in under the time allotted for the purpose.

Tacita was right behind him, tears streaming down her face. Without even pausing in her flight, she kicked Picinisco in the stomach and grabbed her pet. Then she stood there, sobbing into Rosamunda's fur and aiming kicks at exposed areas of Picinisco's body as he rolled this way and that, trying to avoid her and being unsuccessful more often than not because he'd been bound up so tightly.

Once he had ascertained that Rosamunda and Tacita were all right, Jed turned his attention to Prince Albert. He was satisfied to note that the prince was attending to parts of Picinisco's body Tacita couldn't reach with the pointed toe of her boot.

"Good for you," he said. Turning, he noted with disdain that Jeeves still lagged behind, his mincing run enough to make any red-blooded American male gag. And Tacita was going to marry him? Jed's stomach turned over at the thought.

"Prince Albert! Prince Albert!" Edgar's voice was squeaky, too. Jed's disgust was complete.

However, since the fellow had finally arrived to take possession of his pet, Jed turned his at-

tention to Tacita. Very carefully, as he didn't
fancy that pointy toe of hers connecting with his
own shin, he went behind her and put an arm
around her middle. Gently, he tugged her away
from the miserable Picinisco.

"Come on, darlin'. Leave the poor man be
now. We've got him and he ain't—er—he isn't
going anywhere."

It took Tacita a moment to comply with Jed's
wishes. When she did, she whirled around and
flung the arm not holding Rosamunda around
his neck.

"Oh, Jed! Oh, Jed! That horrid man tried to
steal Rosamunda! Again!"

He patted her back. "I know, sweetheart, but
everything's going to be all right now."

Wrenching sobs from the creature at Jed's feet
belied his words. Jed harbored no sympathy for
Picinisco, though, and he did not amend his
statement.

He did, however, spare a smile for Rosamunda, who managed to wriggle herself out
from between Tacita and Jed's chest at that moment. She emerged in a fluff, popping up past
Tacita's shoulder and gasping for breath.

"Good girl, Rosie. You did good today."

Rosamunda stared at Jed, wide-eyed.

So did Tacita, pushing herself away from him
as if she needed to see his lips move in order to
be sure he'd said what she'd heard.

Both mistress and pet wore expressions of absolute shock, and Jed was embarrassed. He
shrugged and muttered, "Well, she did."

Suddenly, his hand was grabbed. He spun
around to find Edgar Jevington Reeve pumping
it as if Jed were a spigot. He frowned.

"Oh, sir, how can I ever thank you for rescuing my darling Prince Albert?"

*You can start by leaving go my hand,* Jed thought sourly. He refrained from saying so aloud, out of deference for Tacita. He did, however, pry his hand out of Edgar's grip.

"Seemed to me your dog was doing pretty well on its own, mister."

He heard Tacita come up behind him and felt her little hand on his shoulder. It made him feel better.

A miserable groan from the floor recalled the three humans and two dogs to their reason for being gathered together this way. They all looked down at Cesare Cacciatore Picinisco, trussed up like a calf for the branding.

"Please, sirs and madam," the wretched Picinisco said. "Please forgive me."

"What in the name of God did you want to take and grab these two dogs for, Mr. Pickerslicky? Both of 'em together aren't big enough to make a meal."

Prince Albert growled. Rosamunda lunged for Jed's throat, but Tacita held her back. Jed lifted a brow, surprised that Rosie had turned on him again. And here he'd been harboring almost tender feelings for her.

Picinisco turned over onto his back so that he could more fully view Jed. The position thrust his hands and feet into the air, since he was hogtied, and Jed might have been amused if he'd been in any mood for humor. He wasn't, so he maintained his stony glare and shook a fist at Picinisco for good measure.

"Oh, Mr. Hardcastle, I know I violated your

hospitality in the forest when I stole Miss Grantham's dog—"

"You drugged us, too," Jed reminded him unsympathetically. The humiliation of having allowed himself to be fed drugged brandy still nagged at him.

Picinisco's eyes closed and a spasm passed over his features. The spasm might have been accounted for by all the little doggie wounds that he had recently sustained, the tightness of his bonds, or the large carpet burn on his chin, but Jed suspected shame.

"I'm sorry. I'm so sorry."

Tacita gave a haughty sniff. So did Rosamunda. Prince Albert snarled. Jed shook his head and wondered how he'd ever survive two of these animals. Then he remembered that he wouldn't have to, as Tacita was self-destined for the Englishman, and he got mad again.

"Sorry don't pay any tolls, Picklefickle. Why'd you take the dogs?"

"For the money," crept from the floor, sounding as miserable as Picinisco looked.

"Figured as much." Jed was thoroughly disgusted. He'd never bought the philosophy that money was the root of all evil because he knew how important money was in this imperfect world. He knew very well, however, that greed had caused more than one good man to go bad. And, from what he'd seen so far, this Pickerficker fellow hadn't been very good to begin with.

"You stole my dog for the money?"

Tacita sounded incredulous. Exasperated, Jed suppressed the "I told you so" that battered against his teeth to get out. He did exchange a glance with her, but since she looked quite huffy and still wore those pointy-toed boots, he decided not to press his luck, and remained silent.

"Y-yes," lifted to their ears.

"But both dogs together wouldn't bring three hundred pounds," Edgar said, plainly puzzled.

"Three hundred pounds?" If Edgar had sounded surprised, Jed was staggered. "The damned animals can't weigh six pounds each!" He shifted his angry look to Edgar, who blinked back at him.

"Er, he's talking about pounds sterling, Jed," Tacita told him, eliciting a frown for her efforts. "It's what the British call their money."

The furrows already wrinkling Jed's frown deepened. He felt silly not to have known that. "It's a stupid way to talk about money," he muttered.

Tacita murmured something soothing and patted his arm. Then she turned to stare down at Picinisco, her own brow wrinkling in thought.

"Mr. Picinisco, Rosamunda and Prince Albert are wonderful examples of the Yorkshire terrier breed and are worth a good deal of money for that reason. In order to sell them, however, you'd have to show them to other people who are interested in the breed. One does that primarily by entering his or her dog in a show put on specifically for the purpose. Where on earth did you expect to find a Yorkshire terrier show out there in the middle of New Mexico Territory? Or here in San Francisco, for that matter? The only Yorkshire terrier shows I know about thus far are in England. Perhaps New York."

Picinisco stared up at her, his eyes wide, unhappiness radiating from his every pore. Several seconds ticked by before he admitted, "I—I didn't think about it."

Tacita said, "I see."

Jed snorted.

Rosamunda and Prince Albert both yipped.

Edgar said nothing, but continued to hold Prince Albert tightly. Jed suspected he was deriving more comfort from the dog than the dog was from him. The prince had already demonstrated that he could take care of himself a hell of a lot better than that fancy-pants dandy could.

Nobody said a word for several moments. Jed didn't know what to say. Anyway, he didn't suppose there was much left *to* say. He'd as soon let the police deal with this Pisklefisky varmint. The muffled tattoo of Tacita's toe tapping against the carpet was the only sound in the place.

At last Tacita said, "Well, I think you behaved very badly, Mr. Picinisco."

Huge tears filled Picinisco's eyes. "I know I did," he whispered. "I'm so sorry."

"You're sorry, all right," Jed muttered. Tacita smacked his arm. He scowled at her.

"However," she continued, ignoring Jed's black expression, "I hope you have now learned your lesson."

Picinisco nodded as fervently as he could in his present state. "I have, Miss Grantham. Oh, yes indeed, I surely have."

Jed snorted again. Tacita ignored his snort as effectively as she had his scowl. "Well, then, if you truly repent your dastardly deeds, I believe we should let you go."

"*What?*"

Jed's roar precipitated Picinisco into a little ball on the floor. He tried to roll away from them. Tacita covered her ears. Edgar Jevington Reeve trembled. Rosamunda barked. Prince Albert howled.

"Really, Jed, I wish you wouldn't do that." Tacita sounded like a schoolteacher admonishing a rowdy student.

Jed hardly noticed. "You can't let this man go, Tacita. He's caused us no end of trouble."

"I know that, Jed, but he repents his sins. He said so. Anyway, I believe Mr. Picinisco's primary sin is misguided money lust. Until he learned that Rosamunda was so valuable, he'd seemed rather friendly and benevolent. He shared his food with us, don't forget."

Jet uttered something inarticulate and said, "He shared his damned brandy with us, too. Don't you forget that."

Tacita's expression went sour for a second. "Yes, yes, I've not forgotten. But that was afterward."

"Afterwards, whatever! He did it!"

"Of course, he did it. But at least he didn't try to hold us up at gunpoint or anything like those other terrible men did." She glanced down at Picinisco and offered him a faint smile. "I believe Mr. Picinisco is merely misguided."

"Misguided? Oh, for—" Jed was too overcome by disgust to finish his observation. He turned around as if he couldn't bear to watch.

"So, Mr. Picinisco, do you promise not to kidnap any other sweet doggies in the future?"

"Grrrrrr," leaked from Jed's throat. Tacita paid him no mind.

"Yes, ma'am. Yes, Miss Grantham. You're a kind and gracious lady. A kind and gracious and wonderful lady. A kind and—"

Jed whirled around again. "Oh, shut up!" He bent over Picinisco, his hunting knife in his hand.

"Really, Jed!" Tacita exclaimed.

Picinisco squeaked and tried to roll away.

"Really, my hind leg," Jed muttered. More sharply, he said, "Stop it, damn your eyes. I'm trying to cut the rope."

"Oh." Picinisco sagged in relief.

Once Jed had removed his bonds, Picinisco had to flex his fingers and wiggle his feet to get his circulation going again. He kept his gaze firmly on Jed, as though poised for escape should it prove necessary. At last he managed to crawl up onto his hands and knees.

"Honestly, Jed, I don't think you should have tied that rope so tightly. The poor man's been punished enough."

Jed said nothing. He even kept his lips together when Tacita balanced Rosamunda on one hip and dug into her little pocketbook. He did, however, exchange a disgruntled look with Rosamunda.

"Here, Mr. Picinisco, I'm going to give you some money—"

"*What?*"

Tacita turned her head to scowl up at Jed. "Must you shout so loudly, Jed? I believe that's quite enough of that."

Jed gave up and lifted his hands in a gesture of defeat and distaste. This was more than his mortal soul could stand. He wasn't going to utter a single 'nother word, not even if the varmint snatched the pocketbook out of Tacita's hands. Jed wouldn't put it past him.

Picinisco quivered like a hound on the scent.

"As I was saying," Tacita resumed, "I shall give you some money. I want you to go away and never bother us again. Use this money to establish yourself in a legitimate business somewhere. Turn away from the dark path, Mr. Picinisco. Seek the light. Pursue goodness and right. You won't be sorry."

A stifled noise crawled from Jed's throat. Tacita shot him a look.

"Th-thank you, Miss Grantham. Thank you." Picinisco grabbed her hand in both of his, much to her surprise. "I'll never forget you. You're the greatest lady who ever lived."

"Please, Mr. Picinisco," Tacita said repressively. She tried to regain control of her hand, but Picinisco wouldn't release it until Jed took a menacing step toward him. Then he scuttled out of Jed's reach.

"I'll never forget you." As Picinisco ran for the door, limping and bleeding, he called over his shoulder, "I'll never forget you!"

Tacita lifted her hand in a gesture of farewell. "And I'll never forget you, either."

Rosamunda's teeth snapped together. Jed could imagine what she was feeling because he felt the same way himself. Then he shook himself. This trip must have been even rougher than he thought if he was beginning to think like a dog. Especially *that* dog. Even if he had come to admire her. Sort of.

Tacita had a big smile on her face when she turned around. She looked like somebody who knows she's done a good deed and is proud of it. Jed thought she'd been a big fool, but he knew she'd just argue with him if he said so, so he didn't. Instead he turned on Edgar Jevington

Reeve, who shrank back clutching Prince Albert.

It did not escape Jed's notice that, while Jeeves seemed afraid, Prince Albert bared his teeth. He guessed these Yorkies had guts, even if guts were all they had.

At the moment, however, that didn't matter. Jed had other matters to take care of, and he intended to take care of them right this second. He pinned Edgar with a glacial look in preparation for asking him something of vital importance to Tacita and, therefore, to Jed.

"All right, Jeeves, I want to know what your intentions are."

Tacita tugged his sleeve. He shook her off.

Edgar gulped audibly. "M-m-my intentions?"

Prince Albert uttered a horrible growl.

Rosamunda looked curious.

"Your intentions," Jed repeated, his voice hard. He barely glanced at the furious Yorkie in Edgar's arms.

"I-I'm not sure I understand you, Mr. Hardcastle."

"Intentions," Jed repeated. "In-ten-tions. Intentions! What's not to understand? I want to know what your intentions are toward Miss Grantham, damn it, and I want to know 'em now!"

Edgar seemed to become smaller and smaller as Jed's fury increased.

Tacita tried again. "Jed—"

"Later," he growled down at her. To Edgar, he snarled, "Well? Spit it out, Jeeves."

"I—I—"

"Jed—"

Jed roared, "Damn it, Tacita, shut up for a minute!"

"Well, really!"

"Now, tell me, damn it, Jeeves! *What are your intentions toward Miss Grantham?*"

Edgar's terrified glance darted between Jed and Tacita. He looked nearly hysterical. Prince Albert had taken to barking out a shrill warning at Jed, who refused to pay attention. His focus was strictly on Edgar Jevington Reeve.

"P-please, Mr. Hardcastle, calm yourself. My intentions are strictly honorable."

"And they are?" Jed's hands had bunched into fists. He lifted them now, ready to strike if Edgar gave any indication of having intended to trifle with Tacita's affections.

Tacita, red-faced with frustration and embarrassment, tugged Jed's sleeve again. "Jed—"

He shook her off, still glaring at Edgar. "Well?"

"I—"

"Jed—"

"*Well?*"

Edgar seemed to collect himself. He squared his shoulders and stood up straight. "Well, really, I should think it's perfectly obvious what my intentions are. The only reason I came to this heathen city in this heathen country was to mate!"

Jed's bellow of rage rattled the crystal chandelier in the Palace Hotel's lobby.

# Chapter Nineteen

"It's not what you think!"

Forsaking dignity and nearly everything else in her panic, Tacita threw herself onto Jed's back, dog and all. This was all her fault, and she had to prevent Jed from murdering Edgar Jevington Reeve.

"*I'm going to kill you!*"

Edgar Jevington Reeve was too terrified for words. Short, shrill, high-pitched shrieks issued from his throat as Jed bore down on him. Prince Albert, hackles high, went into full-fledged attack mode, barking out a terrible warning as he poised to strike.

Tacita shrieked into Jed's ear, "It's the *dogs*, Jed! It's the *dogs*! We're going to mate the *dogs*!"

Rosamunda, finding herself flung against Jed's back, bounced to the floor. Immediately, she attacked his foot, hanging onto his trouser cuff much as she'd done that very first day in Powder Gulch. Only today, she didn't plan on being thwarted. She was going to deal with Jed Hardcastle once and for all.

"Stop it! Stop it!"
Tacita's fear for Edgar's safety was almost too great and she failed to perceive that Jed had at last heard her. Gradually, though, she sensed her words had finally penetrated his blind rage.

Her throat scraped raw from screaming, she repeated more softly, "It's the dogs we plan to mate, Jed."

Jed had been bent nearly double as he reached for Edgar. Now he stood up suddenly, almost tumbling Tacita to the floor. She clung to his back so she wouldn't topple into a heap. Rosamunda still tugged furiously at his trouser cuff.

He said, "The dogs?"

Tacita sighed. Edgar whimpered. Prince Albert's grotesque yapping faded into a menacing growl. Rosamunda remained undeterred. Tearing sounds lifted to their ears. They ignored them as unimportant.

Tacita said, "Yes."

Jed lifted his hands and pried Tacita's away from his neck. He turned around, still holding onto her arms. She didn't like the look on his face.

"You made me bring you all the way from Powder Gulch to San Francisco so you could mate your *dogs*?"

She considered fibbing, but knew in her heart that he wouldn't believe her. Besides, she guessed she'd fibbed enough already. This was all her fault. Since she didn't quite trust her vocal cords, she nodded.

"You . . . wanted . . . to . . . mate . . . your . . . dogs." Jed shook his head, as if to clear it of cobwebs.

Tacita nodded again.

"The dogs."

Another nod.

"Not you."

A shake.

Still holding her by the shoulders, Jed looked hard into her eyes. Tacita held his gaze, but with difficulty. She wanted to cry and beg his forgiveness for deceiving him for a thousand miles and entirely too many adventures.

Dreadfully worried, she finally found her voice and started to babble with it. "You see, I knew that if you suspected the reason I wanted to get to San Francisco was to mate Rosamunda to Prince Albert, you wouldn't undertake the job because you wouldn't realize how important it was because you didn't like Rosamunda at first. I knew you didn't; there's no need to dispute me." She forced a rather sickly smile. "But now I'm sure you understand the importance of the trip. Now that you've come to understand how noble and wonderful a goal it is to breed these two perfect examples of Yorkshire terrier-hood. Now that you've seen them in action and—"

Tacita's words dried up when Jed opened his mouth. She flinched, dreading what he'd say.

"Does this mean you don't love this fellow?" Jed shrugged toward Edgar.

Surprised, as she'd expected an explosion of wrath, Tacita shook her head again.

"And you didn't come here to marry him?"

"No," slipped past her teeth, tiny and soft.

"And you never wanted to marry him?"

"No."

Jed took several deep breaths. Tacita didn't know what he intended to use them for, but she'd never been more frightened in her life. He'd hate her for sure now. She'd always feared he would when he found out, but she thought it would kill her to hear him say the words out loud. His hands were tight on her shoulders and they hurt, but she didn't dare say anything for fear he'd break her in half like a dry twig. He was so strong.

*The dogs. She'd hired him to take her to San Francisco so she could breed the dogs. It wasn't her and Jeeves. It was—the dogs.*

It was almost more than Jed could take in, but he tried. Tacita didn't love Jeeves. She hadn't come here to marry him, but to mate Rosamunda to Prince Albert. They'd traveled over a thousand miles, endured heat, cold, hardship, her Uncle Luther, Farley Boskins, Stagecoach Willy, Avinash Agrawal, Pickleflisker, and about a million other perils so that she and Jeeves could mate their dogs and create another four or five snot-nose terrors.

Jed's heart rose like a hot air balloon. Elation filled him.

Rosamunda had worked her way from his trouser cuff to his boot. Jed didn't care.

Miss Amalie Crunch be damned. Jed Hardcastle was going to ask Tacita Grantham to marry him!

He dropped Tacita's shoulders as if they'd caught fire and fell to one knee before her.

Tacita squeaked in terror.

Edgar backed up another foot or so.

Prince Albert snarled.

Rosamunda fell off his boot, hit her head, rolled over, and landed on her feet. She shook her head, too stunned to resume her attack. She glowered at Jed and Tacita.

Jed lifted Tacita's hand.

"I love you, Tacita." His voice sounded funny. He didn't care. He didn't care, either, that by asking Tacita Grantham to marry him he'd be breaking the hearts of his parents, his aunts and uncles, Miss Amalie Crunch's parents, and Miss Amalie Crunch herself. Plus, he might be making a big fool of himself.

Tacita squeaked again.

"Will you marry me?"

Her eyes almost bugged out in astonishment. Tacita opened her mouth and nothing came out. She closed it, swallowed, and tried again. "You want to marry *me*?"

He nodded, his heart too full for words.

"You"—Tacita poked a finger at Jed's enormous shoulder—"want to marry me." Her finger veered away from Jed and landed over her heart.

"Yes."

"Me."

"Yes."

"You."

"Yes."

"Oh, Jed!"

Tacita flung herself into Jed's arms and burst into tears. "I'm the happiest woman in the whole world!"

Flabbergasted, Jed could only hold her, his heart near to bursting. "Y-you mean you'll marry me?"

"Oh, yes! Oh, yes!"

"You—you like me?"

"*Like* you? Oh, Jed Hardcastle, you silly man, I've loved you for weeks and weeks!"

Tacita's declaration shocked Jed so badly, he had to sit down. He took Tacita with him and cradled her, not daring to let her go until he made sense of all this.

Still holding onto his dog as if to give himself courage, Edgar Jevington Reeve took a step closer to the couple who had just collapsed onto one of the lobby's elaborately upholstered sofas. He peered at them with unbridled interest. So did Prince Albert. For that matter, so did everybody else in the lobby.

Rosamunda stared at the ecstatic pair for several seconds, as well. Then she turned away, crawled under an overstuffed lobby chair, and curled up into a knot of absolute disgust.

"I don't think I could be happier, Jed."

"No?"

"No."

He squeezed Tacita tight. "Me, neither."

Jed lay on his back, Tacita melted on top of him. They'd just made beautiful love on the most comfortable feather mattress Jed had ever had the honor of lying upon. He'd just told her the absolute truth, too. His mind and heart were at peace.

Except for one tiny little particle of guilt remaining about having jilted Miss Amalie Crunch.

He tried not to let it spoil his mood, which was, all things considered, superlative.

Tacita sighed happily, which made her body, slick with perspiration, rub against him, which made him happy. "I can't wait to see Busted Flush, Jed, and to meet your family."

"They'll love you, too, Tacita, just like I do." And they would, too. Jed knew it. Even though they'd also blame him for breaking his promise. Jed wracked his brain, but he couldn't think of another single instance in which a Hardcastle had broken a promise. He shook his head, trying to dislodge the unpleasant notion.

Tacita peered into his eyes and he smiled because he couldn't help it. She had the prettiest eyes he'd ever seen.

"Is something the matter, Jed?"

"No. No, not really."

Brushing his hair away from his forehead, Tacita murmured, "It's Miss Crunch, isn't it?"

Surprised by her perspicacity, Jed hugged her. Lord have mercy, he loved her. "I reckon I jilted her, Tacita. That's not a very honorable thing to do, jilt a lady."

"Well, you couldn't have known we'd fall in love, though."

"No. I couldn't have known that." He scarcely believed it yet, in fact.

Tacita's finger traced his jawline. He gave her precious rump a little squeeze.

After a moment, Tacita asked, "Did—did you give her a ring, Jed?"

Her voice sounded unusually small, as though she were embarrassed to be asking her question.

Surprised, he said, "Criminy, no! What do you take me for, anyway?"

A little frown pursed her lips. "Well, you said you were engaged."

352

"Yeah, we were promised. It wasn't official or anything yet, though. It was understood."

"Understood?" She pushed herself slightly away from him. He hauled her back again.

"Yes. Everybody expected us to tie the knot. We had an understanding."

"You had an understanding."

"Well, yes. Kind of like you and that Jeeves fellow. Or, I mean, kind of like I figured it was between you and that Jeeves fellow."

She pushed herself away again. "You mean to tell me you've never asked her to marry you?"

"Not in so many words."

Tacita stared at him for a full minute. Then she shook her head, heaved a sigh, and flopped down onto his chest again. Jed was pleased.

Rosamunda's revulsion at the state of Tacita's affairs lasted the remainder of that day, overnight, through the following morning, and even during luncheon. It ceased abruptly when she was carried into Edgar Jevington Reeve's suite at the Palace Hotel, and she was wed to Prince Albert.

Their union was sublime. Rosamunda's ecstasy was so profound, she barely noticed the long journey back to Busted Flush. Of course, it helped that the return trip was accomplished in the luxury of private stagecoaches, trains, and padded wagons and took less than half the time their trip to San Francisco had.

She was not particularly taken with Busted Flush. On the other hand, Jed had a large home—indeed, it was almost as big as the one Tacita's parents owned in Galveston—with a big yard that even boasted a flower garden. Eyeing it critically, Rosamunda decided it would do.

She didn't even glare at Jed the next time he called her Rosie.

After their arrival in Busted Flush, where they were greeted by what seemed to Tacita to be more relatives than one human being ought to possess, Jed left her in the care of his mother. With his heart alternating between heaviness and almost unendurable lightness, he took himself off to visit the Crunches.

Tacita didn't mind being left at his parents' home. Jed's mother, a large woman in her own right, nearly smothered her in hugs.

Two days later, however, Tacita insisted upon being taken to meet Miss Amalie Crunch herself. Jed being the honorable soul he was, Tacita knew why he felt guilty. She figured it wouldn't hurt if she were to apologize to Miss Crunch in person. After all, this was as much her fault as Jed's. More, probably. Jed would never have met her if Tacita hadn't devised her plan to mate Rosamunda with Prince Albert. He'd have dropped her association like a hot rock if she then hadn't fibbed about it.

Now she stared up at the woman before her and gulped. Good Lord, the female was as big as a house.

"M-Miss Crunch?" she stammered. Heavenly days, she hoped Amalie Crunch wasn't a vindictive sort. If she took it into her head to hurt Tacita, Tacita wasn't sure even Jed could stop her.

Amalie smiled, showing a set of teeth that reminded Tacita of a lion she'd seen once in the zoological gardens in New York City. "That's me, all right."

At least she sounded friendly. Tacita decided Amalie's mood was not the issue. It was up to Tacita to clear the air. "I—I just wanted to tell you how sorry I am that things didn't work out between you and Jed."

Amalie's smile broadened. "Shoot, ma'am, that's not a problem. I'm happy as can be for the both of you."

"You—you are?"

Good heavens, what did this mean? Surely Miss Crunch must be heartbroken. Any woman would be if she had understood Jed would be hers and then learned otherwise. Why, it was inconceivable that a female wouldn't tumble head over heels in love with Jed Hardcastle once she met him. Not for a minute did Tacita believe Amalie's heart wasn't broken. And, from the looks of her, hers was an extremely big heart. It must, therefore, hurt a lot.

Amalie slapped her on the back, a friendly gesture that nearly knocked Tacita off her feet. "Why, sure, Miss Grantham. I'm happy as a hog in slop for the both of you."

After she regained her breath, Tacita choked out, "Well, I truly do feel guilty about this, and I know Jed does—"

Amalie interrupted Tacita with a hearty laugh. Tacita blinked in surprise, then continued resolutely. "At any rate, I should be happy to know if there is any way in which I can make up to you for the loss of Mr. Hardcastle."

"The loss of Jed?"

Amalie guffawed again, then stopped laughing abruptly. Tacita braced herself. She even backed up a little when Amalie frowned.

"You mean it?"

355

"Of—of course, I do."

Amalie frowned some more. Tacita took another step back.

Then Amalie said, "Y'know, ma'am, there is one thing."

"Anything," said Tacita quickly. She wanted to reassure Amalie in case her pleasant mood took a turn.

"Y'know, when Jed come to visit me and my folks a couple days ago, he said as to how you come from money."

Money. Well, that was easy. Tacita would gladly pay this creature any sum, although she knew full well that no amount of money could possibly compensate for the loss of Jed Hardcastle. She nodded.

Amalie shook her head and smiled some more. "Must be nice to be rich, ma'am."

"It—it is rather pleasant. I suppose."

"Jed's got heaps o' money, too."

As Jed had sat Tacita down and explained his financial situation to her the very night of his proposal in the lobby of the Palace Hotel, Tacita knew Amalie's assertion to be true. She nodded again, uncertainly. Surely, Amalie didn't want so much money that it would take their combined fortunes to pay her off. Did she? "I—I understand he is beforehand with the world," she said, hedging.

"Beforehand? Why, laws a'mercy, the man's as rich as a king!"

Amalie went off into a peel of laughter again. Tacita wasn't sure, but she thought that was a good sign. As she didn't dare take anything for granted, she decided merely to nod.

"Y'know what I really want, ma'am?"

356

"Er, no, Miss Crunch," Tacita told her honestly. "Actually, I don't."

"Call me Amalie, ma'am. I'd take it as a kindness."

"Thank you, Amalie. Please call me Tacita."

"Well, all right, ma'am. It's an odd name. Don't find many womenfolk called Tacita out here in Busted Flush."

"No. I don't suppose you do."

"Y'know what I want, Tacita, more'n anything?"

Tacita wondered if they'd ever get to the point, but didn't suppose it would be wise to ask. She shook her head.

Amalie sighed deeply. "I want to marry up with Sheldon."

Tacita's eyes popped open. "Sheldon?"

Nodding, Amalie sighed again. "Yup. I've loved Sheldon Fellows fer a coon's age. Feared I'd have to marry Jed, 'cause our folks expected us to get hitched, don'tcha know, but I always had a hankerin' for Sheldon."

"Mercy sakes." Tacita could think of nothing else to say.

"I used to sit on the banks of Luggett Lake with Sheldon and we'd spin daydreams about marryin' up with each other and openin' a bakery shop right here in Busted Flush."

"My goodness."

"Neither one of us had no money to get the business started, though. I figured I'd have me some cash after I married Jed, but that ain't going to happen now. Anyhow, if'n I'd'a married Jed, I wouldn't have Sheldon, but only the bakery shop. What I want more'n anything else in this whole world is to have 'em both: Sheldon and the bakery."

Reaching out to put a hand on Amalie's arm, Tacita said quickly, "Miss Crunch—Amalie—please. I should be more than happy to advance you the money to start your bakery. In fact, please allow me to give you the money as a gift. It would be my extreme pleasure. And I know Jed would want to help, too."

Amalie's eyes sparkled. For the first time, Tacita realized her eyes were really quite fine. That they were located a good foot above Tacita's own head had prevented her from noticing before. She was pleased as punch, too, as she'd never expected her problem to be solved so easily. Money was the easiest thing in the world to give a person.

"You mean it, Tacita?"

"I mean it absolutely, Amalie-eeeeeeek!"

Tacita's affirmation ended in a squeak when Amalie picked her right up off the ground and swung her around. When she was set down again, Tacita gasped for breath and realized Amalie was crying. Since she couldn't think of anything else to do, she withdrew one of her lacy handkerchiefs from her reticule and handed it to Amalie. It all but disappeared in Amalie's large hand.

"Please, Amalie, don't cry. I'm happy to help you and Mr. Fellows establish yourself in business."

"And in life, Tacita," Amalie said thickly. "Nobody ever did me such a good turn before. You're makin' our whole lives possible."

\* \* \*

Thus it was that when Jedediah Buchanan Hardcastle took Miss Tacita Helen Grantham to bride in the biggest Texas-style wedding the town of Busted Flush had ever seen, the couple celebrated their nuptials at a reception featuring a wedding cake almost as large as Jed himself and decorated with more pink sugar roses than anybody present could count. The cake was provided by Sheldon and Amalie Fellows as a gift to the happy couple.

Everybody within a hundred-mile radius of Busted Flush was invited to attend the wedding, and Tacita hardly noticed that she no longer possessed any immediate family. Except, of course, Rosamunda, who watched the ceremony from her basket of honor while nursing her newborns.

Tacita took the expression of resignation on her beloved pet's face as having sprung from the rigors of motherhood.

Five sets of tiny doggy claws clicked across the imported ceramic tiles, down the steps leading into the garden, across the flagstones, and down the garden path to the enormous double gates that separated the splendors of the Hardcastle estate from the vast Texas plain. That plain sprawled in an uncivilized manner just beyond the grounds. Rosamunda wanted to make absolutely sure her children knew what horrors lay beyond the garden gate so that they could strive to avoid them in future.

Not that one was always successful in such an endeavor, and she wanted them to learn that fact of life, as well. Rosamunda strove to teach her two boys and two girls that true success lay in how one fought one's battles, even though the outcome of such battles might not always be what one could wish.

Rosamunda herself, for example, had fought the good fight. She had few regrets, the largest being that everybody in the Hardcastle household now called her Rosie. Including Tacita.

Nevertheless, as she led the way, she held her head high. Truly, if one were to study her situation closely, one might even say she had won. The look on Jedediah Hardcastle's face the first time she jumped up on his lap, dug out a nest for herself, and settled in for a snooze, had been worth all her struggles. The knowledge that he was profoundly shocked and—even better— wouldn't dare thrust her away, not with Tacita watching—made triumph soar in Rosamunda's breast.

So Rosamunda did not regret her new name too much. She didn't even regret the fact that she'd been unable to prevent the romance between Mistress and Monster. After all, the Hardcastle estate was as grand as any she'd seen in Yorkshire, and much grander than Tacita's former home in Galveston.

As she told her children while they paused to mark bushes along their path, living well could indeed be accounted the best revenge.

# Heart's Magic
## Flora Speer

**Bestselling author of *ROSE RED***

In the year 1122, Mirielle senses change is coming to Wroxley Castle. Then, from out of the fog, two strangers ride into Lincolnshire. Mirielle believes the first man to be honest. But the second, Giles, is hiding something–even as he stirs her heart and awakens her deepest desires. And as Mirielle seeks the truth about her mysterious guest, she uncovers the castle's secrets and learns she must stop a treachery which threatens all she holds dear. Only then can she be in the arms of her only love, the man who has awakened her own heart's magic.

\_\_\_52204-7                     $5.99 US/$6.99 CAN

## CORAL SMITH SAXE

**Bestselling Author Of *A Stolen Rose***

Sensible Julia Addison doesn't believe in fairy tales. Nor does she think she'll ever stumble from the modern world into an enchanted wood. Yet now she is in a Highland forest, held captive by seven lairds and their quick-tempered chief. Hardened by years of war with rival clans, Darach MacStruan acts more like Grumpy than Prince Charming. Still, Julia is convinced that behind the dark-eyed Scotsman's gruff demeanor beats the heart of a kind and gentle lover. But in a land full of cunning clansmen, furious feuds, and poisonous potions, she can only wonder if her kiss has magic enough to waken Darach to sweet ecstasy.

_52086-9                                    $5.99 US/$7.99 CAN

# AMII LORIN

## COME HOME TO LOVE

## Winner Of Two *Romantic Times* Reviewers' Choice Awards!

**"Amii Lorin always gives her readers something special!"**
                                                        —*Romantic Times*

Matthew Martin needs a woman to run his home, be his hostess and, of course, share his bed. At any other time, Katherine would refuse such an impersonal offer. But she is a widow and the future looks lonely and bleak. So Katherine becomes Mrs. Matthew Martin—and finds that her marriage of convenience is not as convenient as she expects. She can deal with her children's disapproval and Matthew's meddling sister. What she can't handle is the unexpected yearning of her own rebellious heart.

__3852-8                                        $4.99 US/$5.99 CAN